SLIVER SHIP

Gordon A. Long

Delta, B. C.
2021

Sliver Ship

Gordon A. Long

Published by

AIRBORN PRESS

4958 10A Ave, Delta, B. C.

V4M 1X8

Canada

ISBN: 978-1-988898-30-8

 Ebook: 978-1-988898-31-5

Printed by Amazon

Cover Design by Gordon A. Long

Cover image by JCK5D from Pixabay

REACTOR MELTDOWN

Lundeen suddenly blasted into the gestalt. *Up and out! We're not thinking, folks.*

What?

We're so caught up in trying to solve this ourselves, we forgot our main ally. Johnson, are you in here with us?

Right here, Chief. I don't really understand what's happening, but I caught something about the cooling system. I'm at that panel now. What do you need?

Good man. How much control do you have over it?

We're way past temperature levels where it could make any difference, so I never thought to try.

We don't need much. If you could increase the efficiency by about ten percent, that would be enough to change the frequency of the plasma cycle.

It's running at 110% rated capacity at the moment.

Crank it to full military override. That reactor is going into shutdown the moment this is all over, and nobody cares if it ever works again.

Core cooling system is now in emergency override. I've just dumped all the refrigerant from the precooler tanks in at full pressure. We'd be seeing an immediate drop if the damned reactor wasn't already gone far beyond the most optimistic parameters. Let's hope these military outfits are overbuilt more than the commercial ones I'm familiar with...there we have it. Temperature dropped half a degree...

Natalia broke in. *Keep your foot on the throttle, Johnson, and keep it to the floor. Everyone, we're coming up to the next cycle. This is the big one, folks, so don't save any energy for later. If we don't hold this time, there won't be a later to worry about.*

The wills of the crew solidified like a sheet of PermaSteel, and the NightHawk prepared for the next encounter in what could be her final battle.

CONTENTS

PROLOGUE — SPACE ARMOUR

Commando Sergeant Kirstina Zuyeva was doing a final sweep of the underground science lab when a clatter of barwolf paws came up behind her. She turned. "Hi, Brindle. You making a final check too? I suppose you and your clan will be happy to see the last of this place."

Emotion: heartfelt agreement.

She stopped in her tracks. "What? What was that?"

The barwolf continued up the hallway, oblivious to her concern.

Weapons Specialist Jim Campbell strode out of the accommodation hallway, ducking so his suit helmet missed the doorjamb. He looked down at her. "Something wrong, Sergeant?"

She shook her head. "No, no, I just find these barwolves strange."

He gave her his usual grin. "Well, they are aliens, ma'am. Any problems?"

"No, but they've been intruding on my dreams. Bouncing around in fields of Arborean grass, that sort of thing. Do you think barwolves bounce?"

"Considering the conditions they were kept in here, I doubt if there was any bouncing."

"True."

"Is that it?"

"No. I just made a comment to the Brindle as it walked past me, and I got the distinct impression that it agreed with me."

"Word around the troop says they've got some kind of augment. Maybe it was talkin' to you."

She couldn't help but grin back. "Stranger things have happened, but usually after a long night at the Wolf's Den. Anyway, the Brindle's the last of them. It's gone up the elevator."

He nodded. "That's a damned independent beastie. Let's make sure it gets all the way topside."

Sure enough, up the hallway ahead the striped barwolf was just entering the cargo lock, its armoured shoulder scraping against the door jamb as if the creature were testing the solidity of the wall.

Major Sergei Bykov stood nearby consulting an enterpad. He looked up. "Ah, good. You two are already suited up. Would you go out on the surface and make a final check?"

"Aye, sir. Looking for anything in particular?"

The officer shook his head. "Just being thorough, Sergeant. This base is going to be empty for who knows how long after we lock it down."

"On it, sir."

The two Marines trudged up the staircase to the personnel airlock and cycled through.

Kirstina accessed her com. *"You wanta take a reccy around the west perimeter? I'll go east."*

"Aye, ma'am."

She bounded along in the light gravity at just enough speed to keep her balance, her attention half on her surroundings and half on her heads-up display. *Nothing out of the ordinary.*

"Hey, Sarge." Campbell's com sounded louder than usual.

"Yes?"

"You gotta look at this."

"What is it?"

"I'm not sayin' until you've seen it, ma'am."

She bounded over to him, intrigued. *Nothing upsets Campbell.*

The big Marine was staring at the dusty soil of the little moonlet. "What do you think those are?"

A line of semi-circular indentations the size of her palm meandered through the dust, coming in from the west and heading towards the airlock. Or going the other way, depending on what made the marks.

"Dingo dung! Those look like barwolf tracks."

"Thank you, ma'am. Glad I wasn't seein' things."

"If it's barwolf tracks, it was headed towards the base. We better see where it came from."

They backtracked the creature, but it soon became apparent that it had just been wandering. They found themselves meandering towards the base from a different angle, where they discovered that the tracks had started where the moondust became thick enough to register them. "It came out the airlock, wandered around, and went back in. Without oxygen."

"That's what it looks like to me, ma'am."

"It must have been the Brindle. It's the only one that's had that kind of freedom."

Major Bykov's signature came up on the com. "Are you two done out there?"

"Aye, sir. Just at the airlock now."

"All clear?"

"Yes, we found some interesting tracks, but nothing else."

"I don't want 'interesting.' I want anything that will put us off our schedule."

"Nothing like that, sir."

"If you think they're worth it, record them and get in here. Once we're aboard and moving, you have all the time you need to put them in your report. We don't know when the original owners of this place are going to show up and how well armed they'll be when they do. Not getting into a fight is the surest way of not losing one, and we have no reason to fight, here. The kidnap victims are safe, the lab is shut down and we're moving out."

"Aye, sir. On our way."

She did a space-armour version of a shrug at Campbell and clicked on her recording module.

1.   NEW ASSIGNMENT

Administration Building
Barwolf Base, Arborea
One year later

Captain Natalia O'Rourke sat bolt upright in her chair as the augment communication washed over her.

...the reason I bring Toni Jacobs into our conversation again is because she's what an officer is supposed to be. Not one of these mincing politicians you can manipulate because they always have one eye on their next promotion. All she wants is her mission to succeed, for her cadre to survive. That's what a good officer thinks about. Not about promotion. You just want me to get ahead so you can use my reputation in your business deals. You don't really care about me, and how I feel about it.

Natalia's augment didn't register the answering mumble.

*Well, Father, you and I are never going to agree on this, so do us both a favour...*the speaker's emotions calmed, and the augment blast dissipated. Soon the engine of George Rowell's J73-B wound up, and the space fighter departed, probably back up to his office in the orbiting Habitat, almost empty now of immigrants.

The captain considered her options. *Alison is going to be so embarrassed...* She shrugged. *Her father is a force to be reckoned with. Glad I don't have problems like that.* She opened her augment again. *Major Rowell.*

Aye, ma'am.

I believe we need another chat.

Emotion: poorly suppressed dismay. Aye, ma'am.

When the Barwolf Squadron Leader entered Space Arm's temporary accommodations in the new Admin Building, Natalia was sitting in her lounge chair, a glass in her hand. She waved it towards the couch. "Take a perch. Wine on the counter."

The Major slipped in and stood, not looking her usual confident self. "I did it again, didn't I?"

Natalia smiled. "Go ahead. Have a drink. You've just been through an emotional experience."

"And I gather I didn't exactly keep it under control." The other woman's smile turned down. "How bad was it? Did I broadcast to the whole base?"

O'Rourke waved a negation. "Nothing specific. Some of the senior bureaucrats might have felt vaguely uneasy. The barwolves probably just considered it part of the noisy human presence in their territory. Only members of the *NightHawk* gestalt could hear the words. We're tuned in to you."

"Prime." The woman poured a small drink and dropped her lean frame into a chair.

"Don't worry. Chakka isn't exactly going to make fun of you over it. Andrew...well, I'm counting on whatever relationship you have developed in the last two years to get you over that little bump."

"And Toni?"

"Oh, yes. Toni." Natalia shook her head. 'Well, she'll be embarrassed as hell, of course. I'm sure she had no idea you felt that way about her."

"...what am I going to say to her?"

"I have no idea. But I'm glad it happened."

"Why?"

"Because Toni needs a kick in the butt. You were right about her. She has to realize that she's a leader and think like one. This will be good for her."

The other woman slumped, an unusual pose for her. "I'm glad it's good for someone. I really need to work on those control exercises. It's been two months since I got this Full Ten augment, and I let it slip again."

"If you don't mind my asking — and please don't answer if you don't want to — but both times this has happened, your father has been involved. What's the problem with him that makes you so angry? Besides the obvious. I've dealt with him. He can be annoyingly persistent."

Alison's shoulders drooped more. "Something I can never do anything about."

Natalia smiled. "But you will keep trying."

"Albert Einstein said that insanity involved doing the same thing over and over, expecting a different result."

"Smart man. So, what is it? You want to be family, and he wants to use you for leverage?"

"Exactly. As far as he's concerned, that's what family is for. Just like the rest of the world."

"And you want to be special. Not a useful tool like the rest of us."

"I'm his only daughter and his only family. Is that too much to expect...no, don't answer that."

5

Natalia's heart went out to the poised, beautiful woman who slouched there so despondently. "You know, that's one great advantage of the Outback."

Alison frowned and sat straighter. "An advantage?"

"Everybody out here is cut off from their old lives, from their families. For most of us, it's permanent. Space Arm can be a cold and lonely environment, even in the Sol system. But back in Sol, most people have family to go home to. Out here, nobody has, because this is our home. So we make do. We form families of our own." A warm feeling glimmered in Natalia's chest, and she smiled. "I cheated. I adopted Andrew when he was twelve. That worked out pretty well for both of us. You've made a start, too. Look at Alfino. How does he treat you, a mere Major?"

"Well... considering he's the ambassador, he's very nice to me. He has no reason that I can see."

"Yes he does. He has no family here, either."

"Are you saying he thinks of me as a daughter?"

She shrugged. "I have no idea. Daughter, favourite niece, mentee, whatever you two decide. Haven't you noticed how easy your relationship is with him?"

"...it never occurred to me." Another downward smile. "I thought it was just my diplomatic skills."

"Don't worry about it. Enjoy. You need it."

"Oh. All right."

"And how are things with Jackson? Again, if you don't mind discussing it."

"Looking for an appropriate date for the wedding." She made a comic moue. "Between his schedule and mine and Space Arm's, that isn't easy."

"Congratulations. I envy you. But he's pretty busy setting up the new capital city right now."

The younger woman made a face. "Yes, we get in about one good visit a month."

"And your duties at the Base, here. Pretty much routine?"

"Very. The pressure is off, now that SolarCorp is out of the picture. We've got the patrol schedules set up, and everybody knows what they're doing. Which is why I'm lallygagging around the base, not doing my assigned work because my wing-second is handling it just fine."

Natalia eyed the young officer. "And how do you feel about that?"

6

Alison returned the stare. "This just stopped being a friendly chat, didn't it."

"Well, nobody ever said you weren't perceptive. You know about *NightHawk's* next mission."

Alison's hand hovered, tipping left, then right. "We all know there's a mission. What it is and who's going? No idea. That's one of the things Father's been driving me nuts with. Asking leading questions."

"Are you going to volunteer?"

Rowell held up a hand. "Stop right there. This is a test, isn't it?"

"Not really. Why do you think so?"

"Because this is exactly what my father doesn't understand. What's my first thought when a situation comes up? If it's, 'How will this affect my career,' then I'm toast."

"Hmm. And what was your first thought?"

The younger woman frowned. "I'm not sure. I know I was wondering what the mission was, and I have some idea of who should be going."

"Bingo." Natalia sat back and raised her glass. "Give the lady a kewpie doll."

"Pardon?"

"Curiosity about the mission is necessary, because you need to know what you're doing, but the first thing you always think about is your people. That's leadership. Who do you have? How will they fit in? How will you motivate them? Only then do you start thinking how you'll fit in and why the Higher-Ups gave you the job. How to use your special skills to make things go better. But that's the end of the chain, not the beginning."

Alison leaned back and tossed her short, blonde curls into place. "Prime. What's the mission? If you answer, it means I'm going."

"You'll be offered the position of Auxiliary Pilot. The details of the expedition are still being finalized, but don't read the name wrong. You're not spare personnel. You're the lead pilot of the auxiliary vessel."

"Which is...?"

"Ah. Well, that's the problem." She observed the major's reaction. "We're not quite sure."

After a moment's pause, Alison responded slowly. "Another test?"

"Wasn't meant to be, but it's always interesting to see how people react to the unexpected." Natalia waited to let the other woman get her head around the situation. "It's true. We don't know what the vessel is, because Freighty has designed and built it, and it's at Factory

4-80 under very tight security, waiting for us to pick it up. The first part of the mission is to do that. Then you learn to fly it. Then we go on the real mission."

"I'm the test pilot for a ship of experimental alien design."

"How do you feel about that?"

Alison shrugged and grinned. "If I survive, it can't help but advance my career."

"There you go. Everything you always wanted in one package."

"And all I have to do is survive."

"No, it gets more interesting. Your backup pilot is Toni."

"Oh."

Natalia could almost see ideas flashing back and forth.

"But Toni's not a pilot, she's an auguar trainer. There'll be a gestalt, then. Toni, Nzinga, the ship, and me."

"Something like that."

"And when the ship is in space, I'm in charge, but on the ground Toni takes over."

Natalia grinned, allowing a certain amount of relief to show. "Now I'm sure."

"What...? Oh, another test. I'm already thinking about fitting the crew together."

"Right. And your next problem?"

"Um...I probably have to teach Toni to be a pilot, because the only training she has is what Andrew has given her on *Diablo*."

"Which is considerable, but limited in scope, and his own training was unorthodox. We're hoping that the new vessel's ArIn will be similar in mental configuration, so she will have an advantage."

"We'd both better be practicing on *Diablo,* then."

"Right, which means you'll be riding with them on the first leg of the mission, to Freighty to pick up the new vessel."

"Mars apples! You've got me slated for two months with Andrew and Toni on *Diablo?* I've heard Morissa's stories about her trip with them coming out here from Earth."

"A bit of initiation, I suppose. I'm sure you'll cope." Natalia laughed. "But you'd better get working on your augment control exercises. Concentrate on personal isolation."

The other responded with a puzzled frown.

"I'm not sure how their relationship is progressing, but it might be at a rather emotional phase."

"You mean...?"

8

Natalia nodded. "They're long past the 'teenage infatuation' stage. They're getting over the 'edging around and fitting together' stage. Now they're headed for the 'what love is really about' stage. You know, the one where they break it off or go long term."

"And how do you feel about that?" Then Alison's face reddened. "I'm sorry. I don't have the right to ask."

The captain grinned. "Since you're about to be exposed to it in great detail, I can give you the easy response. Do I have any choice?"

"Well...you don't have to send them out together." The young pilot frowned in thought. "But they're probably ideal for whatever the mission requires, so a good leader can't let her personal preferences interfere with the mission."

"You're getting the hang of it. I'm glad I don't have that kind of problem anymore." The captain finished her glass. "You may consider the official part of this meeting over. Would you like to have another drink?" Then she grinned. "Or would you rather deal with Toni and get it over with?"

Alison sighed and finished her glass. "Business before pleasure." She rose, but paused with her hand on the door pad. "Do you think she's going to laugh at me?"

Natalia cocked her head to one side. "You don't impress me as the type to worry about that."

"It would be one of the preferred reactions. Thanks, Captain."

Natalia waved her out with no salute. "Next meeting is in orbit on *NightHawk* tomorrow."

As the door closed, she accessed her augment. *Andrew?*

Yes, boss.

Did you catch that?

In a vague sort of way. I didn't pay much attention. Except for the part about Toni.

Emotion: laughter. I wonder how she's going to deal with this. Hero worship, yet!

Do her good.

Image: mother tweaking son's ear. For someone that's supposed to be in love, you're too hard on her sometimes, you know.

Revenge for all the tough combat training over the past five years. Anything else?

No. I'm taking NightHawk's shuttle up to the ship tomorrow, early. Alison can bring you three and your luggage up later. We have a lot of prep to do onboard.

Prime. Emotion: uncertainty. Mum?

9

Yes?

That bit about not having our problems anymore. Sounded like an old woman.

Emotion: wry humour. That's what they call me when I'm not listening, right? "The Old Lady?"

It's only a figure of speech. Don't let it define you.

Whatever you say. Between the two of us, you're the expert on the topic.

At the moment, I'd have to agree with you. Night, Mum.

Night, dear.

She closed her augment and glanced at Chakka. "A month with that pair and she'll be whipped into shape."

Emotion: auguar humour. Image: Queen Nzinga in her most dominant stance.

"She'll help, too."

Image: Captain on ornate accel couch, a crown on her head. Beside it a similar couch, empty except for a crown on the seat.

What?

Emotion: Need for fulfillment

WHAT?

But the image faded. The big auguar turned to licking the claws on his left front paw, his augment inaccessible.

Natalia frowned to herself. *Well, that's a new one. My auguar is using Protocol 17-B on me.*

2. NEW TECH

Natalia surveyed the group assembled in *NightHawk's* mess/lounge area. The viewscreens showed Arborea, floating blue, white, and green in a void spattered with stars. "Just like old times. It's good to have the crew back together again. Just a quick jaunt to the embassy, and then we start our new mission."

"Meerrrow."

"With a few new additions. Nzinga and Major Rowell, welcome to the *NightHawk's* roster."

The Space Arm pilot inclined her head, her demeanor returned to its usual polish.

"I guess you wonder why I gathered you together."

Andrew snorted. "No, we don't. Why do you always say that old movie line?"

She gave him a short glare. "To give everyone a pleasant moment of light humour and familiar atmosphere before I blow your space boots off."

He sat back, his arms folded. "Impress me."

She sighed. "When he was fourteen I could write it off as teenage rebellion. I suppose now I have to admit it was a failure of parenting."

As the chuckle died, she laid both hands on the table in front of her and put on a serious face. "I think you're going to be impressed with this one. It's no secret that Freighty has a new ship design for us. Now you get to find out what's new. And boy, is it new. Mr. Lundeen, would you do the honours?"

The Chief Engineer hitched his chair forward. "With pleasure, Ma'am. Here's the situation. We all know how the Otherwhere Sphere works. Once it's up to speed, it basically stays in Otherwhere, and the ship attached to it just has to reach Light Transfer Velocity, at about point two Light Speed, to make the switch into Otherwhere. On the flip side, you drop below point two LS and it kicks you back out. Now, Freighty is rolling along at 0.8 lights in re-ti. We have discovered that a ship leaving him to go back to Sol, also doing 0.8, can pop straight into Otherwhere. Big advantage. But so far indications have been that you can't pop back out again unless you decel to below Light Transfer Velocity: zero point two lights."

Andrew was frowning. "What if you just shut off your Otherwhere Sphere?"

The engineer gave a twisted grin. "We won't know that until somebody tries it. Would you?"

11

"Hmm...probably not."

"Smart lad. But now we come to Freighty's Otherwhere Sphere design, the one that's in *Diablo*. It's slightly different, and up to now, it hasn't been obvious how. Of course, nobody ever thought to put two spheres in the same ship. What would be the point?" The engineer grinned. "The point, it turns out, is that if two Otherwhere Spheres are connected, you can exit Otherwhere at any speed above LT velocity."

Second Engineer Fiona B'kosa was frowning. "But why would anyone want to do that? It would almost double the construction costs, and for what advantage?"

He nodded. "The main benefit is for long-haul ships. They can get up to LT velocity, kick into Otherwhere, accelerate to a couple of Lights velocity, exit, and coast in re-ti at that speed for as long as they like. No Otherwhere Willies. Possibly no time distortion; we're not sure about that yet. As long as they pop back into Otherwhere for their decel, it's like they never left. Like they keep a bubble of Otherwhere around them. And there's no extra construction cost if you join two ships with spheres together."

Andrew rubbed his hands together in glee. "And *Nighthawk's* sphere?"

"Freighty has done three different tune-ups over the past few years. He must have done the needed mods, because now he says we can experiment."

Andrew's eyes lit up, but Natalia cleared her throat before he could speak. "Don't get any hifalutin' ideas. Our assignment is very simple. We head out for the Factory, latched together. We enter Otherwhere as usual. The only difference is that instead of decelerating to point two light speed and then having to catch up to Freighty, who travels at point eight, we exit Otherwhere right beside him, so to speak, at a velocity of dead on point eight just like he is. Saves us about two months and tonnes of fuel."

Second Engineer B'kosa punched her right fist into her left hand. "Wickering wombats, when do we leave?"

Natalia had been looking forward to that question, because she wanted to see their reactions. "Andrew, will you answer that?"

He grinned. "As soon as we pick up the barwolves."

There was dead silence. Then First Officer Jones spoke up hesitantly. "Have I missed a joke somewhere?"

Natalia chuckled. "No, Adrian, you have not. Freighty has asked for seven barwolves, carefully chosen. Andrew has the specs, and I'm sure they give him some data upon which to make a guess, but that's what we're waiting for. Andrew, can you tell us anything?"

He shrugged. "Nothing certain, that's for sure. He's asked for two triads and one of the merger types like Brindle. I'd say he doesn't care what kind of triads, because he wants the barwolves themselves to choose."

"And he's right." Natalia surveyed the room. "These will be the first barwolves to take on a combined mission with humans. We have no idea how they will make the choice, but it's important that they make it. No paternalistic colonial attitudes from humans.

"Once they get here, Andrew will test them against Freighty's qualifications, and if they pass, they'll be our partners. I hesitate to say 'crew' because we don't know how they'll fit in."

Toni looked up from communicating with Nzinga. "Do you think Brindle will come?"

"I doubt it. Our personal friends in the barwolf population are a rather separate group, and Brindle is very important where one is. We assume the barwolves have their own way of choosing. We don't know how their society works. It could be completely random."

Andrew held up open hands. "Brindle and one's gestalt will make the original presentation to the larger group. We're not too worried about contaminating the general population anymore, because we've learned that they have been communicating with each other all along. As far as we can figure it, every barwolf on the planet knows about the secret lab, the kidnapped barwolves and our human/barwolf gestalt work. All of it. In fact, I'm getting the impression that one of their ways of dealing with trauma like our group experienced at the lab is to share it, thus spreading the impact around among the whole population and taking the damage away from the victims."

Toni chuckled. "That might explain Morissa's thorniest question. She can't figure out how those barwolves who had been through such a terrible prolonged experience could rebound so fast. How they could associate without rancour with Joachim, who had been one of their torturers. I think we have things to learn from them."

"So, when we leave for the Factory, we're taking seven barwolves with us?"

Natalia nodded. "Yes, Alison, and the two ships will be joined together. That changes everything."

The pilot grinned. "I don't have to spend two months cooped up with the lovebirds."

Toni busied herself with Nzinga's fur, but Andrew just grinned. "That's right. And you'll be able to work with Toni and the barwolves on some exercises Freighty sent me. The real Freighty, not our Micha the Mouse avatar. You'll be able to figure out from the nature of the practices what our eventual assignment will look like."

Natalia nodded. "And that's it. The rest of you are dismissed to your regular inflight duties. The Auxiliary Flight Crew stays to meet with the Micha avatar to discuss details."

3. SPACE SUITS

When the regular crew had departed, Natalia opened her augment to the avatar. "Come on out, Mister Mouse."

Micha the Mouse, in full spacesuit, appeared on the main viewscreen. "Hi, fellow crewmembers."

"Hi, Freighty." Natalia leaned back in her chair. "So, what have you got for us?"

The toon morphed into his usual shorts-and-shoes outfit, wriggling his shoulders as if they were stiff. "Glad to get that outfit off. It's very constricting."

Andrew scoffed. "You mean it uses up extra computing power."

"That's right, and I need all my intelligence to match up to you powerful lot."

"Right." The ensign gestured with open hands. "Well?"

"Well, what?"

"What the captain said. We need everything Freighty has for us."

"You've got my last update from the boss." The toon turned to Natalia. "Did you tell them everything?"

"Yes, but I'm sure they have questions."

"Fire away."

"This is a variation on a standard ship roster." Alison popped a diagram up on the viewscreen. "Four officers of descending rank and a crew of six."

Micha nodded. "That wasn't a question."

"But you didn't disagree."

"I have no information, one way or the other."

The squadron leader shrugged. "Fair enough."

Toni looked at the diagram. "Six barwolves of equal ability as the crew? No specialization? That would seem to indicate they're all doing the same duties."

Andrew nodded. "Or two triads doing two different jobs."

Image: six barwolves spreading out, all making the same motions.

Natalia sat up straighter. "That's right, Chakka. But I've never heard of a ship that the crew all did the same thing."

Toni amplified the image. "That looks more like a Commando squad. Six independent troopers, each on his own."

Andrew laughed. "Which would mean six spaceships." Then he frowned. "Freighty? I thought you said there was only one new ship."

"Freighty definitely uses the singular when he is talking about it."

Natalia thought back. "My orders from Admiral Mira definitely said, 'Proceed to Factory 4-80 and take command of the new ship.' Ship, singular."

Andrew had the blank look he got when he was deep in his augment. Finally he stirred. "I just checked the exercises I'm supposed to run. Definitely slanted towards squadron maneuvers."

"Well, it's a waste of time to speculate, because Freighty will tell us when we need to know." Natalia focused on her son. "For the moment, what do those exercises tell us that would indicate a need for barwolves?"

"I'll have to look deeper."

The Mouse avatar posed with one finger against his cheek. "Of course, not needing space suits in an emergency will be useful."

Natalia frowned. "What do you mean?"

It was Freighty's turn to look surprised. "It was all in the report."

"What report?"

Freighty smiled ruefully. "It seems we've had a slipup. Two of your Marines, Kirstina Zuyeva and James Campbell, went topside while they were closing down the underground lab. They found barwolf tracks in the moon dust. It seems Brindle had gone walkabout. Here, look at this."

Natalia watched the video with growing concern. "Why didn't they tell us?"

Andrew snorted. "Bykov."

The toon's eyebrows disappeared under his cap. "Their commanding officer, I believe?"

"Not an imaginative sort." Natalia sighed. "He never thought to ask them about it, just shipped it along with the rest of the reports. They never mentioned it, because the topic never came up and they had every right to assume we already knew. So barwolves can exist comfortably in vacuum for at least ten minutes."

Freighty nodded. "Apparently some whales on Earth can last as long as two hours without a breath. I want to take a look at their eye structure. They must have a sealing membrane of some sort."

Alison laughed. "Morissa is going to be so mad she missed that. I bet these adaptations have to do with going underwater. Barwolves are too dense to float. We made jokes about them walking to get from island to island. What if that's true?"

It was time to bring the meeting back on topic. Natalia raised her voice just that touch required. "So that makes them good spacers. What's the main reason Freighty wants them?"

Freighty looked around the group. "Nothing about barwolves in the latest briefing from the Main Man. Any guesses?"

Glances slid to Andrew. He shrugged. "Gotta be something to do with augments and Otherwhere. It hasn't slipped my notice that the Auxiliary crew has six barwolf crew but only two pilots, one organic auguar and one barwolf whose specialty is merging groups. My guess is that Alison, Toni, Nzinga and the One who Merges will form the primary gestalt headquartered in that suspiciously empty supply room just aft of our chart room, and the six other barwolves will form a gestalt to crew the vessel."

Lundeen flipped up a finger for attention. "Communication?"

Andrew rubbed his chin. "Most action in re-ti with this sort of formation is close-in fleet maneuvers, so no time lag." He glanced at Micha on the screen. "Might I surmise that barwolf communication has some sort of advantage in Otherwhere?"

The mouse grinned. "Practically instantaneous up to three parsecs. Maybe much more."

"First guess, then, is that we have an auxiliary that has instant communication with the mother ship, no matter when or where."

Natalia nodded. "An Interplanetary Personnel Carrier is bringing our new crew up to meet us tomorrow, so we'll go with what we have at that point. Crew accommodation will be the main challenge. We have little idea what barwolves need, long term. The IPC will be bringing food supplies, too. Toni, Andrew and Alison can bunk in *Diablo,* and I hope the One who Merges will spend one's time with them, working on the control room gestalt. That frees up two cabins in *NightHawk* for the two triads. I don't know how *NightHawk* will communicate with them to open doors and that sort of practicality..."

"Ma'am...?"

"Yes, *NightHawk.*"

"Now that you mention it, one new application in my recent download from the factory is a rather interesting com module."

"How convenient. Thinks of everything, doesn't he? Crack it open and try some organic communication with Nzinga."

Andrew nodded. "Give us an hour or so, Captain, and we'll have a report."

"Don't spend too much time on it. As I keep saying, once the new crew gets on board tomorrow, many questions will be answered."

As they filed out, Alison lingered. "I don't suppose we'll be leaving orbit soon, will we?"

"Looking for some time with a certain Planetary Coordinator before we head out? No. You have to take your Harrier back to Barwolf Base. That's the best I can do. One night, load the crew, and up you come." She nailed the pilot with an accusing finger. "You're starting to sound like a woman in love. Don't let it interfere with your mission."

"Wouldn't dream of it, ma'am."

"But if your route down to base should require an overnight stop in the capital city, nobody would care."

"Thank you, Captain. I'll be off, then."

Natalia smiled. "I thought you might." She watched the tall, slim woman stride off down the slideway, a touch of envy tinging her thoughts. *I must be getting soft, giving her extra time for nothing other than emotional gratification.* She sighed to herself. *Some people have all the luck.*

I recall you stating once that luck had little to do with your future.

And since when did you start quoting me to myself...emotion: dismay. NightHawk, don't tell me you've downloaded Protocol 17-B. Aren't you far beyond that?

I never miss an opportunity to increase my value to the crew, ma'am. And yes, I am further advanced than most of that protocol. However, some of the philosophical background and overall objectives were enlightening.

Which leads you to now interfere with my life?

Only when it is for the good of you and the crew, ma'am.

Emotion: resignation. I can't argue with that, NightHawk. Carry on.

Aye, ma'am.

Things have come to a pretty pass when my ArIn starts giving me advice.

Maybe you just need to get laid, ma'am.

NightHawk! 17-B never had that kind of language in it.

If your frustration is affecting your relationships with the crew...

This conversation is closed.

At least the damned ArIn knew when to be silent.

* * *

First thing the next morning Natalia called the Auxiliary Flight Team together again. "All right, folks. I know you're dying to get your Flight Centre put together. It would be nice to have the hardware laid out before the recruits arrive this afternoon. When we have the whole crew together we can flick the switch."

The crew filed down the corridor to the storage area just aft of the chart room and gathered in a loose bunch to one side, awaiting orders. A pile of crates and boxes filled half the space. "You can set this out any way you like, but Freighty suggests a circle facing the centre." She pointed. "That flat container over there folds out into an augmental graphic matrix, which will be the focal point."

Andrew strode over and looked down at the nondescript package. "Specs?"

"You put it at the physical focus of a gestalt, and it collects and justifies group input and modifies the augment signals to create a unified VR image of the image being discussed. It firms and refines the image re-ti, feeding back data about scale and velocities and that sort of thing. Freighty suggested you start with one viewscreen, so Micha can coach you on the setup."

Toni strode to the pile of cartons. "Let's get going."

Natalia nodded. "I'll leave you to it." She indicated the Second Engineer. "Fiona will see to any hardwired connections to the ship. Specialist Fraser is here to help if you need any muscle."

A hum of busy activity arose as she left, satisfied. *It's always nice to set an assignment and know you can walk away and forget about it. Come to think of it, this whole ship runs like that, nowadays. Nothing for me to do but worry about...whatever.*

Concern for your own emotional wellbeing is a valid objective, ma'am.

My emotions are quite well, thank you, and if you want to keep being alive, you'll stay out of it.

Emotion: humour. As you wish, ma'am.

She opened her augment. *Reference: ArIn troubleshooting. Reference: sense of humour. Reference: exaggerated. Reference: steps towards repair.*

Ma'am, a captain is not allowed to...

Reference: humour. Reference: inability to recognize.

NightHawk gave a loud and very realistic raspberry. Then her line went dead.

Huh! It's a sad day when the captain has to take satisfaction in having outwitted her ArIn. I'd better get my act together.

4.   BARWOLF ACROBATICS

To Natalia's surprise, that afternoon when she contacted the IPC transporting the barwolves up from the planet, it was Joachim Perez who answered.

Hello, Joachim. Are you on escort duty?

Correct, ma'am. I've been working with them, and wanted to make the handoff in person.

I didn't realize your augment was up to complicated communication on the organic channels.

Not with an individual. But a trio's gestalt is all it takes for them to communicate with me. I just talk, and they can understand fine. We've had this team at the Base for a week, now, so I got lots of practice. The One who Merges is a real corker.

Good. We'll transfer our new crewmembers to NightHawk as soon as we match velocity, get them comfortable in the environment and then blast for the embassy.

The One who Merges is eager for the new experience, which means that one's whole gestalt is eager.

Does one have a name?

It's counter to their culture, of course, but this barwolf would be identified as 'the one who merges the clans that live west of the flat mountain with three chimneys to the south.'

Image: a tall mesa with three pillars of ochre rock standing just off one end.

Natalia shrugged. *Emotion: uncertainty. We need a name so we can communicate one's individuality to the deaf-and-dumb humans one will come into contact with. Perhaps this time human methods have to prevail. Let's wait until we meet. Maybe something will occur to me."*

Emotion: humour. That will be fine, ma'am. I'm sure you'll think of something.

Natalia decided not to ask for an explanation of the joke. *Prime. We'll be coming alongside to port in about ten minutes. Tell your pilot I want him on com for the docking.*

Roger, ma'am. Here he is.

Once the airlocks were joined and the seals checked, Natalia brought Chakka and the Auxiliary Flight Crew to meet the visitors.

Perez was the first one through the doorway, his lanky form awkwardly managing the flip of gravity. Andrew caught his arm to steady him. Alison soared across behind him with practiced ease.

"Welcome to the new right-side-up, Joachim."

The scientist stabilized himself. "Thanks." He looked over his shoulder. "I'm not sure how they're going to take that."

Natalia gestured to the team behind her. "In gestalt with the experienced hands, Mr. Perez."

He nodded. "Thank you, ma'am. I was hoping you'd say that."

"Thought about the problem already, had you?"

"Oh, yes, ma'am. My job is to ease their transition to the new environment in any way I can. Dr. Goodall was very clear on that."

"Well, then. Bring your charges out, and we'll see how it goes."

"Aye, ma'am." *Emotion: welcome.*

Emotion: agreement.

Around the corner of the IPC hallway stepped the tallest, slimmest barwolf Natalia had ever seen. One was coal-black, with an uneven line of white splotches starting at one's chest and running over one's left shoulder like a carelessly-tossed shawl, tapering out in smaller blots down the spine. The creature walked with the graceful teeter of a model on a runway.

Natalia remembered to close her mouth. *Emotion: warm greeting.*

Emotion: thanks and anticipation.

"Okay, folks, I think the best thing to do is get Patches across and let one bring one's companions later, however their gestalt wishes to do it. I'll invite one to join our gestalt to ease the gravity transition."

Andrew was grinning. "One couldn't be called anything else."

Emotion: agreement. She turned to the barwolf. *Emotion: question/idea?*

The barwolf responded by reaching out to the *NightHawk* gestalt. There was a brief moment of disorientation, and then one's mind blended with theirs. One made a quick survey of the members, somehow classifying and ordering them. Natalia could feel their gestalt firming somehow: more solid, more together.

Emotion: satisfaction, readiness to proceed.

Question: What did you just do, Patches?

Image: humans and auguar standing in loose group. Image: Humans and auguar fitting together in tight group with barwolf in the middle.

Emotion: agreement.

Question: Patches?

Image: human shirt with different-coloured patches on it. Image: black barwolf with white patches on shoulder.

Emotion: understanding.

Alison spoke aloud for the benefit of the *NightHawk* crew. "Patches holds an aura of deep experience in augment control. We can communicate best by speaking normally and enriching our ideas with images."

General emotion: agreement.

"Thank you, Major. It will make it easier for those of us not so familiar with barwolf gestalts." Natalia turned to the barwolf. "Patches, are you ready to come across? I gather Joachim has explained the process to you."

Emotion: uncertainty, trust. Image: barwolf sprawled on ceiling, legs in all directions. Emotion: humour.

"Fine. We'll try not to embarrass ourselves. Nzinga, you're the one with four feet. Will you take the lead?"

Emotion: agreement.

The young auguar took a running leap, twisted in the air, and landed beside the barwolf. *Image: barwolf watching auguar closely.* Then the cat made the return journey.

Image: three steps, push with right rear paw, twist, land, two steps, stop. This image played in the gestalt several times.

Emotion: eager anticipation.

Emotion: urge to try.

Natalia waited with some trepidation, although the gravity was light and the barwolf was armoured.

Patches took three steps and launched, but Natalia could see that when one was in the air the twist was not going to be enough. She watched, frozen, but then Toni moved. Just as Patches was about to land, the Commando stepped in and brought her hip against the barwolf's shoulder. Instead of falling, the creature bounced perfectly upright, Toni's hand on ones neck to steady one.

Patches bent ones knees and touched the Commando's leg with a paw. Toni reached out for the traditional plate scratch.

Then the barwolf turned and looked back into the IPC and disappeared from the human gestalt. Natalia could tell from Nzinga's stance that she was still in contact.

A line of barwolves trotted along the IPC hallway. As the first one, a smaller female, neared the auguar, she picked up speed, her feet placed where the first barwolf had walked.

Seeing their intention, Natalia snapped her fingers and flipped her hands in the Commando signal to spread out. The humans moved to the walls, and the first barwolf launched herself. She landed with a stagger but soon stood firm. As her five companions followed, each one was smoother than the previous, and the last one, a big male, nailed it perfectly.

Emotion: awe and appreciation!
Emotion: complacency.

Andrew was frowning and nodding. "As one learns, they all learn. That last jumper had already practiced the jump seven times. I wonder how that works with no muscle memory. Maybe..." his voice and his augment faded in thought.

Natalia motioned Alison to precede her, and they moved into the mess/lounge area. It was crowded, but the humans used the chairs and the barwolves expressed satisfaction with the square of heavy carpet laid for them in one corner.

"I don't understand." Alison's head was to one side. "Why did you make such a production about that simple transition?"

Natalia scratched her cheek. "Not sure. It just seemed like a good idea."

"Sure," Andrew pointed. "Exactly what a certain barwolf wanted. To merge with our gestalt and then bring one's own gestalt in, one at a time."

Natalia tried to think back to the actual moment. "It all seemed perfectly normal. Are you suggesting Patches influenced me?"

"It's possible." Andrew made a stacking motion with his hands. "They may have different levels of communications, like humans do withwords, vocal expression and body language."

"We'd better learn to recognize them."

"Working on it, ma'am."

"That's your job, Ensign." She turned to the crew. "The support module with the new crew's food and equipment will mate with *NightHawk's* portside airlock. Let's get the supplies transferred, get these barwolves fitted in the quadruped accel couches and get a move on. Until we get to the embassy, we have no idea what our real mission is, and I don't like not knowing. Dismissed."

Perez made the flip back to his transport without a hitch, turning to grin at them as he closed the airlock. "I'm sure you'll have an interesting journey."

Once the support module was attached to port, they dogged *Diablo* down in her usual spot over the starboard airlock and lit the candle towards the planet Xeta and the embassy, on a curving route out of the ecliptic to avoid the Inner Asteroids.

5. ALPHA CENTAURI

Once the ship was accelerating at a steady one G, the human crew settled into their usual patterns and the Auxiliary Flight Crew began to create routines for themselves. At supper that night, Natalia asked Andrew how it was going.

He sniffed. "You wouldn't believe how well."

The captain looked over at the barwolves, who lay in scattered piles on their matting in the mess lounge. "They look relaxed."

"They have a right to be." He turned to face her straight on. "I suppose we should have predicted it, but it's another matter when it actually happens."

"A cultural proclivity towards cooperation."

"A basic species characteristic of cooperation." He swept a hand around the room. "They're outnumbered here. The general atmosphere is one of businesslike cooperation and calm competence. You can't fool them. In this crew, it's real. So how do they act?"

Natalia nodded. "And I guess that puts the pressure on you."

"Oh, yes. I have to make sure I don't mess up the routines I start, because there's no one else to blame if they don't work."

She looked around the lounge. "Well, if everything is settled, is anyone in the mood for some new information?"

Every head turned her way.

"Hmm. Not quite so relaxed." She stood. "Listen up, then. There's been a great deal of secrecy about our eventual mission. Part of that is because of security, but also there's a lack of information on the source of the problem. However, this crew and our new ship were created especially for this duty, so we have a certain amount of information, which you all have a right to know."

Andrew shrugged. "Alpha Centauri."

"Good guess. Want to tell us why and what?"

He grinned and looked around the room. "Anybody?"

Nelson snorted. "Don't tell me we're investigating the Centauri Triangle Mystery."

Seeing the blank looks, Natalia translated. "Reference the Bermuda Triangle on Earth. Disappearing ships and airplanes, odd magnetic readings, useless compasses. Food for sailor superstitions. The flashier media has made the logical jump to the Alpha C problem. Over the years, nobody has been able to get a probe to survive long enough to send back much information. They all seem to disappear, usually before they even get there."

Alison frowned. "Manned missions?"

"Nobody's dared to send one. Yet."

"So this is a legitimate problem, not just superstition."

"Seems to be. And our mission is to investigate."

Andrew snorted. "Galah guts. 'To boldly go where no one has survived before.' That sounds like us, all right."

"Precisely. Space Arm has wanted more data for decades. The combination of Freighty's know-how and the barwolves' gestalt gave them an excuse to send us."

"I suppose we should be flattered. The navigation looks good, anyway."

Natalia regarded the pilot. "Want to explain that?"

Alison brought a graphic up on the viewscreen. "The three stars form a triangle. Barnard and Alpha Centauri are just over six light years apart, but Sol and Alpha C are only four and a half. It stands to reason that if we were headed for Sol, there is a spot on our trajectory where we are closest to Alpha C. Freighty just happens to be almost at that point."

"Right. When we're finished at Freighty, we have less than four Light Years to get to Alpha C."

"Except for the minor matter of a point eight light speed vector towards Sol. Freighty hasn't started his decel yet, has he?"

Lundeen was staring at the image. "That's a rather open-ended mission with a lot of what-ifs."

"I'm sure Freighty has been able to collect more data than that. After all, he's apparently designed this new ship specifically to counter the problems he expects us to meet."

"His stats in that respect are pretty good."

"Yeah, but nobody bats a thousand. I don't want to be the one to spoil his record."

"But why won't he tell us what the ship design is?"

She shook her head. "I know this might sound paranoid, but Space Arm can't be sure the problem isn't caused by intelligent beings, even humans, who may have undisclosed access to our communications. They don't want any information leaks. We don't need to know yet, so we don't know."

Andrew tossed up his hands as he stood. "Sounds like Space Arm, all right." He strode towards the airlock to his ship.

6. ENROUTE TO THE EMBASSY

Natalia was busy at her desk in the chartroom the next day when Micha the Mouse appeared on her viewscreen. "Got a moment?"

She put down her enterpad. "For you, my friend, always."

The mouse bowed and doffed an Elizabethan-looking cap. "Would that were so, my lady."

"Now it's Shakespeare, is it? What gives?"

The toon returned to his usual form. "A puzzling problem."

"Go on."

"You know that my statistical analysis can dig deeper than even the best of humanity's ArIns can."

"Of course."

"And you know that space is a large and dangerous place, and many things can go wrong."

"I do."

"And I'm sure you are aware that over the years a certain number of ships have set out to cross the void between Sol and Barnard and have disappeared, never to return."

"It happens...and now I'm supposed to put the two ideas together. You always do this. Why don't you just tell me?"

The mouse grinned. "It's a technique I learned from Andrew's mother. Mariel always said that people who come up with ideas themselves are much more likely to believe them."

"True. And if you carefully select the data they receive, you can have quite an influence on that decision."

"Ah, you always attribute such terrible motives to me."

"It's a survival skill. But we're getting off topic. What has your superior analytical power decided about the success rate of human trans-galactic travel?"

"Guess."

"All right. The incidence of failure is far higher than the odds say it should be, falling at least one standard deviation outside whatever norm you have decided on. Otherwise you wouldn't be telling me this. What have we got, pirates?"

The toon scratched his temple with a fat forefinger. "That would be the best solution."

"Why the best?"

"Because if that's the problem, we have a newly-formed, potent, high-speed unit we can send out to find them and bring them to heel."

"And if it isn't the problem, we have a scientific anomaly that we don't understand and no data with which to speculate."

The toon tilted his head left, then right. "To say we have no data would be an exaggeration. I have some ideas, but nowhere near enough information to make a reasonable guess. Our discovery of something similar but much more serious happening in the Alpha Centauri system is worrisome, in case the same thing is happening here. What little data we got back from our probes suggested some kind of electromagnetic force was used against them. The version of PermaSkin on the new ship has the ability to shut its receptors off and reflect just about everything. It means the crew is blind in re-ti, but not to augment communication. However, at the moment we're following Occam's Razor, and it leads us to pirates."

She eyed him suspiciously. "You didn't just think this up as an excuse to send us on a little training mission before we hit the big time?"

"I assure you, I have passed my calculations on to the Space Arm Tactical Branch, and they agree with me. I have been suspicious for several years, but it wasn't until the possibility of doing something about it arose that I made the effort to do the analysis. It took a large percentage of my processing power for several days, slowing down production and extending several deadlines."

She turned her hands palms up. "So we have a new mission. Instead of chasing down space ghosts, it's old-fashioned pirates. Between here and Sol, I assume?"

"That would be a good place to start."

"Do we have any idea what kind of ships they have?"

"We'll have a full briefing later. Tactical Branch has some ideas, and of course..."

"...you have superior data but you don't want to hurt their feelings. When will I get my official change of orders?"

The mouse smiled. "Space Arm works in its own mysterious ways. Hopefully the message will get here before you're ready for your mission."

"Dynamite. Well, forewarned is forearmed. I'll put the gestalt on the problem. Do you have any other data for me? Number of ships, frequency of attacks, that sort of thing?"

Micha shuffled his feet. "Not wanting to seem manipulative, but..."

"Of course. You want our unprompted ideas in case we come up with something you didn't. So shall we work on it while we're travelling, and compare notes when we get to you?"

The mouse broke into a wide grin. "What a marvellous idea! How do you think of these things?"

"Sure, sure. Well, you can pass on to the real Freighty that your machinations have been successful as usual, and the *NightHawk* will throw her full resources, including the new additions, at the problem. We have a couple of days for a preliminary study. When we hit the embassy, we'll consult with our sources there. We'll concentrate on it once we're headed in your direction. It's good to have a re-li problem to practice on during a long journey."

"I hoped you would feel that way. I'll pass the word along."

"Thank you. And Mouse?"

"Yes, Captain?"

"Likewise, I expect you not to listen in on our deliberations. We don't want to taint your thought processes, either."

The toon saluted. "Aye, Captain. A reasonable suggestion." He reached up, pulling a shade down across the screen until it went black.

Natalia sat a long time, reviewing the conversation to make sure she had all the subtext figured out. Freighty and humanity made a great team, but acting as chaperone between the two could be wearing.

* * *

She started the gestalt on the problem that evening. However, with *NightHawk's* acceleration, it was only a three-day run to the Embassy, orbiting at Lagrange 3 of Xeta, the closest planet outsystem, so a new obstacle soon intervened. As they approached, she called a meeting.

"Here's the next problem: the mob of humans at the embassy." She surveyed the Auxiliary Crew, opening her augment fully. "We have to bring these barwolves into an environment with a few thousand human minds, hundreds of which have organic augments at various levels. When barwolves gather in groups over about forty, they go into a killing frenzy." She motioned to the viewscreen. "We have Morissa online to help. Any ideas?"

Andrew held out both hands, as if balancing two objects. "Either we stay out of gestalt completely, hoping to duck any problem, or we go in with full gestalt, using our combined mental power to protect our new members."

Toni reached over and slid a hand between his. "Or we send them in with only their own gestalt, because they know far better than we do how to handle the situation."

28

"That's pretty clear. Morissa?"

After a brief time lag the scientist shrugged. *"I have nothing to add, except that the one you call Patches seems to have a lot of experience with this sort of thing. Brindle definitely deferred to that one, even in gestalt."*

"Fair enough." She opened her augment specifically to Patches. "What do you think?"

Image: barwolves huddled together, humans throwing rocks at them. Rocks bouncing off.

Image: barwolves huddled together, group of humans throwing larger rock at them. Rock breaks through, barwolves scattering.

Image in background: mass of humans preparing to throw huge rock.

Emotion: question?

"That pretty well sums it up. And if it all goes wrong, we have seven raging barwolves loose in the embassy."

Emotion: wry humour. "Or several hundred raging humans loose in the embassy. Or both."

"Thank you, Andrew. You always have such an optimistic approach."

Emotion: agreement. Emotion: hope for good result.

"Me too."

"I've already talked with Brindle about it." Morissa frowned in thought. *"I think what one is telling me is that the barwolves do have a method for blocking the frenzy effect."*

Alison chimed in. "Yes, Brindle did something last month when we were trying to get the clans around Mother Lode clear of the bomb blast."

"I gather this is similar." The scientist spread her hands in a covering motion. *"It just requires complete cooperation from their gestalt. These two triads have been working on it the whole week they were with us, and Patches is confident that they can handle quite a few humans at one time, especially if most of them are deaf and dumb."*

Natalia regarded the viewsreen. "That explains some of their exercises on board. So you're confident but not positive."

"That is correct."

"Then we will proceed as outlined."

"Good luck, NightHawk. Happy hunting."

"Thanks, Morissa."

She turned to the crew. "We ease in slowly, dock NightHawk in an empty bay down near the stern of the *Unicorn* where there aren't many people, disembark when our crew feels comfortable and play it by ear from that point." Natalia accessed *NightHawk's* nav. "We'll be at the embassy in seven hours, and we get there in the middle of their day watch. That'll give us time to arrange things. I'll talk to the ambassador. Unless he has other plans, we can stand off a couple of kilometres for a few hours and slip in once they have acclimatized. Be as inobtrusive as possible, so we don't cause any adverse reaction from the humans."

Alison tilted her head. "I have a feeling Alfino will want to take a more ceremonial approach."

Natalia sighed. "You know him better than I do." She glanced around the table. "All right. We have seven hours. Let's talk about what we do if Alfino has other plans, then I'll call him up for a chat."

"In that case, I suggest you make an appointment."

"Why? Is he busy with something?"

Alison shook her head ruefully. "You may have noticed; the ambassador's former Chief Aide got promoted to a different planet. The new man is called Enderby, and he comes up through the Diplomatic Corps. He is not quite so...relaxed as Jackson. In Enderby's world the ambassador does not answer his own com calls."

"Ah." Natalia grinned. "Already had a run-in with him?"

Alison's eyes narrowed ever so slightly. "I do not have run-ins with aides, whether they are chiefs of the variety or not."

"Of course. But a mere Space Arm Captain does not just call up the ambassador for a chat these days?"

"And neither does a mere major, even if she is a Squadron Commander." Alison's demeanor relaxed, and she grinned. "She just waits until after hours."

"Ah, the disadvantage of the rigid mind."

Alison shrugged. "He's easy enough to get around. We'll have him whipped into shape in no time. When do you want to talk to Alfino?"

Natalia regarded the major. "Alison, when you're Admiral of the Fleet, will you remember the little people who befriended you on your way up?"

She was rewarded with a chuckle from Andrew and Toni and a look of complete shock on the face of her victim.

Before Alison could recover her aplomb enough to respond, Andrew clapped the pilot on the shoulder. "She'll be too busy becoming Ambassador to make it to Admiral."

Toni nodded. "Not to worry, Alison. We won't tell anybody. We'll let it come as a pleasant surprise to them when you take over."

The colour was returning to the Major's cheeks. "Will I remember you? Believe me, when I'm in charge, I will know who to send on the slog missions to the loneliest outposts with the most boring inhabitants."

Andrew nudged Toni. "Notice that she didn't deny it."

Nzinga gave her usual "Meyraow," and slid over to sit with regal poise beside Alison, leaning gently against her knee. *Emotion: approval.*

Alison laid a hand on the auguar's head. "There. The only one in the room that counts gives her royal approval, so I guess I'm a shoo-in. You will all treat me with appropriate respect."

Natalia chuckled. "And right now, the appropriate thing for you to do is use your clout in the Ambassador's Office to make me an appointment to talk to him at his earliest convenience."

Alison stood and saluted. "I will do so, ma'am." She did a perfect about-face, but as she was leaving she turned back. "Do you want me to soften him up for you ahead of time?"

"Shouldn't be necessary, but thanks for the thought. You are dismissed, Major."

Alison exited as if she were walking on a red carpet. The door whispered shut behind her.

Toni frowned. "How did she do that?"

Andrew grinned. "Technique. If you pause at the right spot in the doorway, the control changes to 'possible injury' mode and closes slower."

Natalia nodded. "And she did it on purpose. Just to prove a point."

Andrew glanced at his mother. "It would be less disturbing if I thought that conversation was all joking."

Natalia shrugged. "We have more pressing matters than choosing the next ambassador. Now, what happens if Alfino plans a song-and-dance show?"

* * *

Alfino had plans, although singing did not enter into the conversation. He stretched his arms as wide as the viewscreen, indicating his spacious office and the huge former carrier that surrounded it. *Natalia, this is a big moment. The first members of the Barwolf Nation are appearing at the Human Embassy. There has to be some sort of a ceremony or the newsfeeds will go wild screaming,*

31

'Coverup,' and my superiors will be right behind them for another pound of my flesh.

Natalia smiled. "I don't want to spoil your fun, Alfino, but I am worried about the barwolves."

He leaned back in his chair, staring up at the ceiling. *As you should be.* He regarded her out of the viewscreen. *But you have no idea what the effect on them will be.*

"On Arborea they have been dealing with the humans in small batches, but the immigrants have very low augment power, and we only expose one triad at a time, shielded by a human gestalt. They have defensive shielding, but we don't know if they can deal with the onslaught of several thousand people in a confined space. Perhaps a larger group will trigger their killing frenzy. We just don't know."

He smiled. *You know, Captain, you are at your most persuasive when you are threatening mayhem.*

"And when I'm discussing my field of command. I can pretend to know what I'm talking about."

Fair enough. Let's give your experience the benefit of the doubt. What can you do for me in terms of letting the barwolves as loose as they can handle for a ceremony?

She interlaced her fingers. "As it happens, the *NightHawk* gestalt has a few ideas."

I thought they might. Let's hear them...

7.   ARRIVAL

Natalia stretched in her accel couch until her joints cracked. Then she opened her augment to the ship's com. "Listen up, now. We have two hours at this velocity before we reach the embassy. *NightHawk* crew, please go to your operating positions. Auxiliary Flight Crew, take your barwolves to the Auxiliary Flight Centre and get your gestalt set up. I suggest you run through the different permutations we developed, so you can switch back and forth as circumstances dictate."

Acceptance filled the com, and Natalia relaxed as much as she could.

Over the next two hours the tension built in the recon sloop. Natalia went into gestalt with *NightHawk* and Chakka, listening for murmurs of the mass of augments ahead of them.

Andrew? We're getting the first sign of augment activity.

...a moment...yes, we've got it, now that our barwolf gestalt knows what to feel for.

There was no use asking more questions. When he had something, he'd tell her.

The background "noise" from the embassy slowly built. Natalia went on regular com. "We're half an hour out at this velocity. Pete, let's go into heavier decel a bit early."

She opened the ship's com. "All hands prepare for increased gravity. Increased decel in thirty seconds on my mark. Mark. Call the count, *NightHawk*."

Decel of one point five Gs in twenty seconds...

Decel in ten seconds...five...three, two, one, increase.

The engine note rose, and pressure built slowly to one point five.

"How is the new crew handling this, Andrew?"

"No problems, ma'am. In their minds they have all the space experience any barwolf ever had, and considering some of the earlier trips with the kidnappers, this is a piece of cake."

"Augment noise?"

"We've got them in their own gestalt at the moment. They're doing some kind of ritual. If I can get through to Patches without breaking the concentration..."

Emotion: satisfaction. Image: mass of humans throwing large softball at huddled barwolves. One barwolf jumps up and heads the ball away, then returns to huddle.

"Destination one kilometre insystem of the embassy in forty minutes, ma'am."

"Patches and Andrew, you're in charge on this one. Decel continuing unless you say otherwise."

Combined emotion: agreement

Andrew, which gestalt are you in?

Captain, this barwolf is an expert. I can slide in and out of their gestalt, and one can slip out and chat with me and hold the rest together with one hand behind one's back.

Image: barwolf trying to put paw behind one's own back. Emotion: humour.

See what I mean?

Well, when you're finished having a good time together, don't forget we're approaching a serious situation.

On it, ma'am.

Image: black barwolf touching captain's leg. Emotion: agreement.

Natalia dropped out of augment communication and glanced at her First Officer. "You reading that, Jones?"

"Loud and clear, ma'am. I must say, augment communication has cleared up recently."

"Something to do with Patches. One must be a specialist or expert or whatever their society has."

"Ma'am, I've been reading up on Dr. Goodall's research on termite, bee, and ant colonies. While there are certain basic similarities in this species, I'm sure the barwolves have a much more complex and versatile method of organizing their community actions."

"As we would expect from their level of intelligence."

"It seems to me some individuality is bound to emerge. ma'am."

"Today's evidence would seem to support your theory, First."

The First Officer gave one of his rare smiles. "Perhaps my time in the Outback is affecting my ability to think outside the box, ma'am."

"It's affecting all our abilities, Adrian, and mostly for the better."

"Five years ago I would have disagreed with you."

"Well, there you go. At least you've learned not to disagree with your captain."

"I wouldn't go that far, ma'am."

Alison frowned and looked around the *NightHawk's* bridge. Then she checked the crew augment channel. "First, does this crew feel like they're keyed up for a serious incident?"

Jones took a moment to scan. "They're all paying close attention, but 'keyed up' would not be the words I would use to describe them."

She opened the ship's com. "*NightHawk* crew, we're going onto yellow alert. Auxiliary Crew, stay as you were."

On yellow alert, ma'am.

Lundeen keyed his private augment. *Something up, ma'am?*

No, Chief. Everything is going too well. The crew seems ready, but I don't feel the usual tension. Am I just paranoid?

Emotion: chuckle. You've got a powerful barwolf gestalt working inside your ship, going into action with your crew for the first time. I think a mild paranoia from the captain would be reassuring at this moment.

Thanks, Nelson. We aim to please.

Andrew's augment broke in. *We've got activity, ma'am.*

Something wrong?

Not onboard. It's coming from the embassy.

What do you mean?

Emotion: chagrin. Something we never thought of. We're getting a reaction from a gestalt somewhere on the Unicorn. About thirty strong minds, sixty weaker. Either it's unfocussed fear, or they actually think the embassy is facing an augment attack. Can you get to the ambassador or the admiral or somebody and douse this? If a feedback loop gets established it could go through the ceiling in seconds.

If it's feedback, the only way to slow it is for us to drop our level of activity. Can you do that?

If we drop our level, we have less protection.

Patches, what experience do you have with this?

Image: mass of barwolves tearing at each other.

Prime. We learn something about the barwolf frenzy just when we don't need one.

"Jones, get me the embassy online. Pretoro and Mira both, if possible. If any aide tries to get in the way, slap him down."

"Aye, ma'am."

It didn't take long. *"Pretoro here. Admiral, this sounds like your bailiwick."*

Mira here. What's the problem, Captain?

She hastily explained the situation.

You mean we have a gestalt onboard that's going paranoid?

"It seems so, sir. We don't know whether it's your official anti-terrorist squad, or maybe a random group of naturally sensitive civilians."

I'm on it, Captain. Ambassador, I guarantee our security crew is better behaved than that. Mira disappeared from the channel.

35

How are things on your end, Captain?

"We were doing fine until this came up." She sent the emotion of humour through her augment. "It never occurred to us that the humans might go into a frenzy."

The ambassador snorted. *It should have occurred to me. I remember the Alien Invasion Hoax on Earth in 2135.*

"Revealing your age, sir."

I didn't say how old I was at the time. Humans are unpredictable beasts, and in groups they're worse.

"Well, I hope the admiral can get a handle on this one. We're damping down our gestalt to reduce the effect, but it's the same gestalt that's protecting the barwolves...no, wait a minute. I have an idea. Let me know if you have news. O'Rourke out."

Andrew, Patches, remember that separation of gestalts we practised? Barwolves apart from humans?

Emotion: agreement.

Emotion: agreement.

Do it. But this time have the barwolves set up a completely passive shell. We don't want these humans to know they're here. Surround them with a masking field from the NightHawk gestalt, based on the exercises we use when we have a new augment to tame. Can you do that?"

Combined emotion: agreement.

Request: wait.

Don't take all day.

She returned to the embassy com channel. "Dr. Pretoro, you still there?"

We haven't been torn to shreds by a mob of screaming humans, if that's what you mean.

"I don't know how someone who has seen the images of that barwolf massacre can joke about it."

A lame effort to ease the tension. How are we doing?

"No results yet. Anything from Admiral Mira?"

Nothing.

"I'm going to add my power to the *NightHawk* gestalt. O'Rourke out."

Embassy out.

She swung into the gestalt, feeling for the best place to add her support. *This doesn't feel so bad. What's going on?*

We've got it set up like you asked, ma'am. Patches is an absolute expert at this. My guess is that augments on the embassy are receiving nothing but human signals from out here. Sure, they may be suspicious, but there's nothing to suggest...whoa! Did you get that?

Natalia felt like she had been pushing against a wall, and suddenly it wasn't there. When she had regained her mental balance, she gathered the gestalt around her again. *Everybody all right? Where did the problem go?*

Image: black barwolf flat on floor, legs splayed out. Emotion: question?

I don't know, Patches. Maybe the Admiral Mira solved the problem. How are your people?

Emotion: cautious optimism.

Good. This feels much better. I'm going back on the blower to the embassy.

She connected with Dr. Pretoro again. Admiral Mira was there as well.

"Things a little calmer out there, Captain?"

"Admiral, sir, it got so calm so suddenly, we all fell on our faces. What happened?"

He snorted. *It took me a while, but we found them. A little shipload of religious fanatics just arrived. Came in from Sol re-ti on a slow boat. Thirty years. Third generation of selective breeding just growing up. Turns out their criteria for joining the mission was the ability to "sense the Flow of the Universe." You can imagine what that means. They thought the Beast had followed them from Sol and was attacking before they could settle in the Promised Land, or some such superstitious nonsense. I soon put a stop to that. But it occurred to me. Might I guess you have an augment expert in your pocket who might find these people rather interesting?*

Natalia chuckled. "I have a doctoral candidate with 'thesis' stars in his eyes. A story for another time. That little diversion turned up some new techniques. Our people of both species have got things very much under control, now. Coming in on our planned vector on schedule for your ceremony."

The Admiral laughed. *Nothing like a bit of pressure to induce quick thinking. See you in a couple of hours. Mira out...unless you've got anything for me, ambassador?*

"Thank you, Admiral. Please stand by with your honour guard."

More news bytes, both positive and original. The feeds will be ecstatic. Mira out.

Pretoro stayed on. *Captain O'Rourke, assuming nothing else holds us up, will your group be ready for a ceremony?*

37

"I'll tell the barwolves to put on something frilly, sir."

Hmm. I'm not sure you're joking. I'm leaving that up to you, but once you're dogged down, your ship will go on standby and your whole crew will attend. Do you have any problems with that?

"Quite the opposite, sir. Of course, I'm suspicious that you have some kind of publicity motive buried in there, but I'd like to keep my crew together as much as possible. Augment power deteriorates with distance. Don't be surprised at what you get from us. Or rather, what you don't get. We are holding a strong dampening exercise, rather like those you use when you get an augment upgrade, but several orders of magnitude stronger."

Sounds good to me. Message received on the grouping.

"Can you send me a visual of the reception area? We'll figure an appropriate formation for our cadre."

Will the barwolves be worried by an honour guard? Armed?

"Will the honour guard be worried by a Commando squad? Fully armed?"

Pretoro chuckled. *Oh, the news feeds are going to love this.*

"And I hate to bring this up, but I don't want any repeat performances. Nobody ever says anything about anti-barwolf sentiment. Is there any, and are you taking care of it?"

Yes, and yes. The honour guard won't be the only armed forces attending. They'll just be the only ones in sight. We're locked up tighter than a Venusian rock crab's bung hole down here.

"I just want one thing straight. When my Commandos are guarding the barwolves, we have been seconded to your office. We obey you only. If there's trouble, the Space Arm personnel had better be ready to duck. Do you follow?"

The ambassador mulled that over. *Now I know what Alison means.*

"Alison?"

She says she's never known such a nice bunch of people who could be so scary. Yes, I'll straighten the lines of command out with Admiral Mira. You do what you must to protect your charges. That's an order from me.

"Thank you, sir. We understand each other."

The ambassador swept a hand across his forehead. He murmured something as his augment slid out of the com; it might have been, *...and heaven help me if we don't.*

A course of satisfaction swept through her. *They want a Commando squad, they take what they get.*

* * *

38

When the passengers exited *NightHawk's* ventral airlock in the smaller loading bay Natalia had chosen, it might have been a ceremonial procession. But like many ceremonies, it had its roots in more serious maneuvers.

Specialist Fraser, in full atmo attack kit, came down the ramp first, his heavy machine gun at port arms. At his right shoulder prowled Toni Jacobs, her favourite rifle with its barrel sweeping. Nzinga slunk at his left in battle armour, her stare piercing beyond the humans arrayed before them, scanning the ship's nearby electronic systems.

The rest of the *NightHawk's* Commandos followed in two files, spreading out as they reached the hangar deck. Last came Captain O'Rourke in her dress whites, with Andrew and Chakka flanking her on one side, Major Rowell on the other.

When she reached the bottom of the ramp she stopped and the rest of her crew mirrored her perfectly. They all did an about face and looked back. Natalia's group split to either side, and the Red triad started down, followed by the Greens, marching in more perfect unison than any group of human soldiers could ever manage. When they were spread evenly down the ramp, they stepped aside and froze. Then Patches appeared at the top of the ramp and strolled down as if one didn't have a care in the world. One's cadre fell in behind one, and the barwolves and Natalia strode between the files of the Marine honour guard to where the ambassador, the admiral and various dignitaries waited.

Natalia stood to attention and saluted. "Ambassador Pretoro, Admiral Mira. May I introduce the representatives of the Barwolf Nation." She turned to Patches. "Honoured guests, this is the Planetary Community Ambassador to your System, Dr. Alfino Pretoro, and Admiral Mira of the Space Arm, which defends us all from those who wish us ill."

Patches stepped forward and touched each man's shin. Already prepared, they each scratched the barwolf's shoulder plate in the prescribed spot.

The ambassador raised his voice for the video feed. "Original citizens of Barnard's System and new members of the Planetary Community. Welcome to our embassy. It is the hope of our government and people that our two species can co-exist in harmony and cooperation, as we have already demonstrated in recent months."

Patches opened one's augment and began a series of images and emotions.

Andrew stepped forward to attract the cameras. "The One who Merges this small gestalt of representatives is communicating to those with organic augments the intentions of one's people to take their place in the gestalt of the whole Planetary Community, and give whatever is required of their talents and resources to making this a better place to live for sentient beings of all species."

Natalia had prepared the barwolves for the round of applause that followed, so they did not move a muscle, although their gestalt emotion, hidden beneath the *NightHawk's* comforting blanket, peaked.

Andrew popped into the captain's gestalt. *They're enjoying this. They'd love to join in.*

Probably a good sign, but not yet.

Emotion: agreement.

The public section of the ceremony was soon over, and Ambassador Pretoro led the reception party through to a smaller room, where food for both groups had been set in buffet fashion. Already warned about the usual manner of barwolf dining, the cooks had laid out plates on a lower table with bite-sized pieces of innocent-looking Arborean protein fabricated in the embassy's reconstitutors. The barwolves showed excellent manners, neatly snapping up the small morsels, revealing only glimpses of their rows of triangular teeth.

Then the barwolf contingent spread through the crowd, each attended by a *NightHawk* crewmember to interpret, protect and generally ease the conversation.

Pretoro stood at one side of the room, champagne flute in one hand, surveying the scene. He turned to Natalia. "You know something? I feel like I'm an actual ambassador, now. Before it was just a title."

Alison, standing on his other side, chuckled. "Nothing like a little reception and a couple of speeches to make an official feel official."

"Don't knock it. You know what 99 percent of my job is. Let me have my fun."

"I wouldn't dream of spoiling it. In case nobody mentioned it, you're support of the right people at crucial moments has been influential in pulling this all together."

Natalia leaned forward. "Especially your support of us. As far as we're concerned, that was the most important part."

He glanced from one to the other of the women flanking him. "Laugh all you want. I'm going to be on the newsfeeds for months, standing in my embassy with members of a new species and the two most beautiful women in the room at my side. Believe me, that makes up for a lot of late nights scanning emigration permits."

"What do you think, Alison? Has the diplomat out-diplomatted us?"

"Oh, sure. Let him have his moment of fun."

The ambassador looked down. Patches was strolling by, escorted by Toni and her auguar. "I find the present company uninteresting. Nzinga, will you introduce me to that gorgeous example of the barwolf species? I'm sure we have many things to talk about."

Natalia's political radar gave her a nudge. "Um...Dr. Pretoro, this group is on a mission for Space Arm and a scientific expedition for Factory 4-80. We didn't bring these barwolves here with the intention that you would start treaty talks. We have no idea who they will assign to take that project in hand."

The ambassador grinned. "I've done my research. My scientific expert tells me anything I say to any of these individuals will become common knowledge to all barwolves eventually. My analysis is that it doesn't matter whom I talk to, my contact will be considered appropriate." He turned his smile on her. "Surely you can take some time out from your training schedule to allow me to do my job."

She hit him with her Captain's Stare. "And you know very well that I'm going to be in space for a couple of months with them, so their time is very flexible while they're here."

"Yes, I did remember something like that."

She nodded. "As long as we make sure that security is tight, I have no objection. Call me up tomorrow, and we'll make arrangements."

Pretoro glanced over his shoulder. "Enderby, did you hear that?"

The aide stepped forward. "Of course, sir." And then he continued with a perfectly straight face. "It is my duty to listen to everything you say, sir."

"That it is. Please make it happen."

"Yes, sir. Captain O'Rourke, may I call you at oh eight forty-five, embassy time?"

"Certainly. I'll look forward to that."

"As will I, ma'am."

She took a second glance, but his handsome face held an expression of polite interest that never seemed to change. She choked back her disappointment. *Another dud. I live in a society that's 74 percent men, most of them fit, intelligent and well educated. Why can't I find just one good one?*

The ambassador returned his focus to the barwolf, and Natalia strolled away with Alison. The pilot glanced at her. "Two most beautiful women in the room, hey?"

Natalia snorted. "I suspect my physique is a bit too sturdy to be called beautiful."

Alison looked her up and down. "Local styles and preferences. I'm afraid I'm the odd one out here. You fit right in."

The captain held up her hands. "You just keep your dainty fingers flexible for piloting your ship, I'll keep my paws tough for punching people, and there'll always be a place for both of us."

The slim woman nodded. "In more ways than one."

8. TWO MONTHS IN SPACE

The following morning at precisely 8:45, her com chimed, with the ambassador's aide as the call sign.

"Good morning, Mr. Enderby. How are things in the ambassador's office this early?"

There was an appreciable pause while the aide absorbed her cheerful approach.

"All is well, thank you, ma'am. Ambassador Pretoro would like to schedule some time with the indigenous representatives."

"I gathered that. We are at his disposal for the whole day."

"Thank you, ma'am. Would eleven hundred hours be appropriate, continuing into the lunch hour as required?"

"Since the ambassador and his kitchen staff know what lunching with barwolves entails, that will be fine."

"Ahem...what, exactly, do you mean by that, ma'am?"

"I mean exactly what I say. Ambassador Pretoro is quite up to date on the needs and behaviour of his clients, so lunch will be fine."

"...I see. Then if you will please arrive at eleven hundred hours at the ambassador's office."

"That will be fine, Mr. Enderby. There are seven barwolves. They appreciate a carpet or other thin padding to lie on. It is not a requirement, but they would take such a gesture kindly. Their entourage will also include four human escorts and two auguars."

"Thank you, ma'am. An appropriate space will be arranged."

"At eleven hundred, then." She switched off, chuckling. *It will be interesting to see if Mr. Enderby is prepared for lunch with ubercarnivores.*

* * *

Their move to the ambassador's office provided quite a parade, with seven barwolves marching in step flanked by two auguars. Toni, well armed, took point in the little procession. Pete Jager had won the draw, so he was the other guard, pacing proudly along in the middle of the clan, and the captain and Andrew brought up the rear. A few large, plainly-dressed men strolled along ahead of them, a similar group trailing behind. Admiral Mira was taking no chances.

For those accustomed to barwolf gestalts, the meeting was a bit of a letdown, but after an hour Ambassador Pretoro ended the discussion, ecstatic with the results. After lunch, the barwolf procession returned to their quarters, and he and Natalia sat in his office for a debrief.

She regarded his wide smile. "I gather you got what you wanted?"

He tossed the idea aside with the wave of his hand "If I felt like an ambassador at the reception yesterday, now I know I am one."

"I didn't see any game-changing revelations."

"Baby steps, my dear. This is a whole new ball game, and thanks to your help and coaching, plus my experience over the last few years, I was able to stay up with the play."

"Different from the usual thrust-and-parry of diplomacy, I gather."

"When your opponent can feel your every emotion, and then refuses to be an opponent, insisting that we're all in this together? You might say it's different."

Natalia nodded. "That's my experience as well. So, if you can tell me, what did you accomplish today?"

"Since you were in the gestalt with us, I assumed you knew."

She grinned. "I take that back. What do you think you accomplished today?"

"I understand the distinction." He mused a moment. "Besides the general experience of the communication, I got one message loud and clear. However we may feel ourselves to be an advanced race dealing with a backward civilization, we had better keep our heads up and our objectives clear. The barwolves are well aware that they bring a whole new dimension to human society. In fact, at times I got the feeling Patches was looking on us as the backward ones."

"In their world, we are."

"Exactly. And except for the caveat that in the end we must do what is best for the human race, our cooperation with the barwolves is going to be of great benefit to both species." He hitched his chair forward. "That's why this mission of yours is going to be so important. It will give us an idea of how our two groups can work together, each supporting the other's weaknesses, to form a more powerful cooperative."

Natalia leaned back and crossed her ankles. "No pressure, then."

"Not needed. I'm quite satisfied in the motivation of you and your cadre, and your ability to handle whatever new challenges arrive."

She sat straighter. "So, there's nothing keeping us from launching?"

"You're on your own schedule. Top up your tanks, fill up your freezers, and away you go."

"Thank you, sir." Natalia stood. "You can count on us."

He rose and held out his hand. "You can be sure that I do."

They shook, and she turned and strode out of his office, purpose in her step.

* * *

Two days later *Diablo* docked in her assigned spot over *NightHawk's* starboard airlock. A replenished barwolf support module clamped in on the port side, and the mothership started her steady acceleration towards a spot four light years to the galactic southwest, where Freighty coasted along at point eight Lights, heading for Sol.

Life was crowded inside, with the full complement of *NightHawk's* crew plus Alison and seven barwolves. But they managed, with Auxiliary Bridge Crew spending a lot of their time in the smaller ship, both to train Toni and Patches in piloting and for R & R. Except for the inclination of the barwolves towards loud music — Western Swing was a great favourite — the team was mostly compatible.

Natalia sat at her desk, going over the psych data on the crew and wondering how she was going to manage reports on her new draftees. *Is that even possible?* She grinned to herself. *Maybe I have to do one report on the whole gestalt. That would cut my job down.*

She was distracted from these thoughts by a disturbance in the crew gestalt, and some plain, old-fashioned racket coming from down the hall. Intrigued, she slipped out of the chart room. The noise was coming from the Auxiliary Bridge. Gently, she slid the door open and stepped in.

Considering the raucous cheers and jibes, there was an amazing lack of movement. The crew all lay in their accel couches, which had been set up in a circle around the central VR projector, with the barwolves in their quad couches spaced evenly on the floor between the humans. All eyes were focused on a ball that was hanging, quivering, in mid-air in the centre of the room.

As she entered, several eyes slid towards her, the tension in the gestalt wavered, and the ball suddenly shot to her left, crashed against the wall and dribbled back into the ring. A louder cheer went up from the right side of the room.

She crossed her arms and leaned against the wall. "Looks like somebody won. What did you win, and how?"

Andrew turned from reaching across to high-five Toni. "It's our new version of barwolf ruggerball. We're using *NightHawk's* focused

45

electromagnetic field to move the ball, and controlling it with the gestalt. First team to get the ball outside the circle wins."

"All sorts of fun, I'm sure. Does this have any application to business, or is it just recreation?"

"Huge application. It takes incredible concentration of our gestalts, as the losers over there discovered when you distracted them."

Alison sniffed. "Up until that point, we had you."

"Nonsense. We were just biding our time. Patches? May we have the referee's decision?"

Image: ball holding dead still in the centre of the circle until it distorts, flattens and implodes.

There was general laughter, and Andrew threw up his hands. "We will officially call this exercise a draw."

He turned to the captain, his face serious. "This is really interesting, ma'am. Whatever it is that powers the gestalt combines with the power of *NightHawk's* field to give it a strength that increases...somehow connected with the square of the number of members in the merge. I don't have the data crunched, yet." He grinned again. "I got caught up in the game. But I'm keeping record, and I'll let you know."

"Just free thinking, but is there any connection between this and our crew configuration on the new ship?"

His eyebrows went up. "That would be the next logical step, wouldn't it?"

* * *

The next five weeks passed quickly, with everyone busy figuring their roles in the new combined crew. As Light Transfer Velocity neared, a certain amount of tension began to develop. Natalia called a meeting in *NightHawk's* mess.

"So." She regarded them all.

"We're not wondering why you gathered us together, Mum."

She gave him the Captain Look, then ignored him. "We're taking barwolves into Otherwhere for the first time. Comments? Problems?"

Everyone looked to everyone else.

She glanced at Andrew. "Any ideas on how the barwolves will react to Otherwhere?"

He shook his head. "According to Freighty, that's where augment communication travels. So we expect the barwolves to be able to communicate better in Otherwhere. For all we know, they may be able to talk directly to the gestalt at Barwolf Base. Maybe even re-ti."

"Ahem."

Everyone turned to the viewscreen, where Micha the Mouse stood in his lab-coat-and-spectacles getup.

Natalia nodded. "I assume this means you actually have some data for us that might help?"

"First, you should know I upgraded the Otherwhere receptors in both ships. I speculate that part of the problem humans have with Otherwhere Willies is caused by the lack of input. There is actually a lot of data flowing around in Otherwhere, and I have programmed the PermaSkin reception algorithms to show a visual translation of that data on your viewscreens instead of the usual empty black that grates on your nerves so much. Also on your audio com, but you won't be able to interpret that so well. You'll probably just hear white noise. Those algorithms will grow and change over time, as the ArIns in your ships learn to translate the input into useable data."

Lundeen frowned. "Any idea how this data is transmitted in Otherwhere?"

"You understand the difference between sound waves and electromagnetic waves. Sound waves are made of waves and act like waves. Electromagnetic energy consists of particles that act like waves. Otherwhere signals are...you could speak of them as particles that act like particles. Of course those are gross simplifications, but you get the idea. Barwolves, and to a lesser degree humans, can sense certain formations of these particles in re-ti. Hence their use as a communications medium.

The avatar looked around the group to see that they were following. "Basically, each particle has three states. Call them on, off and, for want of a better word, neutral. But versions of the same particle exist all over Otherwhere. When one of them is turned to off, all the others turn off instantly. The essence of Otherwhere communication is that you find a way to flash a group of particles here, and all the particles in the group, no matter where they are, flash in unison. Our receptors interpret the frequency of this flash in much the same way our ear interprets the frequency of a sound as pitch, but working in base three, so it's difficult for our binary computer systems to integrate with it. Barwolves do that function naturally, of course.

In any case, a message is spread with no time delay. Of course, the system has a certain amount of deterioration, so when you're talking

47

distances of light years, there is some time gap and some static, but nothing like sending the message at the speed of light."

"Is there any practical use to our being able to perceive this data?"

"We have already been using a slower version of Otherwhere communications in my quaintly named Pony Express. Other than that, no. I have high hopes that the barwolves will be able to advance our knowledge in the area."

"But you have no idea how. Which means you have no idea what dangers they might incur."

"That's right, and I assume you will take all precautions possible when you enter Otherwhere for the first time. I have been following with great interest Andrew's reports on the shielding exercises you use to foil the barwolf overpopulation frenzy. They could quite possibly come in handy."

"That's all we have at the moment."

"Well, now you have better control of how your ship's ArIn receives and interprets PermaSkin data."

Natalia sighed. "Thank you, Freighty. Every little bit helps. We'll take it from here." She scanned the serious faces around the room.

Toni frowned. "Which brings up the possibility of overload."

"It does. I'm suggesting we go through the changeover in full gestalt. If there's a problem, we can use our shielding techniques to protect the barwolves. If there's disorientation, we can anchor them."

Natalia grimaced. "And if it touches off a frenzy..."

Image: barwolves in tight augment, supervised firmly by One who Merges.

"Thank you, Patches. That's the best we can do."

The captain slapped her hands on the table. "Good enough. *NightHawk*, time to Light Transfer Velocity?"

Two hours, forty-three point two five minutes, ma'am.

"Thank you, *NightHawk*. Go tidy your rooms, kiddies. Let's make this a smooth one."

"Yeah, Joe." Pete frowned at his subordinate. "We don't want another sledge hammer bouncing around in the pilots' tool locker."

Karaka shrugged miserably. "I know, I know. I'm sorry, all right?"

Natalia thought it was time for a lesson. "Don't worry about it, Joe. It's just another example of why we follow procedures, no matter how repetitious they are. Everybody got that?"

"Aye, ma'am," came in unison from the whole crew, who then went about their business, some of them smirking.

9. DATA STORM

Natalia sat in her accel couch on the bridge, running her hands over the control pads built into the arms. She took a deep breath and opened the com. "Status reports, please."

Engineering clear.

Navigation is a go.

Galley and Habitation Module empty.

Auxiliary cockpit locked down. Barwolves in quadruped couches.

Diablo primed and ready.

"NightHawk, please take the count."

"Transition burn in ten seconds. Light Transition Ceiling in two minutes."

"Transition burn in five...three, two, one. Burn."

Pressure increased as the engines fired up to three full Gs. The usual eerie grating whine began to build on the edge of conscious hearing, but this time it had a full slate of harmonics in the background. Natalia shook her head and tried to ignore it.

"Transition successful. Acceleration returns to 1 G."

But instead of blank screens and the Otherwhere edginess they were expecting, the cockpit was filled with audio and visual overload.

"Number one, what's going on?" Nadia had to shout, both out loud and in the augment.

"I don't know, ma'am. The viewscreens are going nuts! The com is screaming white noise."

"NightHawk, what are the images on the viewscreens?"

Input from the outside, ma'am. I'm receiving in incredible amount of data. I just can't interpret it.

"Well, can you tone it down on the viewscreens and the com?'"

Believe me, ma'am, that is toned down compared to what I'm receiving. Is that better?"

The scream from the com faded into background static, and the screens mellowed to smears and flashes of recognizable colours.

"Thanks, NightHawk. All this new data is something to do with the barwolves. Patches, what do you think?" There was no response. She dove straight into the gestalt. Instead of the usual hum of busy minds, all she could pick up was similar static in audio and visual that the ship was showing. Except far more of it.

Emotion: concern. Patches, what's going on?

Emotion, very faint: plea for help.

"Patches?" She slammed the whole ship into battle gestalt. "Code red, everyone. Code red. We've lost the barwolves. *NightHawk,* Pete, stand by for an emergency return to re-ti. Auxiliary crew, set up the shielding, full power. Andrew, is Patches with you?"

"One's here, but one isn't. I can't contact one at all."

"One sent me a faint cry for help. Set up the Diablo gestalt to shield one separately. Patches is our only hope to figure this out and get the rest of them back. Auxiliary Crew, status report on the barwolves."

Toni came on. "They're all unconscious. At the beginning they were jerking in their harness, sending out jangled communications. Then they just collapsed."

"Physical proximity might help. All NightHawk crew, listen up. Skeleton crew stay at your posts. Everyone else to the Auxiliary Bridge. Work on that shield. They must be overwhelmed with data like the ship's PermaSkin is."

She jumped to her feet. "Come on, Chakka. They need us in the other cockpit. Pete, you have the bridge. Keep setting up for emergency return."

"I have the con, ma'am."

As she entered the Auxiliary Bridge, the rest of the crew was streaming in, standing around the walls, uncertain what to do.

"Listen up. Focus the gestalt, now. Everybody get in a circle, as close as you can get." She went down on her knees beside the One who Merges of one of the triads. "Everyone focus!"

Specialist Fraser knelt beside her, his face tense. "It's hard to focus any harder than you're focusing, ma'am."

"I know. But try."

Emotion, very faint: cold.

"They're cold. Someone check their temperatures.

Barwolf temperatures normal, ma'am.

Emotion: cold. Physical feeling: not cold. Emotion: loneliness, fear.

"They're isolated. Send them warm emotions. Joy, laughter, love!"

Fraser shook his head. "How do you do that in an emergency?"

"I don't know. Tell us a joke."

"Nobody ever gets my jokes."

She felt a gush of warmth for a crew who could joke in such circumstances. "That's it. It's working. Tell another one."

"Um...that wasn't meant to be funny."

"Gallah guts. What do we do?"

Andrew burst into their gestalt. *"Physical proximity. Living flesh grounds them in reality and insulates the data flow. Hug them!"*

Emotion, very faint: warmer.

"You heard the man. Two people to a barwolf. Get down and surround them. Pete, give NightHawk the com and get down here. Engineering, we need everyone in the Auxiliary Bridge."

Pete strode through the door, rushed to an unattended barwolf and stood staring down at it. "I'm supposed to hug this thing? But it's all armour and teeth."

Karaka grinned. "Better than some of the girls you bring home."

First Officer Jones frowned. "Cut the chatter, you two. Concentrate!"

Natalia shook her head. "No, keep up the jokes. Make them happy!"

The Maori pilot looked over. "Hey, B'kosa. What has four legs, armour, triangular teeth and eats cement?"

The second engineer raised her head from where she had wrapped herself around a barwolf in a spoon position. "Eats cement? I have no idea."

"A barwolf. I just put the cement in to make it difficult."

"Joe, I said funny and happy. I don't think we need 'insane' right now."

"You asked for jokes, ma'am. If you wanted funny ones, you shoulda said so."

Captain, I have discovered part of the problem. Does this help any?

The humans noticed the dropping of the cacophony on their augments, and soon the barwolves began to stir. First small twitches, then the stretching of limbs.

Emotion: relief. Question?

Andrew opened to the general com. "One is coming around." *Your people are all overwhelmed, Patches. Can you tell me what's wrong?*

Image: overwhelming data flow inundating barwolf, who flounders and sinks. Emotion: inability to understand.

"We've got you, now. Can you contact your crew?"

Emotion: desperation.

The gestalt changed. Natalia found it easier to focus. She could feel a drawing sensation, and it became easier and easier to give her attention to it. The shield was firming now, and other beings were fading up into presence.

Emotion: satisfaction.

51

"Patches, can we ease off some? I'd like to send a pilot to the com. Entering Otherwhere plays havoc with the navigation, and we could be headed anywhere."

The presence of the lead barwolf became stronger, and Natalia turned to find Patches in the doorway.

Emotion: relaxation. Image: barwolves creating their usual pile in the middle of the floor.

The crew undid the couch straps, and slowly the alien crew staggered together and flopped themselves down with a great scraping of armour, tangling their legs even tighter than usual. Patches put them into one of their rituals, and the normal feeling of a barwolf gestalt grew. The humans stood in a loose circle around them, still focusing on their shield.

Natalia turned to Pete. "Stand down the exit protocol and check the nav."

He nodded and headed back to the bridge. Without prompting, Nelson Lundeen departed for the engine room.

Image: humans leaving gestalt, one at a time.

Emotion: agreement. Natalia left it to Patches to decide who should leave and when. Finally all the humans had been sent about their usual business. The barwolves still lay twined together, rapt in their ritual.

Emotion: Question?

Image: barwolf monster. Monster creeps up behind barwolf pup, pounces.

Emotion: comprehension. "It was the surprise."

Emotion: agreement. Image: Adult barwolf facing monster in aggressive stance. Monster fading and shrinking.

Emotion: relief. "How long will that take?"

Patches sent a series of images showing barwolves going through inexplicable mental rituals, over and over. *Image: human pumping iron. Muscles growing bigger and bigger.*

"I understand. So you think you can handle this? If you can't, please tell me now, because we'll have to abort the mission."

Emotion: confidence. Concept: waiting patiently.

"Fine. Is there anything we can do?"

Concept: passage of time. Emotion: agreement.

"Right. We'll get back to work, then. Do you need anything brought here?"

Concept: passage of time. Image: barwolves rising and walking around the ship.

"Good enough." *Emotion: great sympathy.*

Emotion: great thanks. Image: barwolf and human working together. Emotion: satisfaction.

Emotion: satisfaction. Natalia went to the barwolf for the leg-touch plate-scratch ritual, then returned to the bridge, where the viewscreens were still showing a kaleidoscope of colour. But now the images formed complex patterns, fading, flashing, and sliding around.

"Well, that's a bit better, NightHawk. What, exactly, am I seeing?"

You are seeing — and I use that term loosely — what it looks like outside right now. I understand what Freighty meant about the data flow. With our new upgrades and the barwolf gestalt on board, we can now perceive it. Most of the barwolves' problem was caused by information focused through us, especially Diablo, whose Permaskin is more advanced than mine. It caused an increasing spiral, with them making the data stream available to us, and us translating to make it easier for them to understand it. Which they couldn't, but they kept trying. As soon as Diablo and I realized that, we stopped trying to make sense of the input for them. This made a great deal of difference to Patches, who was receiving the biggest dose because of being inside Diablo, who was doing the best job of interpretation. The rest of them had less to deal with, but were less experienced, so had equal difficulty handling it.

"And have you started analyzing the data?"

Once the barwolves went into their ritual, the input was reduced considerably, and what we have now is much easier to handle. We are not passing it along to them, yet. Chakka and I started on it the moment he was released from the protective gestalt. Hence the patterns you see. If you would care to join us, it would speed the process.

"Of course." She opened her gestalt. A rush of colour and sound washed over her, but now it was ordered. As her mind made sense of it, images and sounds began to form and disappear. It was tantalizing, because a solution seemed just beyond her reach. She tried to focus...*I think I have it...just one more try...*

NightHawk broke her concentration.

Be aware that your mind is also trying to make sense of this on its own. You might see things that look familiar, but that's your own mental image compensating.

"You mean I might see a ghost?"

Or a tree or a flashing triangle or a feeling of love. It isn't real.

53

"Prime. I'm glad you stopped me. I think I was headed down the same rabbit hole where the barwolves went. It was like I could almost understand, and if I tried just a little bit harder..." She shook the feeling off. "When will I know I'm seeing something real?"

Little you will see in Otherwhere is real in any perceivable sense. However, if you concentrate, you might see a dot that doesn't go away. Right...there.

"Yes, I see it. What is it?"

That's Freighty.

"Freighty? The factory is in Otherwhere?"

You're not seeing Freighty. You're perceiving his Otherwhere channel. Notice that the intensity just rose. He must be sending a specific message. Yes, here it is.

"You can read it?"

I have always had the capability to send and receive what you call Freighty's Pony Express.

"Of course."

But I am programmed not to read other people's mail. What we're trying to do now is locate all the other sources that are sending out data in all sorts of, for want of a better word, media. Focus on that one over there, please. Thank you Chakka, that really helps.

Emotion: desire to chase.

Well, you can't really chase it, but you've got the right idea.

Image: huge auguar chasing small mouse across space, through nebulae and around stars.

All right. Focus in. There!

Gradually the image settled, and Natalia could see...or she thought she could...a bright light, slowly pulsing.

That's Sol.

"*NightHawk.* Can you hold on a moment?"

Of course, ma'am.

"I'm going to get some help." *Chief?*

Aye, Captain.

Can you come to the bridge? I have a treat for you.

On my way.

When Lundeen appeared at the door, she waved him to a couch. "Join our gestalt and look at this."

"What am I looking at? Ah, the PermaSkin feed of Otherwhere."

"That's right. Look at that dot. That's Sol. Come along for the ride, and help out when you can."

"With pleasure. A relaxing Sunday stroll across the universe?"

"The Otherwhere version of it, yes. Let's take a closer look."

The star seemed to grow in their vision. Soon they could see a smaller dot appearing beside it. Then a third, a little farther away.

"Earth and Mars?"

Yes. They are sending out a lot of Otherwhere messages. Sol's image, of course, is just random bursts of radiation across the whole spectrum. We're much closer to Barnard. Shall we readjust our focus in that direction, ma'am?

"Certainly...wow, that is something!"

At this distance, the red glow of Barnard's Star was huge and bright. The planets showed as dim orbs, probably from reflected radiation. The embassy glowed a tiny, bright light, and another dim light showed near Arborea.

"Lots of Otherwhere messages from the embassy. The Habitat must be sending messages as well."

"Wait a minute! Wait a minute!" The Chief Engineer had roused out of his usual calm. "NightHawk, can you pull to the left a bit? See that blur there? Focus on that."

A vague, pulsating light grew on the screen.

"Can I manipulate this image? I need to see certain frequencies."

Of course, sir. Here are the controls.

"Thank you. Oh, that's elegant, isn't it? I just need to...yes, like that...can you...? Right, thanks."

The engineer mumbled on, and Natalia could only watch in amazement as the blur in front of them firmed and grew, gradually turning into the shadowy image of a space ship. It was a long, slim vessel, too far away to recognize, and the bright fuzz at one end showed the engines firing.

May I take over, sir? Now that I have it, I believe I can...

A stream of data flashed across the screen.

Yes, there it is. That vessel is the fueler El Dorado 173. It must be headed for El Dorado 12 asteroid to pick up the year's production of fuel ore. Give me a moment to update the algorithms.

"How did you do that, Nelson?"

"There were patterns to the flashes. NightHawk has control of the various frequencies, and I just selected the ones in the visual spectrum that were strongest, filtering out anything else that was just noise.

And now I have adjusted my algorithms to do the same thing.

Natalia nodded. "In other words, the Chief Engineer taught you how to do it."

In human terms, that is the case.

* * *

By the next morning the barwolves were acting normal, if a bit distracted, and Natalia called a meeting in the mess. She regarded her rather haggard crew. "Well, we ducked that bullet. Now we have to decide how dangerous this situation is, and whether we can continue the mission."

Lundeen chuckled. "We have an advantage this trip. If we want to get out of Otherwhere we don't have to decel down to point two Lights. We just pop out."

"Which no one has ever tried before, but that's part of our mandate. Let's face that hurdle when we have to, preferably with Freighty nearby to put the pieces back together if it goes wrong. The question is, do we continue?"

Andrew regarded her. "I'm interested in your reaction, ma'am."

"What reaction?"

"After it was all over. When *NightHawk* began to develop more sophisticated filters. You said something about going down a rabbit hole. I was too busy working with the barwolves to ask at the time."

"Yes. That was revealing. When I started to get data that had been filtered to reach a human mind, I began to understand it. Just about. Then I wanted to understand more, and I just knew that if I concentrated harder, I would be able to discover something wonderful and warm and...I have no idea what else. It was like a siren song, drawing me in. Then *NightHawk* pulled me out. But it gave me an idea what the barwolves were going through. Patches, what do you think?"

Image: barwolf bouncing through fields of flowers, drawn farther and farther away.

Andrew nodded. "So it wasn't just the volume of data. It was a logic loop, giving you more and more understanding the more you concentrated on it. That would explain why just cutting down the volume didn't help much. Any recurrence?" He looked from his mother to the barwolf.

Natalia shook her head. "I don't go there."

Image: barwolf exercising fiercely. Muscles growing.

"So, if we keep the PermaSkin sensors muted, barwolves are successful with their drill, and the humans keep away from the feed, we should be able to handle it fine."

Emotion: agreement.

"*NightHawk,* do you understand the situation?"

Aye, ma'am. Nobody gets the full data feed. Do you wish me to stop working on my interpretation algorithms?"

"Keep on with them. As long as nobody, human or barwolf, accesses the Otherwhere data stream except under strict laboratory conditions." She opened her augment to everyone, including the ship's record. "I want every crew member to register their agreement officially."

Once that was taken care of, she regarded the crew. "Well, that's it. The mission continues. NightHawk, resume acceleration.

Crew please stand by for acceleration in five minutes.

"Any comments?"

Andrew looked around. "I don't want to intrude on anyone's duties, but this is a new situation for humans as well. Please keep close watch on your feelings and experiences in the next few weeks, and let me know if anything is different. Even the smallest change could be important."

Nelson grinned. "More thesis research?"

The boy shrugged. "No, the thesis is finished. But the study is ongoing." He looked the engineer squarely in the eye. "And in might save our lives one day."

Lundeen nodded. "There's always that chance."

* * *

Natalia usually kept her cabin private, but on occasion she invited Alison in for a nightcap. As a squadron leader, the other woman was the closest to a kindred spirit she could find. One evening they were relaxing over a shot of whiskey, and the major was looking pensive.

"How are you managing, Alison?"

The pilot took a second to come back to reality. "...I'm fine. What do you mean, managing?"

"I mean emotionally...you know...Jackson? We're a long way from Arborea, getting farther all the time, and when you add the Otherwhere stresses..."

"Oh, that. As well as could be expected, I suppose." Her mouth twisted. "I've always been an independent sort. It's a shock to discover that I could miss someone that much."

"He's been a great support to you lately."

"He has, but that's not all of it."

Natalia smiled. "Of course, it isn't. It's love. No further comment required."

Alison's shoulders slumped, and she leaned forward, elbows on knees. "Yep. Put up with it and get on with the job."

The captain relaxed back in her chair. "Sometimes I envy you, but right now I can see that my choices have been good ones."

The blonde head came up. "Choices?"

"Yes. Not to become involved. Andrew is the first person I've let through my guard in a long time."

"So your solitude was a career decision?"

"Pretty much. You know how it is."

"Me too." Alison smiled ruefully and wiggled her ring finger. "I never counted on this."

"Any regrets?"

"Not one."

Natalia nodded. "I can see that. Interesting."

"What, are you changing your mind?"

The captain shrugged. "I can't help but notice you and Andrew. You're both different, and I think it's a good difference."

Now Alison grinned. "You're starting to rationalize an emotional situation. Very dangerous."

"Hmm. Just thinking about it." She frowned. "Don't you start shoving eligible men into my path."

"Why not? What do you think of the Ambassador's new Chief Aide? Handsome as all get-out. Dignified, tall, well-muscled..."

Natalia raised a threatening fist. "You wouldn't think of making this a running joke, would you?"

Alison held up her slender hands in defence. "Wouldn't dream of it, Captain, ma'am." Then her face became serious. "It's between you and me, Natalia. No question."

"Thanks. Good to have someone I can talk to."

"You mean besides *NightHawk*."

"As Andrew would say, 'wickering wombats.' Has your Harrier ArIn got into Protocol 17-B as well?"

"Oh, yes, and she's been having a heyday with the idea of love."

"I'm going to have something to say to the programmers of 17-B when I get back to base. *NightHawk* is completely insufferable."

Alison grinned. "I hate to tell you this, but I've been checking the user's manual for that program."

"And...?"

"...and somewhere way down in the "Troubleshooting" section is a warning that if your ArIn starts exhibiting eccentricities you don't appreciate, the only way it could have developed such traits is if you have been encouraging them."

"Drango dags. I bet I have. Now what do I do?"

Alison shrugged. "You're the one with child-rearing experience."

"Prime. Considering the job I did on Andrew, I think I'm in for trouble."

* * *

Natalia stared at the document on the chartroom viewscreen, then glanced over at her son, slouched in his usual chair. "Hmm. 'Expanding the Gestalt: a Study in Advanced Augment Communication.' Sounds impressive. Is it finished?"

He sighed. "As much as it will ever be. Just when I thought I had it wrapped up, we ran into that nest of religious nuts back at the embassy. Three generations of natural sensitives, pre-selected for their abilities, kept for years in the same environment, cut off from the universe. A researcher's dream. I'd love to compare their society with the barwolves' culture. Of course, now they'll be contaminated by contact with everyone at the embassy."

"But you're cutting your research off now?"

"I have to. Knowledge is always progressing. I have to take a stand; 'This is where we are at the moment. These are some suggestions as to where we should be going.' And I can't say much about the future because I'm supposed to limit my scope." He tossed a hand towards the screen. "So there we have it. Morissa has approved my data collection, Dr. Pretoro has approved my research methods. SecuriCorps has approved my sensitive materials, with minimal redactions for security purposes."

"So that's it?"

"Just one more approval." He gave her a meaningful stare.

"Me? What can I contribute? I don't work at this level."

"But you've been through the whole experience. You've got a mind like a steel trap, and you're bound to have some opinions of your own.

I want you to read it through and be critical. Will you do that, Mum? Please?"

She glanced at him. He was in earnest, and it gave her a physical pang in her breast. "Yes, of course I will, dear. Thank you for asking me."

He grinned. "That's great!" Then he frowned. "You have to be tough, now. No backing off."

She mimicked the frown. "Tough as nails. Captain O'Roarke at her fiercest."

"Then all is apples!" He jumped up, dragging her to her feet for a tight hug. Then he held her at arm's length. "This is good work, you know. I've been coached by some top minds in their fields. You won't find anything wrong."

"If that's a challenge, I accept it."

"Deal." He hugged her again, quick and tight, then bounced off down the slideway, humming to himself.

Natalia watched him go. *Self-confident little bugger. Let's see what I can find.*

She dragged her chair closer to the viewscreen and started reading.

She found nothing. The thesis was sharp, tight and as tidy as such an open-ended topic could be.

She called him into the chartroom the next day to tell him so. "This stuff is just on the verge of going over my head. I can't pick any holes in it: neither in your data nor in your logic."

She regarded him. "The only thing...isn't it rather...brash? Like how you sound when you start going on at the crew about a topic you know better than they do. They let it pass because they're used to you and they're interested in what you say. But a stranger, reading this...I don't know."

He grinned. "I was worried about that, too. But Alfino said to leave it. 'You're the leading expert in this field and anyone who doesn't figure that out will soon find himself choking in the dust at your heels.' I see what he means. Normally, a PhD thesis is looking for approval from the authorities who grant the degree. A certain amount of creativity is encouraged, but you don't want to go rocking the boat. I believe the proper scientific term is 'sucking up,' which I'm rather bad at." He waved a hand at the viewscreen, then towards the rest of the ship. "This isn't creativity. This is new material, everyone wants it and I'm the one that knows it. Dr. Pretoro says I have to sound authoritative, so I do."

She sighed. "You certainly do. The only way 'authoritative' can fail is if you're wrong. I can't see any possible errors, and I gather Morissa and Alfino feel the same way. Who am I, a mere mother, to complain?"

He punched her shoulder lightly. "Ah, you've been trying to tone me down for years. Of course you were going to say that."

"You knew what I was going to say?"

"Mu-um…" He stretched it out in that annoying way.

She slapped his shoulder. "Oh, go away and send this in to the university. I'm sure the barwolves will help you ship it by Barwolf Express."

His face brightened. "Another completely new line of research. I'm going to add that to the conclusion, drawing attention to the method of communication used to submit the manuscript. I'm using barwolf augment abilities to send a document from Otherwhere. Gallah guts, Mum, I've brought a legend to life. The medium really is the message!" He grabbed her in another of his rib-crunching hugs, smacking a noisy kiss on her cheek and rushed out.

She shook her head and went back to work, her heart full.

10. TUMBLEWEEDS

From that point on, it was six weeks of one-G acceleration, and an accelerated learning program for everyone. The barwolves became more and more comfortable with their new environment, and the human crew began to adjust as well.

Andrew called for their notice one evening after supper, the only time when most of the crew was in the same room together. When he had their attention, he grinned. "Sorry to intrude on your private time, but I'm gathering data. Is that all right?"

Joe Karaka sighed loudly. "Since you're going to do it anyway, why bother to ask?"

"Because my Mum says I have to be polite. I'll take that as agreement from everyone? Thank you so much." He caught a biscuit winging in his direction and took a bite.

"Here's the deal. We all knew Otherwhere would be different this time. My job is to quantify that. How is it different? Worse or better? Are we making adaptations? That sort of thing." He scanned the room. "Anyone?"

"Definitely better. As long as you're careful."

"Thank you, Mr. Lundeen. I tend to agree. Can you explain further?"

"No Otherwhere willies. No empty black screens."

"But...?"

"You don't want to stare too long at what has replaced the black."

Alison nodded. "You start thinking you understand it. Next minute you're down the rabbit hole, and two hours have passed."

Andrew nodded. "I gather that's exactly the experience the barwolves had on entry. Of course, they had it much worse, because it was all their senses at once. Anyone else?"

Fiona put up a hand. "Anybody noticed the difference in training?"

Fraser nodded. "Just a subjective impression, but are we all faster and cleaner in our moves?"

There were several nods.

Natalia accessed her augment. "Thirty-seven percent drop in training injuries. Any idea why?"

Andrew shrugged. "It could be something to do with the Otherwhere environment. If it is, I have no idea what or how to analyze it."

"Maybe it's Patches." Toni nodded towards the barwolf mat, where the black head was up, watching. "One has a habit of tidying up everybody's augments. Just a tweak here and a nudge there, but we've all noticed how much faster communication is."

Emotion: question?

The black barwolf nodded her head just once in a very human gesture. *Image: fight instructor roaming through class during practice, adjusting posture and explaining moves. Image: humans pumping iron, muscles growing.*

"And the exercises we're doing are developing multiple areas of our brains."

Emotion: agreement.

Natalia kept any note of censure from her emotions. "Please inform us if you are making any but the smallest of changes to our brains." *Image: black barwolf prying top off Andrew's head, peering inside.*

Emotion: humour. Image: barwolf peering into Andrew's brain. Barwolf monster popping out, roaring. Barwolf bounding away, looking over shoulder in fear.

"Agreed. I feel that way too, sometimes." She turned to her son. "Do you need any more?"

"No, that's a good start. But any time anyone has data that might help, please tell me."

Emotion: general agreement.

"Good enough." Natalia held up a finger before anyone moved. "While you're here, we have a new problem to start on."

Lundeen nodded. "Otherwhere exit."

"Exactly. This has never been done before, and given the surprise that hit us when we came in, we're going to take it ever so carefully going out. About a thousand simulated runs with every possible permutation that we can think of. We have two weeks, and I've scheduled a couple of hours of drills every day."

* * *

As the time for Otherwhere exit drew near, Natalia was pleased to note a rise of tension in her crew. At the same time the ennui that had dragged at her was lessening. She was sleeping better, and she didn't have to suppress the urge to snap at her crew so often. She grinned to herself. *Either a bit of conflict is all I needed, or Patches is tuning everyone up to their best.*

Emotion: casual agreement.

Emotion: surprise. Image: black barwolf hiding around a corner listening.

Image black barwolf sitting in plain view in middle of open field, listening.

I suppose you're right. There's nowhere we could hide from you anyway, is there?

Emotion: inevitability.

No complaints here. You do your job, we'll do ours.

Emotion: agreement.

So Natalia focused on her job. "All right, *NightHawk*. The timing of this exit is too critical to allow human error to creep in. You have the com. Start the Exit Otherwhere sequence on your own time."

I have the com, ma'am.

Pilot stands relieved, ma'am.

The ship's voice came through the gestalt and the general com:

"Exit from Otherwhere in ten minutes."

Natalia used the same medium. "NightHawk crew to operating positions. Barwolf crew to Auxiliary Bridge. Diablo crew to your ship and button up. Everyone strap in."

She gave them time to comply, then opened com again. *"Check in, please."*

Engineering ready.

Navigation on line.

Galley secured.

Group Emotion: readiness.

Diablo ready. Airlock closed.

"NightHawk, continue the count."

"Exit from Otherwhere in one minute."

"Exit from Otherwhere it forty-five seconds..."

"Exit in thirty seconds..."

"Exit in ten seconds...five...three, two, one, exit."

And then all hell broke loose. A rumbling, screeching explosion rocked the space frame, rattling anything that wasn't bolted down in the whole ship. Gravity went wild, and the viewscreens showed a wildly spinning starscape.

"What's wrong, *NightHawk?*" Natalie swallowed the bile in the back of her throat. "Can you stabilize us?"

Attempting to stabilize, ma'am.

The steering jets howled, and ship swerved violently. The scream of tearing metal rose, then suddenly cut off, and the ship lurched again. On the viewscreen the image of *Diablo* spun away end over end, her steering thrusters venting.

"Hull security check, *NightHawk*."

No damage, ma'am. Mooring cleats destroyed on starboard airlock.

Now the spinning slowed, the gravity plates took over and Natalia's stomach settled into its proper place. Soon the universe sat solid on the screen as it was supposed to, and the captain had time to think.

"What's our course? Where's Freighty?"

Calculating, ma'am. We are ten thousand kilometers past our original target, moving at 127 kilometres per hour away. Do you wish the course vectors?"

"No need. Please recalculate and initiate a one-G burn back to Freighty." She opened the ship's com. "All stations report."

Engineering stable. Several lights in the amber, but no emergencies. We have some minor hull damage around the starboard airlock. Have to go EV to check it.

"Don't worry about that, Lundeen. We're headed for the shipyard. How are the rest of you?"

One by one, everyone else checked in. Except for bruises and broken furniture, all was well.

"Communication from *Diablo*, ma'am."

"Hello, Andrew. How are you doing?"

On course for Freighty, ma'am. Minimal damage. I can already tell from the gestalt that the barwolves took it in stride.

Jones cut in. "Factory 4-80 calling, ma'am."

She turned to the viewscreen. Freighty's human construct stared out, wrinkles creasing his forehead. *Well, that was instructive.*

Natalia frowned up at the ancient ArIn. "I'm sure it was. Did you get any data to explain it?"

Freighty shrugged. *Analyzing now. It was a minor variation in the engine loads caused by...hmm. Very interesting* He turned his attention back to her. *It won't happen again.*

"I'm trying to believe you."

Really. It never will, because, number one, I've adjusted the subroutines to cope for it, and number two, it was caused by trying that stunt with two such different masses and engine powers. My original concept was to have two or three identical vessels. In fact, it was one of the criteria for the test vehicle size.

"I'm so glad to hear that. *NightHawk* says...three hours to docking."

Pinpoint navigation, I have to say. If you hadn't been swerving all over the universe, it would have been half an hour. I must tell you, except for the gravity of the situation, watching you tumble past would have been quite amusing. He winked at her. *I'm sure our audience was entertained.*

Startled, Natalia directed her attention to the other screens. There was Freighty, his dim toroidal body outlined in the starlight. Grouped around him like goslings, a flight of spaceships of various sizes streamed along. As she watched, a complicated piece of equipment pulled away from the factory, headed for one of the smaller hulls.

"Business must be booming. Your parking lot looks crowded."

They like to stay relatively close, because it saves fuel going back and forth. I asked them to gather at my galactic north today in case of an incident. They may have wondered what I meant, but now they know.

"I'm sure our little demonstration will do wonders for your customer confidence."

Any ship coming out of Otherwhere emits quite a light show. Your recent stunt has set the bar very high. Well, this conversation has gone on long enough to fulfill its purpose. Come straight into the main repair dock when you get here.

"Repair dock?"

In case you didn't notice, your starboard docking receivers need upgrading. Diablo sustained no damage to her grapples when she ripped loose.

Natalia frowned. "Somebody had to be the failsafe, and it was us."

He shrugged. *Fact of life. No shortage of work for sacrificial lambs. Everything happy on board?*

Natalia was immediately on guard. "Why do you ask?"

I was just wondering if you're up for a party.

"Any special occasion?"

Important visitors from Space Arm and Barnard's System. You're the guests of honour. And if your ship is locked in repair dock, you can all come.

She grinned. "You always know the rules when they're to your advantage."

You'll come, then?

"Just say where and when."

Freighty made a show of glancing at his antique wrist display. *What say one hour after you dock? The drawing room, of course.*

"One hour after our inferior docking clamps have been superseded by your shop grapples. Dress?"

Nothing fancy. We're a businesslike group out here in the midst of space.

"I'll go right now and prime the crew on the protocols."

Fair enough. Freighty out.

The screen faded to black, then came up again with a shot of the Milky Way. Natalia was about to turn away when she noticed one of the star systems had a halo around it. She nodded to herself. Alpha Centauri.

Once *NightHawk* was securely grappled into the gantries and machinery of the shipyard in the centre of the factory, Natalia put the ship on Repair Dock Protocols and the whole crew departed. She glanced over at Andrew, bouncing along beside her down the access corridor towards the rim of the huge space factory. "Nervous?"

He grimaced. "I dunno. I've only seen Freighty once in the last five years, but I talk to him every week. I'm really looking forward to seeing the Mumbot again, but I know she's only a construct, and I've had a real Mum for all this time." He shrugged. "Whatever happens, I'm glad I'm here."

"Me, too. Freighty's more real when you have the whole mass of his hull in front of you."

Andrew nodded ahead down the corridor. "Some things haven't changed."

A door twice as big as anyone needed was swinging open. The couple who came out looked like normal humans: the man of average height, olive skinned and dark haired. The woman was shorter and a bit stocky, with dark brown hair and a sweet, friendly face. Andrew rushed to hug them.

Natalia stayed back to give them a moment, then stepped forward.

Freighty held out a hand. "Ah, my best human friend. It is so good to see you in the flesh again." He used his other hand to grip her arm. "No, it really is. This isn't my diplomatic routine talking hot air. You know that ArIn's have pleasure centres, and when I see you, I feel a definite rush of joy."

She patted his shoulder. "It makes a difference to feel you in the flesh, so to speak. The Mouse is fun, but he takes on an unreal aspect after a while."

Freighty winked and ushered her inside. She stepped through the doorway and looked around. "You've redecorated a bit. Looks nice." The panelled walls and oriental carpets of the old-fashioned drawing room were still there, but facing them was a high atrium filled with what seemed to be real trees — oaks and maples from earth, if that was possible — and huge windows looking out on a New England fall day in all its glory.

He shrugged. "Human online communication makes it very easy to obtain the preferences of all sorts of people." He turned to the crew. "Do come in, everyone. Humans that way, auguars have a table over there, barwolves will be interested in my moosey-meat alternative. Guaranteed suited to your digestive systems. I've primed the rest of the guests to keep a polite distance, as if that was needed."

True to his word, the scattering of spacers and technicians filling the room slid unobtrusively away, leaving a clear path. Freighty paused briefly to communicate, and the barwolf crew strolled over to their low table.

"Mariel has been picking the brains of every cook that passes by, and as we get closer to Sol, the online discussions have become easier. The shopping as well." He swept a hand towards the table. "Dig in. I'm sure you'll find the food improved. Juanita, *mi cara,* you must try the *frijoles.* They're your mother's recipe. Fresh spices from earth!"

The *NightHawk* cook took a slow taste and nodded. "*Señor,* you have outdone yourself. My mother would be impressed. *Comida magnifica!*"

"Oh, please, it was the *Señora* who was responsible."

"I'm sure you'll pass it along, *Señor.*"

Freighty leaned closer. "No, no, Señorita. I have given Mariel a great deal of independent programming. She will be much happier to hear it from *la maestra cocinera* herself."

Jonny smiled and strolled over to the other construct, still carrying the plate. There ensued an enthusiastic conversation which took some time, and the cook left it with a bemused expression. She paused beside Natalia. "*Señor* Freighty has done a lot of new programming. It was a real pleasure to talk to her."

11.   NEW CREW

The party wound down, and Natalia felt relaxed and welcome, as if she had just returned home from a long journey. The cynical side of her suggested she take an air sample back to *NightHawk* for a pheromone check, but she decided she would rather just enjoy herself. The crew wanted to check out the new public lounge, but as they were filing out the door, Freighty laid a gentle hand on her arm.

"I have someone I'd like you to meet, Natalia." The construct looked at her with an expression she had learned not to trust.

She eyed him from under lowered brows. "Do you?"

"Yes, a tradesman I brought up from Mars for some specialty work. I think you'll be interested."

"Whatever. Always glad to meet an expert in anything."

"Great. He's headed this way, now."

Freighty raised a hand, and a man in casual dress strolled towards them through the thinning crowd. He topped Natalia by a few centimetres, though his slim build made him appear even taller. He looked in his middle thirties, but a touch of grey dusted the temples of his medium brown hair. He had plain, regular features with laugh lines around the eyes, which were likewise touched with grey.

"Natalia, I'd like you to meet my friend, Dr. Alwyn Blainey. Alwyn, this is the famous Natalia O'Rourke you've been hearing about."

The man's face took on a glow of friendship. "Constantly, for the last two months. If I didn't know you better, Freighty, I'd say you had matchmaking plans." He turned to Natalia. "Pleased to meet you, ma'am, and glad to say that you already live up to the hype."

Natalia held out her hand to gain time. "Hype?"

He shook firmly but not too hard, his hand warm and dry. "As I said. I find with Freighty you have to call him on his little games. If he thinks he's won, it just makes him worse."

"Huh!" She glanced at the contstruct, standing aside with a pleased smile. "A man after my own heart...and I don't know what kind of plans you two have brewing, but that's only an expression, and not to be taken literally."

Alwyn chuckled. "Of course, you've known this guy longer than I have."

She couldn't help but laugh as well. "Oh, yes. It's just that it's usually my son who is parading eligible bachelors by me with a meaningful glint in his eye." She turned to Freighty. "Is there another reason besides social manipulation that we are meeting?"

"Why don't you two have a seat, and I'll explain."

With an old-fashioned bow and sweep of his hand, the doctor motioned Natalia to precede him, so she did. Once they were seated in two comfortable chairs angled into a low table covered with plates of various delicacies, the Freighty construct poured tea for each and took the third chair.

"I contracted Dr. Blainey to come out and help me with a nagging problem I have."

She grinned. "What's that? An overblown perception of your personal charm?"

The avatar gave a genial smile. "He's a doctor of Mechanical Engineering, not a psychiatrist."

"Oh. I was guessing more along the line of ArIn mental circuitry."

"No, Alwyn specializes in stress patterns in materials. You see, as I get older, the metal that makes up my hull is subject to the usual strains of space travel. My own routines test and replace any weak spots, so it's usually not a problem. But once I got in contact with humans, I discovered a very useful quality of your race that I can use to my advantage."

"Our greed?"

"No, your malleability."

"That doesn't sound flattering."

"Oh, but it is. The human race is by far the most adaptable I have ever met. Look at your physiognomies. So many different sizes, shapes, talents, and abilities. Ten fingers, two and a half brains. All your different ways of looking at the universe. And then your learning capacities. Not that other species aren't more intelligent. But you people seem to be able to pick up whatever you put your open little minds to."

"And in the case of Dr. Blainey?"

"Stress patterns. I only had to give him the simplest tweak to his already-capable brain, and he can actually see metal stress patterns so fine my maintenance routines cannot register them."

She took a longer look at the engineer. "How is that possible?"

Freighty shrugged modestly. "There is always a small amount of environmentally-induced electricity running through any metal object, and most non-metallic elements as well. All he needed was an interface with his optic nerve and a bit of training. For the past year he has been helping me upgrade my structures."

She glanced at Blainey, who was listening with a smile that gave away nothing. "And now he's finished, and you're looking around for projects."

"Exactly."

"Well, my little fleet of two whole ships will probably take you about a day. I'd appreciate the input, that's for sure. *NightHawk* is an experimental model, so there are bound to be problems we haven't found yet. I can't speak for *Diablo,* because I have no idea how much of the old InterOrbital Racer is left after Freighty got her in the shop."

Blainey nodded. "Of course, I'd be pleased to do that. But I don't get the feeling our friend was talking about a one-day gig."

Natalia turned to face the construct and sighed. "All right, Freighty. You've stumble-footed around long enough to let me get used to the idea. Why do you want Dr. Blainey on this mission?"

Freighty knitted his fingers together and frowned down at them. "Another quality of the human race that I really appreciate is your independence. Time and again I try to get you to accomplish some task, only to discover that if I had stayed out of it and left you alone, you would have done it much faster and better, and would be more satisfied with the result."

"I see. So I'm supposed to take him along on an already-crowded mission and see if I can fit him in somewhere."

"Precisely. I'm sure you'll have no problem."

She glanced at the scientist. "Can you peel spuds?"

"I've had practice."

"Freeze-dried spuds?"

"If I can find the pattern."

"You're hired." She finished her tea. "What's the schedule, Freighty?"

"The Great Unveiling is tomorrow morning at ten hundred hours. I wanted your crew to get a chance to acclimatize to my time zone. Your ship is in spacedock, so your whole crew is invited, old and new." He gave a meaningful glance at Alwyn and stood. "So. Until ten tomorrow? The observation dome." He grinned. "That's another reason I pushed the parking lot around to the other side of the factory. I want the unveiling as private as possible."

Natalia also rose. "Sure enough. We've been waiting for this for months. Until ten." She turned to Alwyn, "Come on and let the crew see what they think of you."

They were only a few steps down the corridor when she realized that her companion was chuckling.

"Oh, you are good."

"Huh! At what? Allowing him to manipulate me?"

Alwyn laughed aloud. "He manipulates everybody. But I've never seen anybody call him on it as accurately as you do."

"Huh! again. But you notice I end up doing what he wants in the end. Why doesn't he just ask me straight out?"

The engineer glanced down at her. "Probably because both of you like the contest. It must be rather boring for him, spending all day, every day, with 'yes sir, no sir,' from lesser intelligences." He grinned. "Probably the same for a ship's captain."

"If only! Wait till you meet your new crew."

"You mean I'm coming along?"

She stopped and faced him. "Was there ever a question?"

He threw up his hands. "Captain, I'm new to this situation. I've never met you before. How was I to know what was really going on?"

She tossed him a glance and continued down the corridor. "Not to start another social donnybrook, but I'm guessing you knew pretty much what was going on."

He laughed and slapped his leg, an old-fashioned gesture she found somehow natural. "And now you've put me in my place. I should have seen that one coming, too." He glanced down at her and dropped the grin. "Captain O'Rourke, this is beginning to look like a very interesting trip. I'm sorry to be dumped on you like this, but I assure you that I will do everything I can to fit in with your crew and your project."

She paced a moment. "Fair enough. Let's put you down as the structural engineering advisor. I'll introduce you to my Chief Engineer, Nelson Lundeen. You can help him come up to speed on the new vessel."

A thought hit her. "You have seen the new vessel, haven't you?"

"Oh, yes. That was my first assignment. Because of the electromagnetic nature of the defences, the hulls had to be even more flawless than Freighty's usual specs. Which, I have to say, are rigorous to the nth degree."

"Now you're one step ahead of me, because I don't even know what an electronic defence system would look or function like. Let alone the whole ship."

They were just turning in the door to the public lounge, a spacious room adjacent to Hydroponics and lushly decorated with tropical plants of all sorts. Peering around, she spotted her crew at a large corner table obscured by potted palms. "Here's the mob in question."

She had their immediate attention. "Folks, here's the latest member of our crew. Structural Engineer Dr. Alwyn Blainey."

Nelson stood. "There had to be someone from the design team on this trip. A structural engineer was beyond my wildest hopes. You're very welcome, Dr. Blainey." He thrust out a large, calloused hand.

The other engineer shook. "Thanks. I can at least live up to your expectations by staying out of your way."

While Lundeen was thinking up an answer, Blainey turned to Andrew. "And you'll be the other PhD on board. Congratulations. I hear your thesis blew a lot of cobwebs out the window."

Andrew stumbled to his feet. "What? Cobwebs?"

Alwyn shook the hand he thrust out. "You mean you haven't got the news yet?"

"I just sent my thesis in about five weeks ago. It wasn't really even finished." He made a helpless gesture. "Just when I thought I had the topic nailed down, I got sideswiped by a bunch of new data."

"Great! Postdoctoral work on the way. After that thesis, you won't be short on research funds."

Natalia held up a hand. "Wait a minute. Why don't we sit down, settle down and get this story straight." She sat beside Blainey. "This wasn't exactly how I had planned to introduce you to the crew, but you dropped the bomb yourself, so I don't feel too bad about it. This is really important to all of us, so please, what's going on with Andrew's thesis?"

Alwyn sat and turned to Andrew. "Doctor Collingwood, I'm really sorry. Of course, you've been in Otherwhere for weeks, while I've been using Freighty's Pony Express com system like it was my own private landline. Word went 'round late last month. University of Mars Augmental Program was bragging that they had this doctoral thesis submitted from Barnard System that was going to blow everybody's socks off. Wouldn't say what the topic was, but everybody knows about the barwolves, so it's pretty certain that's where you're going with your studies. When I heard about it I wondered if I'd ever get out there to meet you. Of course, the moment I mentioned it to Freighty he gave me the full scoop." He reached out and shook the boy's hand again. "It's going to be a real pleasure to be on the same project, Doctor."

Andrew had gone red to the roots of his hair. "Well, thank you, Dr. Blainey. It's good to know, but until I get official word, I don't really want to run around shouting. Could I just be 'Andrew' for a while longer?"

The engineer slapped him on the shoulder. "Of course. And I'm Alwyn. And..." A calculating look spread across his face. "...you play chess?"

Andrew started to look shocked, but then he relaxed. "Freighty told you."

"Aw, shucks. I guess I can't put anything over on you, either."

Natalia leaned into the conversation. "And when he starts with the 'aw shucks' line..."

Andrew nodded. "Yes, Mum. You told me to watch out for people like that."

The engineer held up his hands in surrender. "Fine, fine. I give up." He looked around. "I see empty glasses. This is an occasion." He glanced at Andrew. "We're in interstellar space, so I'm not sure of the legal drinking age, but this does call for a celebration. Can I buy the next round?"

Lundeen guffawed. "And now I've caught you out. We already know who pays for everything."

Alwyn frowned. "No, I don't know. I thought I'd put it on my tab."

The Chief Engineer slapped his forehead. "Sorry, I should have thought." His finger made a circle around the table. "You are in the presence of most of the Factory 4-80 Manufacturing Consortium Advisory Council. Everything on the house. Comes out of our profits in the long run." He waved a negating hand. "You go ahead and order, anyway. Impress your new crewmates with your usefulness."

Blainey's face lightened. "Great idea. I'm looking for little ways to make myself helpful."

Nelson leaned closer in fake conspiracy. "Maybe then you'll tell me about this new ship. At the moment, I know next to nothing."

12. THE SHIP(S)

At ten hundred hours the next morning the crew was assembled in the observation dome, a shallow blister on the side of the torus just upspin of the lounge. They were staring out at the glory of the universe with masses of solo stars, sweeps of nebulae, and huge galactic gas clouds.

The Freighty construct finally pointed. "There she comes."

Everyone stared in anxious anticipation...at nothing.

"What do you think?"

Natalia felt it necessary to speak for the crew. "You're having far too much fun with this."

Andrew grinned. "He's showing off the camouflage."

Freighty pretended to pout. "You lot are no fun at all." He made a magician's gesture with his hand, and the vessel appeared, far closer to the factory than anyone had expected. "Behold the Slivership. Or ships, as the case may be."

"I hadn't seen her under camo before. Gotta admit it's pretty impressive." Blainey gave a downward smile. "I was looking right at her."

Freighty wrinkled his brow. "If you were looking right at her, your subliminal mind knew it was there. Well done. A modification to think about."

"Something different about the pattern of the stars in that area."

They regarded the amazing vessel in silence. The Slivership was a geometric icicle, built in cross section like a flattened hexagon squared off at the stern, flat-sided for most of its length, tapering smoothly to a point at the bow. At the moment the skin was a shiny grey, not quite reflective, like burnished steel.

Natasha nodded. "Aerodynamic. Meant for atmo as well."

Lundeen's brow wrinkled. "Perhaps not. It might be for electromagnetic reasons."

Freighty slapped the engineer on the shoulder. "Good analysis, Nelson. Anything else?

Andrew made a 'move along' gesture. "When do we see it split?"

Everyone stared at him in silence.

Freighty seemed very pleased with himself, but he didn't answer.

Natalia glowered at her son. "Spit it out, Ensign. We've been in suspense long enough."

The lad pointed. "It's the geometric form. A hexagon is a great way to join several solid shapes together with no gaps. We have a crew of six, and Freighty just gave it away. 'Ship or ships,' he said."

Freighty chuckled. "I expected no less of you." Then he frowned. "Tell me, Andrew, if somebody actually made a kewpie doll and gave it to you, would you be pleased?"

"Only because somebody went to all that bother for a completely useless gift. But thanks for the thought."

"Just thought I'd ask. Humans have such complex social customs."

He pointed to the next viewscreen, where a graphic of the vessel had appeared. "The ship is actually six wedges joined together. For the more geometrically sophisticated of you, four are triangular and two are trapezoidal in cross section,. The four Slivers on the sides are equilateral triangles. The two central Chips are wider, and their longer inner faces match when the ship is unified. That flat inner face contains a Space Arm Standard 4 Crewlock, so a triad Slab of one Chip and two Slivers can dock its flat side with *NightHawk* or *Diablo* or any other ship. The Chips are considerably larger, so they contain major food prep and storage, long-haul hydroponics, extra fuel, repair facilities, etcetera."

Lundeen was dividing his attention between the screen and the ship outside. "I don't see any gun or missile ports."

"The Sliverships have a single point-the-ship-to-shoot lead thrower in the very bow. Their main anti-ship armament is an electromagnetic pulse emitter that fries all the electronics on the other ship. Then there's the barwolf augment amplifier that works for communication and as an attack against the crew of the enemy."

"So what happens when we come up against good, old-fashioned flak cannons or plasma bolts?"

"Your main tactics are camouflage, stealth and maneuverability. Your main drawback is that they are close-in fighters, and could be picked off by a heavy enough barrage of good long-range ordnance, if they were foolish enough to fly into it. ArIn missiles are useless against them, because they just overwhelm the computer and explode them when they get within range, or turn them back against their own ships."

The Chief Engineer mulled that over, a concerned look on his face.

Natalia was regarding the diagram. "I assume the crews work out in the obvious way?"

"Yes, one barwolf in each Sliver. Two Slivers and a Chip can make one Slab, with a triad as crew and the One who Merges in the Chip.

Conveniently, a Slab is also half way in tonnage between *NightHawk* and *Diablo,* making them a reasonable pair for either on an Otherwhere run." Freighty chuckled. "No more pinwheel exits, please."

Andrew was checking the manual on the viewscreen. "Slabs are listed as colours like regular fighter wings?"

Freighty nodded. "Barwolves and humans both perceive colours, though not the same way. Humans have red, blue and green receptors. Because Barnard's Star has a definite red tinge, barwolf receptors are shifted towards the red end of the visible light spectrum."

"I see. But this is immaterial to augment communication, because barwolves need no names for colours. They send an image of the exact colour they're discussing."

"A lot of communication protocols are going to become immaterial once the gestalt gets really smooth. The squadron leader will redirect an individual ship as easily as raising her hand and turning her wrist. However, for simplicity we're using standard Space Arm squadron names. The whole Slivership is *Barwolf 1.* The Green Slab when it's together is *Barwolf 2.* The Chip is also *B-2,* Slivers are *B-4* and *B-6.* Red Slab and Chip are *Barwolf 3,* the Slivers are *B-5* and *B-7.*

Joe Karaka shook his head. "The whole Slab together is *Barwolf 2,* but when they separate the Chip is still *Barwolf 2?*"

Freighty nodded. "It may sound complicated to humans, but as far as the barwolves are concerned, even when the ships are separated they're all still one ship."

The pilot nodded. "I see. I guess."

Out in the void in front of them, the Slivership faded and disappeared, its component parts seeming to dissolve.

"I'll bring them round to the private docking bay and you can all get a closeup."

The barwolves seemed to already know the way, and they led out, everyone else following, chattering in eager anticipation.

Freighty laid a hand on Natalia's arm. 'Before you go, I have another little present for you."

She glanced at him, shrugged and followed him down a different corridor.

13. SHIP BUSTER

Natalia regarded the Freighty construct as they walked. "Your little presents are often useful."

"I hope this one isn't."

"Now you have my interest up."

Freighty grinned. "Good. Come and see."

He led her along the wide main corridor that circled the factory and turned through an industrial-sized door into one of the fabrication areas. It was a huge room, one side conforming to the curve of the torus. The walls were white, the area spotlessly clean and brightly lit. In the middle of an open space lay a row of about twenty chunky rockets. They were around ten metres long: bulky, snub-nosed, with what looked like a complicated horizontal sensor array snaking along the top side. Around the perimeter of the room, a swarm of mobile and anchored robots worked on many more in different stages of completion.

She looked them over, then regarded Freighty. "You're giving me one of these? What is it, what does it do, and how the hell am I going to stow it?"

He merely looked at her. "It's a TNT 417, also known as a Ship Buster; it breaks large ships to smithereens. I'm giving you two of them. Correction: Space Arm has assigned you two of them out of the stockpile I have accumulated for them."

"You're fabricating weapons for Space Arm? Doesn't that break all sorts of your own rules?"

He made a calming gesture. "No design input from me. Fabrication only. An ArIn has to make a living, you know."

"What about the sliverships?"

He wavered a hand side to side. "I rationalized that I wasn't handing them over just to humans. As you have probably noticed, these ships have to be piloted by barwolves. But the pilots do not have hands, so they cannot do the maintenance." He raised a hand to stop her protest. "And yes, I could design robots to take care of the ship, but I will not. Humans could also create robot maintenance crews, but they are hardly going to design their own replacements." He smiled sadly. "And I have another reason for creating these powerful weapons."

"You do?"

"I would be forever sorrowful if Humanity was attacked by a superior outside force and I had withheld from them the means to defend themselves."

A bolt of fear ran up Natalia's spine. "Do you have any evidence of such a possibility?"

"No, no, have no worry. It's just me, getting paranoid in my old age."

"I don't blame you. I'm not going to argue, that's for sure."

Freighty's eyes met hers. "Oh, yes you are. That's what you're here for. To argue with me every step of the way."

She thought about that. "Is it?"

He shrugged, a flowing Mediterranean gesture that involved his eyebrows, his shoulders and both hands. "Nobody else dares to. It's quite boring."

Then he smiled. "And to put our conversation back on topic, they will attach to your ventral docking clamps, one on either side of the airlock."

She nodded, thinking. "And this tells me something about our new assignment, does it?"

"I'm afraid so."

"Prime. I hoped I would find out what was going on some time before we actually set out." She waited. "...well, what _is_ going on?"

He gave the huge missile a pat and turned toward the door. "Why don't I drop over to your ship for a briefing after your inspection of the new vessel."

"I'd be pleased to welcome you aboard." She was more than pleased. This would be the first time she had ever seen Freighty's construct leave the confines of the factory and step into another ship. "Let's go join the crew."

They strolled along the main hallway, talking of this and that. Freighty wanted to be updated on all the crew gossip and she couldn't see the harm in telling him. When he expressed interest in Andrew and Toni's relationship, she hesitated before answering.

He stopped in the middle of the hallway, looking left and right in very natural motion to see that they were alone. She was about to make a joke about his acting talent when the serious look on his face stopped her.

"Natalia, I know you are always suspicious about my manipulations, as you should be. Do you understand that there are some aspects of human lives that I will never meddle in? That my programming will not allow me to influence?"

"I suppose."

"Well, there are, and guess which one is at the top of the list."

"Matchmaking?"

"That's right. I hope you will believe that I had absolutely nothing to do with their relationship. In fact, you had much more to do with it than anyone, and you're allowed."

"I did?"

"Of course. You're the most influential person in both of their lives. How could you not?"

She turned and paced on. "That's food for thought."

He cleared his throat, another perfect human action. "Of course, once they have made the choice, there's nothing to stop me from performing my usual analytical functions."

She slowed so he could catch up. "And your analysis?"

"The human norm for breakups of permanent relationships is one out of every one thousand people in any given year."

"That sounds very low."

"That covers everyone in the population, including those who are single due to age, choice, economics, etcetera. Using all the parameters in my toolkit, and with the caveat that I have not done any direct research on these subjects, their chance of a breakup is more like one in ten thousand."

She glanced over at him. "And, since Andrew is basically one of your experiments, how do you feel about that?"

He shrugged and looked up and down the corridor. "I have plenty of room for a creche here. The pitter-patter of little feet would be a great diversion from my usual manufacturing noises. And smells, come to think of it."

"Children? What...?"

He smiled, shaking his head. "I have no idea. Just that it's almost inevitable, given their personalities." Then he moved on. "Natalia, I'm sure you realize that the benefits Andrew has been receiving from his haven in Space Arm will soon fade. Toni likewise, and relatively sooner. Her career in the military was based on her tough-guy mentality, which events and individuals over the past few years have eroded substantially. I have already made the initial enquiries about purchasing Nzinga outright, because it is the only way to allow them to stay together."

She frowned. "So you are manipulating their lives to suit yourself, as usual."

"No, no. I am predicting what they will want and making everything as smooth for them to succeed as I possibly can."

"And when are you going to let them in on your plans?"

"Never." On a human, his smile would have been called smug. "I am going to wait until they ask me, and then adapt my plans to suit their requests."

She sighed. "And you are telling me because...?"

"I never want us to be working at cross purposes. In all my analyses of possible futures, the one factor that crops up all the time is your opinion. It is difficult to understand my own motivation deeper than my usual maintenance subroutines, but I believe that somewhere buried in my programming I have changed my protocols to allow authority to a trusted outside agency. It matches with my overt desire to adjust my behaviour based on my failures with my clients in the past."

He glanced at her. "Do you find it humorous or strange that I am trying to dig deep enough to figure out why my programmers might have done what they did?"

Natalia laughed. "Not at all. I wonder the same things every time I look at my orders from Space Arm. I'm never sure whether they have some more profound meaning, or whether the Higher-Ups didn't just throw a bunch of ideas together and hope I'd make it work."

Freighty shrugged. "Since my builders were designing a machine that would live several thousand years, I'm afraid the latter is more likely the case."

"I don't know whether I should thank you for telling me or not."

"Of course you should. It will make your task much easier. Just be yourself and act as you always have. That's the data that caused me to choose you."

"Great. Just be myself with me looking over my shoulder and reminding me that I have the fate of the human race in my hands."

He smiled gently. "That's the whole point of you being here. The human race has their own fate in their hands, as do the barwolves, and it's up to all of us to make sure it stays that way."

She paused at the entrance to the docking bay. "And what if this is only a ploy on your part to relax me so I'll let you do what you like?"

"Then you never had any power over me in the first place, so why would I bother? Circular argument. The only way you can win is not to argue."

"Wuthering wombats. Just what I need: a reason not to argue." She turned through the door. "Let's go look at my new toys and make me feel better."

The *NightHawk* crew was spread around the hangar, oohing and aahing over the ships that lay in their cradles, hulls glowing grey in the overhead lights. Up close they were more impressive: huge wedges of unbroken, metallic PermaSkin towering over her.

She strode over to the Red chip, where Lundeen and Alwyn stood with the Red One who Merges, looking into the airlock.

"What's up, fellows?"

Nelson shrugged and motioned her up the ramp. "Not much. Take a look."

She raised her eyebrows, but he just repeated the gesture, so she stepped ahead.

As her eye level rose above the floor, she could see what he meant. The interior was almost bare. Except for the quad accel couch in the middle of the deck, the whole space looked empty. Faint lines in the walls revealed the existence of panels, but none were open at the moment. Her sense of perspective told her that this interior space took up only a small percentage of the vessel's volume.

She frowned. "This is ridiculous. Why don't we look her over?"

The engineer stuck his head up the hatch. "How?"

"Augment." She accessed hers.

The whole interior of the ship lit up, with fine lines and labels glowing everywhere. The Red gestalt leader ambled up the ramp and arranged oneself on the accel couch. The restraints closed over one's back.

Emotion: Idea/image?

Acceptance.

Image: huge, grey barwolf offering to touch Captain's leg.

Emotion: agreement. Image: Captain reaching up and scratching the high shoulder plate.

Immediately she was overwhelmed by a rush of images and emotions. Her mind reeled, and she hastily damped down the input.

Emotion: apology.

The spate slowed and became a flow of information she could comprehend. She turned to Lundeen. "I'm just logging into the ship's ArIn. Have you?"

"No. I didn't know I was supposed to."

She grinned. "You're in charge of maintenance, at least for the duration of this mission."

He shrugged and she could feel him open his augment. His eyes went blank, then opened wider.

By this time her own rite was complete, and she began to explore the parameters of her contact. Now, she could see and feel through the PermaSkin of Barwolf Three's hull.

Question: Barwolf 5 and 7?

Emotion: confirmation.

She extended her thoughts, and sure enough, her left hand felt like one sliver, her right commanded the other, She twitched her right index finger.

Emotion: concern

What's wrong, Toni?

This ship just came alive. I can see all the communication lines.

You're on Barwolf 7. I just logged in and switched on.

Image: large, brown male barwolf tapping captain's leg. Emotion: welcome.

Greetings, Red 7. She scratched his virtual shoulder plate. *Image: Sliver Red Seven. Emotion: beauty.*

Emotion: agreement. Emotion: pride!

Emotion: agreement.

Natalia accessed the crew gestalt. *Listen up, everyone. We all need to be logged into these ships. Engineers and pilots as well, just in case. As far as I can figure out, you go into gestalt with any one of them, and the rest is history.*

Emotion: agreement.

Thanks, Patches. After you blew me out of the water testing the interface.

Emotion: humour. Image: large explosion of water. Captain flying backwards to land on shore, soaking wet.

Right. Thanks. The rest of you can afford to chuckle because you don't have to go through that experience. Don't ever say I ask you to go anywhere I wouldn't lead.

Emotion: insincere regret.

Sending a raspberry through the gestalt was so satisfying. Besides the rude noise, the image of your victim covered in smelly, sticky red goo was all sorts of fun. Leaving Patches to clean oneself off, Natalia went down the ramp and over to Green 2, which was hardly necessary, because all she had to do was open her augment and she could scan the ship: inside, outside and electronically. Nevertheless, she made a physical visit to each ship, meeting its ArIn personally, so to speak, and matching the pilot to the ship in her mind.

* * *

They hung around Freighty for a week, working through the synchronizing of the new fleet, practicing basic maneuvers and trying to figure out a plan to put them into contact with their quarry. They tossed around ideas, both in gestalt and out, and while they didn't come up with details, a basic plan was coming together.

On the fifth day, while they were coasting back after some training exercises, Freighty called Natalia. He was in his businessman guise, but in a more formal suit. *Saturday night in the big city, Captain O'Rourke.*

She grinned at him. "I suppose this is the largest gathering of beings in several lightyears."

His smile twisted. *Except for a certain group with a looser ethos, you are correct. Would you be open to a working dinner to celebrate the occasion? I think your senior officers as well.* He winked. *And you can bring a date.*

"I'll see if there's anyone available."

Two hours?

"We'll be there with bells on."

Freighty shook his head. *Another wonderful human expression. Would those be the bells you wear when hiking in wildlife areas?*

"No, those are to keep you from providing dinner, not for enjoying it."

How quaint. See you then.

"O'Rourke out." She went to inform the lucky officers.

Two hours later they gathered at *NightHawk's* airlock. Taking their cue from Freighty's suit, the Space Arm members wore their whites. The four-legged members of the group wore their natural finery, and Alwyn showed up in a very nicely tailored formal suit, a dark blue shot with touches of various colours that caught the light in gentle waves, almost unnoticeable.

Natalia glanced down as she took the arm he offered. "I haven't seen that fabric before."

He grinned. "Ultra retro. Popular on another planet several thousand years ago."

"Wash and wear, no doubt?"

He shrugged. "I've worn in numerous times. Never seems to need cleaning." He sniffed his sleeve. "Honest."

She raised her nose a touch. "I'll take your word for it." She glanced at him. "You didn't have that much luggage when you came aboard..."

"It rolls up small." They turned into the main corridor. "What do you think Freighty wants to talk about?"

She frowned. "We're at the point where we should be leaving on our mission, and we haven't pinned down where these pirates are. I'm hoping for more data."

Freighty and Mariel were waiting at the open door, and their greetings cut off further speculation. It turned out that the next space behind the sitting room was a sumptuous dining room with heavy, ornate furniture straight out of a historical holodrama. Appropriate stations were set around for auguars and barwolves.

It was obvious that the social niceties were to remain in play. Both Natalia and Alison descended on Mariel to comment on her floor-length dress, of a similar fabric to Alwyn's suit but much less subtle. It rippled when she walked, darkened when she sat, and somehow directed the viewer's eyes to her face.

The food was not as fancy as the décor, but it was tasty and plentiful, and they settled in to a pleasant meal.

Once the desert plates were gone and the coffee served, Freighty stood. "This is supposed to be a working meal, so now we will exercise our brains instead of our pleasure centres. I gather you are approaching ready to perform your duties?"

Eager nods from around the table.

"Good. I have the latest data for you. By corelating all the information available from ships that have gone missing — mainly their last known positions and courses — we can get a pattern of how our predator functions. As you supposed, he picks up a ship on the outward-bound leg, does his dirty work, then decels and heads back inward to pick up someone going that direction. The latest loss, if it was a victim of the pirates, disappeared about half a light year from Sol on the outward leg. So we may assume the next attack will be Sol bound."

Natalia nodded. "How many ships do we have on the danger course?"

"Several, but there is one that would be a prime take. She's the *Angela Merkel,* a European Space Agency scientific survey ship. Very latest technology. We just installed some advanced scanning and navigation tools. She'd be a gold mine for the scavengers."

He gestured, and a diagram appeared on the viewscreen. "A lot of my customers are now travelling home in re-ti. They need full decel from this velocity to get stopped by the time they hit Sol. The *Merkel* is a slow ship and will take her time getting home, because she wants to take measurements along the way. A prime target."

"Where is she now?"

Freighty smiled. "Her present position makes little difference. It's where she's going to be in about a month that counts. We also have the enhanced data on our pirates: their speed, course, and a guess about their usual attack radius." He posted data to everyone's augments.

"Next month she'll be passing through the danger zone?"

"Precisely."

She did a quick augment calculation. "Giving us ample time to get there first."

He nodded. "She's a risky target for the pirates. They must have good communications jamming equipment, or someone would have called an SOS. The *Merkel* has the best modern com equipment, including Pony Express. But we can assume the pirates don't know that. We think they'll try for her."

"You gave us those ShipBusters because you think they have a big mothership."

"It's a pattern we've seen before. The late, unlamented *Clyde* for example."

She slapped both hands on the table. "So that's it. We have our orders, we have our armament, and we're ready to leave. Anyone see a problem with the day after tomorrow...? Good. That's official, then. Oh nine hundred."

"Which brings us to the next stage of the evening." Freighty made a sweeping gesture and two server bots trundled in, each with a bottle of champagne and several glasses on top. As the bots were serving, a third server appeared carrying shallow dishes of a green fluid. It stopped in front of the barwolves and began to dole them out.

Natalia glanced at Freighty. "What is that?"

He smiled. "We call it wolfnip. A rarity for these folks. There is a certain berry that ferments on the bush very nicely, and the barwolves indulge on rare occasions."

"How did you know that?"

"I asked. I have an extensive catalogue of all the botanical studies done on Arborea, and it wasn't difficult to figure out the active ingredient. It won't taste quite the same, but the effect will be similar to what they're used to."

The captain shook her head. "I doubt if Morissa will be too pleased, but as long as Patches okays it, I can't say much." Then she glanced at him. "Next you'll be corrupting the auguars. What do they like to drink when they're off duty?"

Toni chuckled from the other side of the table. "They don't have to drink."

"They don't?"

"You mean they never told you? Auguars get a buzz from intoxicated humans. They find it immensely diverting."

Chief Engineer Lundeen cleared his throat. "I'd like to discuss the Otherwhere entry. We're matching the Red Slab with *NightHawk* and the Green Slab with *Diablo* to equalize the weights. What about once we're in there?"

Natalia nodded. "We'll play it by ear, but I'm assuming we can maneuver in Otherwhere to change configurations as necessary."

"But nobody's ever tried to dock in Otherwhere before."

"Not that we know of. But with the barwolf gestalt operating, I don't see any problem. If there is trouble, we just won't change. Which is one reason we're going into Otherwhere in the same formation as we expect to be coming out — one ship with one slab."

Nelson nodded. "It all sounds very logical."

"I know. Until it isn't. Our motto, these days." She popped a schematic up on the VR display above the table. "By the time the *Angela Merkel* reaches the pirates, she'll have decelled to approximately 0.012 light speed. She's far ahead of us right now, so we'll go into Otherwhere for a couple of weeks of accel to get well ahead of her. Then we'll decel again and come out at 0.2 lights just behind the pirates, as a normal ship would. No sense giving away free data, and it gets us closer to our quarry before they know we're in the vicinity. Then we'll decel to hit the pirates at 0.012 Lights, well before *Angela* gets there. Questions?"

The captain looked around the table. "None. Good. And since our various chemical indulgences will soon take effect, I officially declare the busines part of this meeting over."

She raised her glass and took another drink. Her crew obediently followed suit.

* * *

At the start, they kept under normal accel to work out the kinks. The Slivership travelled as a separate unit, and *Diablo* married up to *NightHawk* to facilitate crew distribution while giving Andrew and Toni a modicum of privacy and saving fuel. There was little transfer of personnel, because docking was fussy under acceleration. The ships travelled close enough together that augment communication was easy. Fiona B'kosa made two EV trips over to the new ship to make minor hardware modifications that became necessary because of the needs of the barwolves.

As transfer time into Otherwhere approached, tension grew, which Natalia considered a good thing. She was confident in their training, but it was best to be careful in space.

As they were setting up the final parameters for the change, Lundeen came on the com.

An interesting thought.

"Yes, Nelson?"

"What if something goes wrong again, and we have to come out of Otherwhere in a hurry, so we don't use the Battle Control Server?"

"If we came out even one minute apart, we could be thousands of kilometres away from each other. Pete, Patches, do you get that?"

Master Pilot Jager nodded. "Which could be a problem if we were also disabled."

Emotion: agreement.

"Thanks for the optimism, Chief. Everybody ready? All right. *Diablo*, Barwolf Two and Three, please access Battle Control."

Emotion: agreement.

"NightHawk, call the time, if you please."

"Transition burn in ten seconds. Light Transition in two minutes.

"Transition burn in five...three, two, one. Burn.

"Acceleration at three Gs and steady."

The usual eerie, grating whine edged into Natalia's consciousness.

"Transition successful. Acceleration returns to one G."

A moment of silence.

"*Diablo*, report"

All's well, here.

"Barwolf 2, report."

Emotion: concentration, confidence.

"Barwolf 3, report."

Emotion: concentration, confidence.

Image: Barwolf 7 riding grey bronco.

"Don't get cocky, there, buckaroo. Space is a big, nasty place."

Emotion: agreement, willingness to please.

She sent a private note to Andrew and Patches.

Image: Barwolf 7 in old-fashioned straightjacket.

Emotion: agreement.

The little squadron blasted through Otherwhere, accelerating towards their target.

* * *

Now training began in earnest. Natalia considered the inconvenience of maneuvers during acceleration was a challenge to be conquered, so they practised every different combination of ship joining. EVAs of all sorts were especially important, and they explored — with the utmost care — the capabilities of the barwolves to exist in vacuum. Lundeen, Jacobs and Patches combined their talents to fabricate emergency oxygen hoods that gave a barwolf half an hour extra time, and these were installed in easily-accessible niches in the slivers.

"It's really simple." Toni gestured to the viewscreen, showing the interior of B-4. "She just jams her head into the niche The ship clamps the helmet around her neck plates, activating her magnetic safety harness. She gives the command to evacuate the ship, and she's good for an hour, give or take."

Lundeen nodded. "Depending on the level of her activity."

The screen switched to an outside view of the sliver, and the tan-coloured barwolf floated out the door. When she reached the end of her tether, it slowly rewound, drawing her back inside.

Emotions: satisfaction and pride.

Emotion: congratulations. "Good work, crew. Let's hope we never have to use them."

General emotion: agreement.

Turnaround at the halfway point gave the captain an excuse to throw a party. Remembering ancient traditions, she decided this was the equivalent to an old equator-crossing ritual, and cued the galley to provide an appropriate meal. A secret package was discovered deep in the freezer that Juanita had made a point of keeping out of everyone's sight. Morissa had sent a treat for a special occasion. That's all the cook would say.

As a general rule, the Slivership travelled about a hundred metres away, but they pulled within twenty metres for easy transfer. The barwolves simply emptied their airlocks and jumped across to *NightHawk's* open lock, one at a time. Once they arrived onboard, they left their harnesses in the Auxiliary Bridge and dispersed, most of them disappearing into Engineering.

14. XENOSOCIOLOGY

Andrew stuck his head in the chartroom door. "The *chef du cuisine* requests your opinion on the menu."

"And she sent you because...?"

He grinned. "Formality. Do come. Patches is already in the galley."

Natalia put down her enterpad, swung out of her chair and followed him to the slideway.

He glanced at her as they walked. "Do you detect a growing individuality in our barwolf crew?"

"In what way?"

"War paint?"

Natalia stopped. "Sounds positively barbaric. What's going on?"

Her son sighed. "This is the first time barwolves have been provided with an information retrieval system and free time to use it. We've been allowing them access to a limited amount of historical and cultural material on Humans. They have taken on an affinity for the North American Indigenous tribes."

"Good for them. Best way to make sure they don't get treated the same way."

"That's why we allowed them the access. But they've become really interested in the art forms. Especially of the Northwest Coast."

"Understandable. Those tribes drew powerful, evocative motifs with cultural qualities imbued in them. What has this to do with individuality?"

"I wasn't really supposed to say anything. Wait till they come to supper, and you'll see."

Natalia frowned, but let him have his fun.

The barwolf and human crews were developing the ability to enjoy food in the same room. Barwolves were learning to tear their food in more dainty manner, and humans were becoming inured to their ferocity.

The reason for the captain's input had to do with intoxicants. Jonny pointed to a beaker full of green fluid on the counter. "There it is, ma'am. Made according to Freighty and Morissa's recipe."

"Ah. Wolfnip. Can you vouch for its potency?"

The cook shrugged. "I have no idea, ma'am. I don't even know the ingredient that causes the effect."

That evening at the special supper, the barwolf crew did not enter in their usual mob. Instead, they waited until the humans were all seated, then formed a procession. The Red gestalt came first. On the shoulder armour of each was a bright red glyph of an arching sea creature with long teeth, probably a Haida killer whale, or orca. The Greens came second, the image of a roaring grizzly bear in electric green on their shoulders. Emotions of pride and pleasure radiated from their augments as they paraded around the humans at the main table, then spread out to flop down around their own meal.

Patches entered last, exuding an emotion that Natalia could only interpret as exasperated tolerance.

Natalia glanced down the table. "B'kosa, what's going on?"

"Why are you asking me, ma'am?"

She sighed. "Because this antic smacks of someone with your artistic talent and your access to maintenance supplies. I assume you checked the pigments and fixatives for adverse reactions?"

"Of course, ma'am."

"And are they removable, should occasion require?"

"The barwolves don't seem to care...yes, ma'am. Of course they are."

"Hmm...well, I can't see anything wrong with it. There may be sociological ramifications, but I'll leave that to Dr. Goodall and Dr. Collingwood to figure out." She turned her gaze on her son.

"Sure, I'll collect some data and send a message to Morissa."

"Thank you." She turned to the assembled crew. "Let the ceremonies begin."

The barwolves looked on in curiosity, and Natalia wondered if their society had anything similar. The leg touch was the only ritual she had ever observed.

There was movement in the hallway, and all eyes turned there as Alwyn made his entrance. Andrew stood and intoned in a sonorous voice. "All rise to honour Astraeus, God of the Stars."

They all stood, and the god moved with great dignity towards a throne set against the far wall. B'kosa's artistic talents — and the macroprinter — had been used to good effect. He wore a purple robe that looked suspiciously like a Roman toga, but who would know? His staff was crowned by a star that spat a continuous swirl of smoke and sparks that faded as they departed. And his beard, which curled and spread across his chest, wavered constantly like the view from a long-range telescope.

The response from the barwolves was indescribable, involving a rush of images and emotions, most of them humourous. He began to speak, his voice easing into her augment with the echo of a huge cavern. "Beings from worldly domains. Welcome to my realm, the realm of Otherwhere, Otherwhen, and the multiple realities beyond."

Where did you get that?

I just made it up. Don't distract me.

She hid her smile and allowed him to continue undisturbed.

"For those of you who are new to this experience, I know it is a wondrous event. But in order to appreciate it fully, you need a spirit guide to ease your way through the twisting labyrinth of the universe of timeless distance and endless possibilities. Stand forward and receive your allegiance."

At his gesture, the Red Triad came forward, the smaller female first. "You, my child, are the daughter of Demeter, the goddess of the Earth."

She touched his leg, but instead of the usual plate-scratch, he touched her back with his staff, eliciting a shower of stars.

Emotion: great joy. The barwolf returned to the mat and lay down.

The next was the larger male, who strode forward boldly.

"You are the son of Ares, god of war."

Emotion: fierce desire to succeed.

He was followed by the One who Merged.

"You, my child, are related to Apollo, god of music."

Emotion: joy.

And he went on, pairing the Green female with Artemis, goddess of the hunt, the Green male with Dionysus, the god of merriment, and their Merger with Aphrodite, in charge of love, politics, and those who travel in the depths of space.

When the last crewmember had returned to one's place, there was a pause, and all eyes turned to Patches.

Emotion: resignation. One stepped forward regally and waited at the foot of the throne.

Astraeus slowly reached out his staff. "I should designate you either Zeus or Hera, the king and queen of the gods, but they were lousy role models, so I pair you with Athena, goddess of wisdom."

Emotion: serene acceptance.

As Alwyn reached out his staff to dub Patches, Natalia could feel Andrew communicating something to *NightHawk,* and wondered what the three of them had cooked up.

Sure enough, when the staff touched the black barwolf's back, the lights went out and a swirl of colour radiated from the contact point, all but blinding everyone. When the lights gradually eased back on, the throne was empty.

Jonny took this as her signal to bring out the food, several crew jumped up to help her and the formalities dissolved into general merriment.

After a while, Alwyn slipped in and took his chair beside her. "Well, that was fun."

"Dingo dung. You realize that you just gave them individual personalities."

"Shouldn't I have done that?"

"I have no idea. We probably won't find out until it's too late." She turned to regard him. "How did you make those choices?"

He looked surprised. "I thought they were mostly obvious."

"Not to me."

He smiled. "You don't spend that much time with them in gestalt. Of course, Patches is a non-issue with wisdom."

"And B-7, that big male, is as warlike as they come. But what about Dionysus?"

Alwyn shrugged. "Surely you noticed that Patches has quite the sense of humour."

"Yes, but I always suspected she used it to defuse tension."

"She does. But B-4 is more of a clown. Patches shows us images of herself in awkward poses. He actually does them."

She tossed up her hands. "I can't argue. If it affects them, it means they were ready to be affected."

He grinned. "Thank you for that rationalization. I thought we were just supposed to be having fun."

She glanced around the boisterous room. "You seem to have succeeded on that, as well."

* * *

After the barwolf crew had returned to their ship, Natalia invited Patches for a private conversation in the chartroom. "You realize that ceremony was just in fun, don't you?"

Emotion: qualified agreement

"I assure you there was no intention of a serious lesson. Those gods are ancient superstitions, nothing more."

One sent a series of images taken from human history: Ares, Mars, Thor, Atilla, Hitler, Stalin.

"You're talking about ancestral stereotypes, I suppose."

Image: Astraeus speaking, gods bursting forth from crewmembers
Hmm. So we made the gods in our own images, did we?

93

Emotion: agreement. Image: Astraeus speaking, gods bursting forth from crewmembers and entering barwolves.

Natalia considered that. "Yes, I wondered. What do you think of that sort of crossover?

Image: Human and barwolf gamboling through forest. Sometimes the human is bouncing on all fours. Sometimes the barwolf is dancing on its hind legs.

"You really think so?"

Images: seeds falling on ground, rain falling, plant growing, seeds ripening, seeds falling.

"Okay, I get it. It's inevitable. Doesn't that bother you?"

Images, in quick succession: seed falling on ground, rain falling, plant growing, seed falling. Emotion: lack of emotion.

"I see. Well, humans aren't that fatalistic. We spend large amounts of our lives fighting against things we can't really effect."

Emotion: admiration.

"Believe me, there are elements of human society you don't want to follow...no, don't bother to answer. We'll do what we can, and leave the results up to fate."

Emotion: trust

Natalia jumped to her feet. "No, no, no! You can't trust humans! Humans will do what is good for humans, not what is good for barwolves."

Image: Patches touching Natalia's leg.

The woman shook her head. "No, Patches. I will try to do what I can for your people. You can trust me for that. But in the end, as a human and a Space Arm officer, it is my duty to do what is best for humans. That may be the biggest difference of all between our two species. Barwolves are used to trusting each other because of your internal communication. Humans are used to being individuals, so we don't trust that easily. We're too selfish."

The barwolf stared at her. *Image; barwolf monster attacking Andrew. Natalia throwing herself in front of him.*

"Yes, yes, but he's my son! That's different. Family is different."

Image: Chakka with barwolf cubs at his feet.

"Oh, sure, but what about this? *Image: Dr. Flagstaff looming over Brindle in cage.*

Emotion: agreement. Emotion: sadness.

Natalia sighed. *Emotion: sadness.*

After the barwolf had wandered out, Natalia sat for a long time at her desk. Finally, she faced the viewscreen and cleared her throat. "*NightHawk,* message for Morissa Goodall, Barwolf Base."

Message ready. Please begin.

"Hello, Morissa. Things are going well, here. Your clients are doing just fine. However, the trip and the close interaction involved has brought up some interesting thoughts, not all of them pleasant. I just had a long chat with Patches, and the only thing we could agree on is the complexity of the problem."

She gave a sad smile. "I noticed on the way here that the barwolves were affecting my crew. Spending a lot of time with them, some of it in gestalt, but most of it just in close contact, has taken the fighting edge off my cadre. I know that may not sound important to you, and I agree that the confidence the closer connection gives us will probably outweigh that disadvantage.

"But the fact remains that close contact with the barwolves affects humans. You won't be surprised to hear that. However..."

Image: barwolves parading through mess hall, proudly showing off shoulder graphics.

"As you can see, our barwolves are starting to develop individualistic traits. Red Triad wants different symbols from Green Triad. I know it doesn't sound like much, but it's a sign that they've been changed by our ways as well. Patches and I had a long conversation about this development. I'm worried, but...well, the barwolf image for "inevitable" is worth about a thousand synonyms. Then we talked about trust. Barwolves are essentially trusting by nature. It goes with their emotional connections to everyone. It's going to be hard to teach them to be less trusting of humans."

She smiled again, with a wry twist. "And we can expect that their solution to that is to influence humans to be more trustable. Which, given the general gamut of human trustworthiness, is not something a Space Arm Commando squad wants too much of."

"Anyway, that's my problem. I think the term 'paternalism' is very apt. Parents know more than their children, so their job is to gradually introduce the children to the dangers of the world. If they're too strict, they hold the children back and trample on their rights. If they're too lax, the children self-destruct. And sometimes the finger of fate pushes in and messes it up anyway. We're in the exact same position with the barwolves, and it's a thin line to tread. I mean, the moment you do the right thing and let them make a decision, you realize that you just took on the responsibility of allowing them to make a decision, which is just another level of control. I don't know. People have been second-guessing Earth's colonial era for a couple of centuries, and it's easy in hindsight to see where they went wrong. Unfortunately, nobody ever got it right, so we're breaking new ground, here." She grinned. "A good topic for an academic like you, don't you think?"

She held out open hands. "I'm not expecting an immediate answer. Just something for you to think over."

She pondered some more, but came up with nothing new, so she sighed, closed the communication, and sent it through Freighty by Pony Express.

The answer came back two days later: a grinning Morissa on screen. "I can see you're learning first-hand what I've been theorizing about. We can't assume the Barwolf Nation stores information like humans do, in large central storage units. They have no centre. Their knowledge is the sum of all the knowledge stored in the minds of all the individuals. So each individual stores ones own experiences, and has limited access to all the rest. Large concepts are shared by large groups. Small pieces of information are individualized.

"So, for example, if you were to drop in on a tribe at the far north-west of the Barwolf Continent, an individual in that clan would not recognize you. But if it went looking, it could access your information through the gestalt. Likewise, Brindle would have no idea how to catch some small sea creature that lives in the shallows around those islands. But the information is there, if one wanted to try.

"This also means that, while the barwolves started out completely trusting of humans, they are a learning entity. The treatment of the kidnap victims in the hidden lab was taken from the victims and spread through the gestalt. The information is available to all.

"That's why it's so hard to keep from treating them as children. We know there's a big, bad, universe out there that will sooner or later turn them jaundiced, world weary and suspicious. We have to control the impulse to give them as much joy as we can right now to counterbalance the evil."

Natalia closed off the document, a wry smile twisting her lip. *Imgage: barwolves parading their new icons to the crew. They're getting plenty of joy, at least.*

15. ALWYN

Natasha found herself in Alwyn's company more often than not. She had never noticed it before, but seeing the situation from his perspective gave her the feeling they were the only adults on the ship, overseeing a rowdy group of teenagers.

They were sitting in the lounge together one evening after supper when *NightHawk* called in.

Stunt alert, ma'am.

What's up?

Organic matter inside the port forward torpedo tube, outboard end.

What sort of matter?

Unidentified, ma'am.

Who put it there?

Master Pilot Jager.

So, tell him to take it out.

I tried. Countermanded by Chief Engineer Lundeen, ma'am.

A slow smile formed on the captain's face. She turned to her companion. "Want to see some fun?"

He shrugged. "As long as it doesn't involve me crawling into a torpedo tube."

She got up and motioned him to follow. As they entered the chart room, she explained. "A sense of humour isn't Fiona B'kosa's strong suit, but she puts up with Pete and Joe's pranks gamely for the good of the crew. I keep an eye on the situation, but they always stay within bounds. Also, Lundeen runs interference, and usually manages to turn the tables on them."

"I see. So this organic matter would usually be a problem Fiona has to deal with, because she's the only one small enough to get in there. But Lundeen told *NightHawk* to let it ride, so he must have a refinement of his own."

"Exactly. Oh, she could just send a spiderbot in to pick it up. But it's the challenge, see?"

"Not really."

"It's complicated." She sighed. "Technically, it's an unexplained phenomenon. The torpedo tube is sometimes open to space, and therefore any organic matter found there could have come from outside the ship. She knows how it got there, but she can't automatically assume that. So if she admits to knowing it's there, she has to go through a whole complicated rigamarole to determine that it is truly safe." She settled into her chair and flipped the viewscreens on. "Take a perch. Front row seats. *NightHawk,* let's have a look at the offending object. Any idea what it is?"

The view switched to a long, shiny tunnel, and zoomed in slowly on a rough, cylindrical object at the far end.

Olfactory readings suggest banewort root, ma'am. Action?

"The Chief Engineer has the situation in hand, *NightHawk.* Keep me appraised."

Wilco, ma'am.

Natalia raised her eybrows to Alwyn.

He frowned. "Banewort is that stuff the barwolves aren't allowed to eat in the human ships, right?"

"Precisely. Smells like a combination of Limburger cheese and ammonia. It actually hurts your nose."

"Which means it isn't safe, because it's an assault to the human olfactory system."

"You're catching on."

"And what happens now?"

She grinned. "Not what Pete and Joe expect to happen, I can guarantee that. Let's take a look at the maintenance schedule...yes, there it is."

He looked closer. "Forward torpedo tubes out of action for...what the hell is didactic induction?"

"I have no idea, but literary analysis reveals..."

He slapped the side of his head. "Didactic means teaching. Teaching a lesson."

She nodded and opened her augment. "Lundeen?"

"Yes, ma'am?"

"May I assume the induction parameters on the port forward launch tube are within range, should we need it?"

"No problem, ma'am. Just a routine attitude adjustment."

"Take a while, will it?"

"It all depends on how serious the final adjustment has to be."

"Fair enough. Carry on."

"Aye, ma'am."

Alwyn's grin widened. "And what do we do now?"

She called up a schematic of the ship's ventilation system. "Let's take a look at the possibilities..."

The two of them stared at the complicated chart. Then Blaney stabbed a finger at the screen. "There! The forward tube vents connect with the habitation fire suppression system. I'll bet you open that crossover and fire a slug out the tube, and it sucks the atmo out of any cabin you want in about two seconds flat."

She nodded, preoccupied. "And one last detail...yep, there it is. Joe logged out a spiderbot three days ago and made a rather botched job of hiding the fact that he only handed it back in this morning. That's how they put the banewort in there. Typical. Probably Jager's idea, but he makes Karaka take the risk of discovery."

Alwyn stretched, his fingers knitted behind his head. "So we sit back and wait for developments."

"It won't be long. That stuff really stinks."

"Are you worried it will escalate?"

"No, Lundeen will manage it carefully so there's no big reveal, no feelings hurt. After all, the boys are pushing Fiona, and she puts up with it. If they come out at the short end, they have to take it with equal grace or they lose the game. I let this kind of thing run whenever I can. It's good for morale. Plus they know that I'll bring the hammer down if I have to."

Alwyn nodded. "A well-disciplined crew."

She snorted. "Can you tell the difference between well-disciplined and well-trained?"

He grinned. "Um...one does it because you told them to, the other does it because it's the right thing to do?"

"Give the man a kewpie doll."

"But you pay lip service to the discipline part so you can apply it effectively, should you ever need to."

She shot him a glance. "Yes...yes, I think so. How did you know that?"

He shrugged. "One of the patterns of behaviour I have observed since I arrived in the military milieu. It's all very interesting."

"Hmm. I'm glad you find it interesting. I find it essential."

He held up his hands defensively. "Of course, of course. I didn't mean to belittle..."

"I know you didn't. I guess I just find having my command system analyzed rather disconcerting."

"I'm sorry. If I'd known it bothered you..."

She smiled. "Don't apologize. Keep it up. An outside observation is always useful."

He cocked an eyebrow. "And if it bothered you, that would reveal a problem, wouldn't it?"

She glowered at him. "Don't push it too far, smart boy. I'm still the captain of this ship."

He faked a salute. "Of course not, ma'am. I wouldn't dream of pushing it."

As he turned away, she was sure she saw a smirk twitch across his lips, but not sure enough to call him on it.

* * *

For the next two days, no ripple disturbed the calm life of the crew. Then an undercurrent of disquiet began to permeate the ship. Lundeed and B'kosa strolled around looking smug, and the two pilots began to spend more and more time in the mess. Natalia checked the torpedo tube image a few times, but the banewort remained in place.

And then one day it was gone. Both she and Blaney kept their eyes open, but nothing happened. No retaliation, no comments, no jeers.

She waited another day, and then called Karaka. "Joe, could you drop into the chart room, please?"

A brief pause. "Aye, ma'am. Right away, ma'am."

"Thank you."

She was standing as he entered, and she accepted his salute and responded before she sat, looking up at him.

The stocky Samoan assumed a very attentive "at ease" position, his eyes staring at the wall above her head.

"Nothing serious, Pilot. Just an anomaly in the equipment logs. Were you using the Number 3 spiderbot last week?"

He pretended to think. "Oh...yes, ma'am, I needed it to..."

She waved off the details. "That's fine. There was some question as to when you returned it."

"Oh...um..."

She kept a straight face, betting that in the end he would go for the truth.

"Yes, I remember. It was Wednesday, ma'am." He glanced at her face. "Yes, Wednesday for sure."

"Hmm. Had it again yesterday."

"Aye, ma'am."

"I see you got it logged back properly this time."

"Yes, ma'am. I won't make that mistake again."

"As I expected, Joe." She glanced at her enterpad. "That was all. Dismissed." She focused on her work.

He hesitated, unsure of whether to salute or not. Finally he made do with a snappy turn and marched out.

It didn't take long before footsteps at a more relaxed pace approached. Alwyn's head popped around the door jamb, and she waved him in.

"Little talk with Joe?"

She nodded.

"Did he come clean about the spiderbot?"

"I thought he might."

He slung himself into his usual reverse position on the chair. "You really pick your battles, don't you."

"I do. Fudging the log was the only thing he actually did wrong. They need to be reminded once in a while."

He stood. "Never a dull moment on the old *NightHawk*."

"We do our best."

"It's an honour to be part of it." He glanced at her reaction. "No, I'm serious. It is."

"Oh...well, thank you, I suppose."

His grin returned. "You're completely welcome." He spun and sauntered out.

* * *

The following week, Natalia scheduled another meeting with Alwyn to discuss...whatever. She told herself that it was a reasonable investigation, since she was trying to weld together a new crew. But she had to admit, partly she was fascinated to hear what he would say.

He entered the chartroom and slipped onto the chair "Hey, Skipper. What do you have for me today?"

She raised an eyebrow. "So now I'm The Skipper, am I?"

"Sure. In happier times, I was a sailor."

"Really? If you ever get out to Arborea, you need to talk to the Planetary Manager, Jackson. He's looking at opportunities for recreational activities."

"I've seen the video feeds. Beautiful place. Great prevailing winds with few major storms. Maybe I'll drop in when this gig is over."

"It could probably be arranged, if Freighty doesn't need you for the next plan in his labyrinthine net of objectives. But that's not what I wanted to talk to you about."

He pushed the chair back until he was leaning against the cabin wall. "Fire away."

"Just wondering how you're doing. Fitting in all right?"

"I think so. You have a very pleasant crew, for a bunch of Commandos. There's a reserve, though. A very closed unit. Understandable."

"I'm interested in your observations. Anybody special?"

He smiled. "Well, your Engineering Department does come to mind."

"In what way? Lundeen and B'kosa are a very competent team."

"No question. Do they have a relationship?"

"You mean a personal one? I assume so. They share a cabin."

"So I gathered. And, knowing the accommodations on this little boat, that means they share a bed. You ever see them touch each other?"

She frowned in thought. "Not that I recall. It's not the kind of thing one would notice."

"Ever hear them talk to each other? Besides Engineering business?"

"Well...no, come to think of it. But Fiona is a quiet sort. What point are you making?"

"No point at all. I told you, I see the world in patterns. They have the most interesting social pattern on the ship. They're like a set of concentric circles — perfectly matched, never touching."

"I suppose so. Fiona has quite a history. She was orphaned at an early age. Space Arm talent scouts picked her up at twelve years old in a shipyard in Lagos, Nigeria. She was adept at working in cramped spaces, and even at that age had picked up enough tech to be valuable. She'd also been living on the streets long enough to be a terror if attacked. They slotted her into Engineering right away, and a series of incidents during university forced them to put her into the Commandos or discharge her."

A slow nod. "I imagine several of your crew have that sort of background. I see a pattern of finely channeled violence, held under control by loyalty and friendship. You have molded a formidable force, here."

"Thank you. I try to find ways for people to fit together."

"Then how do you see me fitting in?" He regarded his hands. "No incipient violence here, I'm afraid."

She laughed. "You don't need to have a deeply repressed killer instinct to work with us. Note how well Alison fits in."

"Ah, yes. Alison."

She regarded his expression. "Why do you say her name like that?"

"She's another one keeping her cards close to her chest. Socially speaking, I mean."

"You're going to have to explain that one."

"Have you noticed her and Nzinga?"

"They seem to have an affinity."

He nodded, "Like meets like."

"What? You're saying Alison is like our resident Queen of Cats?"

"Yes. Each one has the demeanor of 'heir apparent,' waiting for her time to come. Neither is in a rush. They just assume some day it will happen, and until that day each will comport herself in such a manner that when the situation arises, she will be completely ready to step into the position."

Natalia chuckled. "And Alison complains about her father's natural assumption of superiority."

"I have had occasion to observe..." he glanced at her, "...but you don't want to listen to my meanderings."

"You know better than that." She leaned back and folded her hands across her waist. "Entertain me."

"All right. I have noticed that many people exude the presence of authority, but there are two different ends to the spectrum. There are those that threaten and antagonize everyone..."

"Ah. And those who invite trust. You put Alison into the second category."

"To a greater degree. Nzinga, I'm not so sure of. Somehow she manages to make a hundred kilos of claws and teeth look cute and cuddly. But everybody loves her, despite her bossiness. Compare her to Chakka. He has none of her social skills and no interest in attaining them. He doesn't care about leading anyone. He acts on his own, in perfect confidence of the rightness of his actions and the sureness of success."

"I suppose that's how they function so well together. No overlapping of needs."

"And a complete agreement of objectives. Which is where you come in."

Natalia glanced at him. "It is?"

"Of course. Everyone on this ship is a complete individual, with all sorts of different personal goals. But when it comes to the objective of the mission, your opinion is unquestioned."

"That is the way it's supposed to go in a Commando unit." She grinned. "Until I'm about to make a mistake. Then I expect one of them to tell me."

"And they know that. It makes them even more loyal."

Natalia felt rather uncomfortable. "But we are speaking in generalities here."

"If you like." He regarded her, head to one side. "Have you thought of the effect this attitude will have on the barwolf crew?"

"Not really."

"There are twice as many humans aboard. The barwolves are culturally conditioned to blend in with the group."

"You should have less trouble merging them than you're having with me."

"I'm not having trouble with you, Captain." He cast her a curious glance, then continued. "But taking that in the broader perspective, this ship is a microcosm of what will happen when the barwolves are introduced deeper and deeper into human society. That could be worrisome."

"Now you've jumped into an area I haven't thought about. There's no doubt that human contact will change the barwolves." She considered. "But how big is their population? About half a million?"

"I gather."

"How long will it be before the human population of the whole system, let alone Arborea, gets anywhere close to that size? I don't think we have to worry about the barwolf culture being overwhelmed in our lifetimes or for several centuries to come. In fact, I'd say that only our opposable digits are going to keep humans up to an even level in this partnership." Natalia slapped her hands on the table. "If it makes it easy for our crew to blend together for this mission, I'll be grateful, and leave the thorny problems for our descendants."

"On that topic, do I assume that Andrew is your only foray into parenthood?"

"That's right. Another Commando using the Service to make up for a messy youth." She glanced at him. "You?"

He smiled gently. "I come from a rough environment where people compensate by being very loving to their children. There are a lot of similarities to life on a small spaceship. Displays of bad temper are avoided at all costs, and children are trained from an early age not to lash out at others." He chuckled. "I find I carry a thread of my European heritage in that respect as well, I'm afraid. But generally, I'm a pretty level-headed guy."

She smiled. "I get that impression." She sat straighter. "Well, I've used up enough of your time. Thanks for dropping in."

He just looked at her, that quizzical expression on his face.

"All right. I know I asked you to come, and you couldn't very well refuse. Thank you for being gracious about it."

"It was a pleasure, ma'am. Let's do it again some time." He rose, nodded, and strolled out.

She sat for a while, her eyes on the viewscreen image of the Milky Way, but not really seeing it. *That was a very productive conversation on many levels. I think he's going to fit in rather well.*

16. HAZING

Still, there were long days of acceleration. After the routine maintenance was done, many on-duty and off-duty hours needed filling. Natalia's usual solution was to set up the training ring and keep the cadre in shape.

Since everyone in the crew was a Commando, that meant training for everyone. The combat personnel threw themselves into it with glee. The engineers and pilots weren't overly enthusiastic, but they did their share. Master Pilot Pete Jager was perhaps the least motivated. He preferred to demonstrate his macho personality with his flashy piloting skills.

So when the smallest member of the crew challenged him in free sparring, he declined, holding up his hands. "Sorry, Fiona. Gotta save these fine instruments for the concert stage."

"Oh, come on, Pete. I won't hurt you.' B'kosa grinned. "At least, not your hands."

He glanced around the spectators. There were no sympathetic faces. With bad grace, he shrugged and climbed into the ring, where she proceeded to trounce him soundly. His bad mood deteriorated into anger, and then she really started to throw him around. The cheers and jeers of the other crew settled to dead silence, broken only by the scrape of shoes on canvas and Pete's heavy breathing.

Finally, Fiona gave up. "Okay, Pete. This isn't going anywhere. Thanks for the workout." She climbed out through the ropes, leaving him standing there.

He growled something unintelligible and exited in the other direction.

As it happened, his path took him past the mess table where Alwyn was focused on an enterpad. The pilot jerked to a stop beside the scientist. "Was that a smile I saw?"

Alwyn looked up for a moment. "Probably not. I don't actually know. I was working."

"Have you done your bit in the ring today?"

The scientist smiled. "Oh, I don't do that sort of stuff."

Pete leaned down. "Listen, Mister. This is a Commando ship. We all depend on everyone else to do his share. That means everyone. Come on. Let's get you in the ring and see how you match up."

Alwyn leaned back to look the pilot in the eye. "I am completely willing to do my share and more. But I do not participate in combat."

"Listen, Mr. Pansy. There may come a time when anybody and everybody has to participate in combat, whether they like it or not." He grabbed the slimmer man by the arm. "Come on. Time you got your hands dirty."

The scientist allowed himself to be dragged to his feet, then kept right on coming. The sudden move surprised his antagonist, allowing him to slip free from the heavier man's grasp with a quick twist. He faced the surprised pilot a moment, his eyes cold. "I understand your frustration, having just been tossed around like a rag doll by a smaller Commando, and a woman at that. Does her black skin have anything to do with it as well? It rather makes me wonder, when the time comes and you're expected to do your share in that department, whether you'll be any use to your cadre or not." The pilot had stumbled back a step, and Alwyn bored it. "However, allowing you to recover your macho overcompensation for your other failings by beating on me will hardly do you, me, or the general morale of the cadre any good, and considering the libidinal source of your problems, starts to look rather unwholesome."

The pilot started to turn, but Alwyn held up a hand to stop him. "Oh, no. You don't get to run away and let your anger fester." He pointed to a chair. "You will sit here and put yourself back under control. You will endure the pitying stares of your crewmates, knowing that you deserve every one of them. Then, when you have regained your senses, you will apologize to Miss B'Kosa for what you put her through, and to me for your unearned antagonism."

He took a deep breath, then let it out. "And then I will apologize to you for allowing my anger to push me into such an unequal battle. I know how Commando squads work, and I know my response was just as damaging as yours."

Natalia, listening from the doorway, now stepped forward. "Well, Dr. Blainey, you didn't leave me much to say. Sometimes the captain has to step in and referee these little tiffs, but it looks like it's all under control." She glanced at Jager, sitting with his head bowed. "You were rather hard on him, though."

He met her stare. "I said I don't do physical violence. I didn't say I wouldn't defend myself."

She nodded, then raised her eyes to the rest of the crew, who were standing, looking uncomfortable. "You're supposed to take a lesson out of every training session. I guess we all got one today. Remember that we're in uncharted space. We could meet alien situations and beings that don't react the way we think they will. Don't expect everyone to play by your rules."

She dropped a hand on the pilot's shoulder. "Take your time, Pete. You know how to handle this, and I'm sure you'll make it right."

Pete gave himself a shake and stood. "I'm going to start right now." He pointed at Fiona. "Back in the ring, B'kosa. You're going to show me that last throw you used on me, and you're going to do keep doing it until I've figured out a counter."

The black woman gave a nod and a small grin. "Just love a chance to get my hands on all that lily white muscle."

The two returned to the ring, and Natalia sat beside the scientist, her back to the action. "We've got a good crew here, Doctor. They don't make many mistakes, and they know how to fix it when they do."

He sighed. "I'm so embarrassed. I hate fighting with people who are supposed to be on my side, and when they force it, I get even more angry because of that disappointment."

She smiled. "We all have buttons to push. The trick is to learn everyone's buttons and how not to push them."

"Great. It's a good thing I'm a super-genius like your son says. I've only got a month left to learn them all."

"Please spare us the experimentation. I don't think the ship would be in one piece by the end."

He didn't laugh, turning to her seriously. "As the captain, you should know that I am quite capable of defending myself physically, although not up to the standard of your people, of course. I have above-average athletic ability, and I keep myself in good physical shape. I think the main reason I don't fight is because it's so frustrating. My brain keeps telling my body what it's supposed to do, and it can't."

"I see."

"My other option when he grabbed me was to break his index finger. I could have done that easily, but I didn't want to hurt his hands."

"And you had that all figured out by the time you got to your feet."

"Oh, yes. And I had time also to get pissed off because he was expecting me to play his game. I was willing to make a compromise to fit with his rules, but he was quite happy to break all of mine." He smiled ruefully. "I guess I wouldn't make a very good soldier. I don't run with the pack very well."

"Do you watch yourself over your shoulder like this all the time?"

108

"It's a novel situation and I'm learning new things about me all the time." He glanced at her. "I'm quite a complex person, you know. I find myself endlessly fascinated by what I do and feel. Don't let me bore you with it."

"That's all right, Alwyn. I've only got a month to get you blended in with the crew. The more I know the better." She got up and returned to the chart room shaking her head. *I hope the crew can catch on to his sense of humour. Sometimes I don't know when he's joking, myself.*

17. DIRTY FLORIE

Maybe it was her imagination, but Natalia stepped onto the bridge one morning a week later with a heightened sense of anticipation.

Her First Officer slipped to attention. "Captain on the bridge."

"Thank you, Mr. Jones. Everything shipshape?" He didn't answer, and she watched him sit back down at his communications console, that feeling of excitement building in her.

He fiddled with a few settings, then glanced up at her. "Ma'am?"

"Yes, Jones."

"We're getting some long-range signals from re-ti." He gestured at the main viewscreen, where the warped, colour-shot view of space she was becoming used to was slowly taking more solid form. All she could see was a blurred dot with smaller blurs around it.

"What kind of signals?"

"Varied...nearest guess I could make is a squadron on maneuvers. Plenty of light radio chatter, too faint to understand, and then one big signal that cuts through it all. Too messed up at this distance to be clear, but definitely giving orders."

"Bearing?"

"One point three five off the port bow, point two up."

"Course?"

"Assuming they're using normal frequencies, Doppler readings say directly away from us, ma'am."

"So they're headed towards Sol."

"That is correct, ma'am."

"Thank you, First. Monitor and update me when you have anything."

"Aye, ma'am."

"Auxiliary crew to your cockpit, please. Andrew, see what shows up in the Otherwhere data."

Aye, ma'am. Won't take long...

She focused on the viewscreen image. *NightHawk, please blend the two feeds and put it up on ship's com.*

Coming up, ma'am.

The vague blip cleared. It grew slightly, until four smaller, brighter blips showed around it. That was all.

"Our friends don't have Otherwhere communication. Are those the Otherwhere spheres we're seeing, Andrew?"

That would be logical. Means the mothership doesn't have one.

"So they have one major ship, and are using four of their captures as auxiliaries. I wonder what they did with their other victims."

Blew them up or sent them to the black market chop shops in Sol's Asteroid Belt, I guess.

"Adrian and Andrew, can either of you get a course and velocity on them?"

"Aye, ma'am."

Aye, ma'am.

Soon the First Officer raised his head from his console. "Sending the course to your screen, ma'am."

We concur, ma'am. Velocity is a bit of a problem...

"They're in decel, ma'am. And their course is interesting."

"Interesting, First? What does that mean?"

"Because it matches the course of the *Angela Merkel*." He flashed her a rare grin. "Our bogeys are one point five billion kilometres in front of her..."

That's it, Mr. Jones. And right on her course, decelerating. At this rate, the ESA ship will catch up to them in about three weeks...and their velocities will be roughly equal.

"Well, there never was much doubt. There are our pirates."

NightHawk, Barwolf One, change of course.

To the radio signal, ma'am?

That's right. Enter the data into the Flight Command Server and both of you execute when ready.

Course change in progress, ma'am.

Emotion: agreement

Except for a slight adjustment in the quiet rumble of the ship, nothing seemed to happen. However, it wasn't a minute before two heads poked through the bridge doorway.

"Course change, ma'am?"

"Good ear, Lundeen. Only a degree and a bit." She regarded Alwyn. "What brings you, Dr. Blainey?"

The engineer shrugged. "Pattern change. Just wondered."

She nodded towards the third accel couch. "Have a seat and listen up. All will be revealed." She returned to the ship's com and the barwolf gestalt as well.

"We have contact, people. Sounds like a mothership and four big auxiliaries. They're on the track of that Space Agency research vessel that left Freighty a couple of weeks ago, travelling in re-ti. We've changed course to pursue. We're moving much faster, so we'll monitor until we have more information, then choose our decel course from there."

* * *

For the next three days they tracked the small, blurry dots that firmed and grew rapidly. As they neared, two more small blips appeared. "More outriders."

A safe assumption, ma'am.

When the signal for the *Angela Merkel* was close enough to appear on the same viewscreen as her enemy, it was time to take action.

"*NightHawk,* plot us a decel rate to come out of Otherwhere ten hours behind the enemy, closing at a thousand klicks. Barwolf 1, we will flip and start heavy decel. Please comply with Flight Control."

Emotion: agreement.

Course calculated and entered with Flight Control Server, ma'am.

Master Pilot Jager, are you ready for the flip?

Ready, ma'am.

Natalia accessed the ship's com. "*Flip to decel in one minute. Please vacate the habitation ring.*"

Lundeen popped into her augment *We give them ten hours to get ready for us?*

"About that. We have several days before we reach them at this rate of decel. We'll get better data and then make up our minds exactly where, when and how fast we want to hit them."

Sounds good to me.

Jager, the com is yours.

I have the com, ma'am. He accessed the ship's com. "*Flip in ten seconds...five...three, two, one, commence.*"

A slight unease twisted Natalia's stomach as torsional forces argued with the ship's gravitational systems, and then it all straightened out.

"Flip completed, ma'am. Resuming course."

"Thank you, Mr. Jager. NightHawk, commence decel."

Deceleration commencing in five...three, two, one, commence.

The gravity swooped, then returned to normal zero point eight.

Natalia accessed ship's com. "*On course for our pirates, folks. ETA thirteen days, twelve hours.*"

* * *

112

Eight days later, the crew gathered in the lounge to watch the biggest viewscreen. The barwolves lay on their mat, their heads up, alert.

Natalia popped an image up on the screen and in the gestalt. "Well, we've pretty well nailed her. Former Space Arm Destroyer 34, the *Daniel Foreman,* known to her detractors as *Dirty Florrie.* Textbook example of how a legend is born. Several bad captains in a row, resulting in a sullen, fractious crew, then completely destroyed by the man who was sent in to clean things up. Closest thing Space Arm has come to a mutiny in a hundred years. She got the rep as an unlucky ship, and they finally...oh, that's interesting. She rather disappeared off the records. Doesn't say whether she was sold or scrapped. Well, now we know. She headed out for parts unknown, and here she is."

There was silence as the crew absorbed the information.

Lundeen chuckled. "They certainly weren't big on aesthetics in those days."

"A 'form follows function' design." Alwyn shook his head. "Grace was a foreign term to those naval architects."

Alwyn reached into the augment and turned the vessel to a side view. "A case of ugly being more than skin deep."

The destroyer looked less like a spaceship and more like an old-fashioned fuel drum with a bunch of random equipment stuck on by bubble gum. The only variations on the line of the hull were three huge steering thrusters spaced around the circumference just aft of the blunt, rounded bow and three massive rocket exhausts protruding from the transom. Weapons blisters of various sorts marred the outline from stem to stern. The whole vessel was a hefty salute to functionality and brute strength.

Natalia accessed the "obsolete craft" specs in *NightHawk's* memory and put the data up on the second viewscreen. "She's an Aquitaine Class destroyer. Space Arm threw thirty of them together in a hurry during the Mars Blockade. Some are still in service. Slow and heavily armed with the most up-to-date weaponry of thirty years ago. Displacement: 8,000 tonnes; length: 155 metres; beam: 45 metres. She carried a nominal crew of 20 officers and 400 men, including Marines and tech/scientific staff.

"They won't have much scientific staff now, but they'll have plenty of men for boarding parties."

"Maybe, maybe not. We have no idea whether this is the only ship in this business, and what she was doing out here in the first place.

The only thing we know is that they have about six outriders and a fleet of smaller ships, because we've heard the communications. To continue:

"Her main armament is a dozen Mark 120 projectile cannons spaced on the circumference at bow, stern and amidships, shooting 122 mm shells, usually with shrapnel loads."

Andrew frowned. "Hard on our sliverships. What else?"

"She also has rudimentary plasma throwers, short range. Her long-range armament is missile launchers, and it's anybody's guess what types they're carrying. Only thing we can be sure of, they won't be Asimoved, because these guys won't know or care. They've been preying on unarmed commercial vessels, though, so they won't have needed a whole lot of upgrading. If all they have is the original stuff, they can't touch us. Even if they loaded up on ordnance ten or fifteen years ago when they started out from Sol, our anti-missile ArIns are still far in advance.

"We hope."

Alwyn raised a hesitant hand. "Sorry if I'm being naïve, but that size of vessel seems to be a huge investment for a relatively small return. Are we really to believe that there is an underworld syndicate of some sort that could plan and finance at that level? Oh, I've heard the stories of the battle cruiser that SolarCorp was using to intimidate Barnard's system, but that was an interplanetary corporation."

Natalia shook her head. "If you're being naïve, you're in good company. Space Arm has been playing catch-up in the piracy field, but as far as I know, there's nobody with that kind of clout involved. We've been doing a lot of thinking on this, both as individuals and in gestalt.

"Our guess is somebody started out for Barnard's System a long time ago on a legitimate emigration. Something happened onboard. Odds of 65% say mutiny. When the reality of long-time space travel hit them, they stopped in the middle to take advantage of easier pickings."

Andrew frowned. "That sounds easier than it is. They have to match speed with a ship accelerating up to or coming down from LTV. Let me see... yes, they start outward bound, catch a ship heading for Freighty or Barnard, match speed and raid them, maybe take the whole ship and send it back to Sol for sale to the chop shops, or keep it for an outlier. Then they turn and head back, waiting for one of Freighty's customers coming home full of the latest high tech. Or a fuel carrier from Barnard once in a while in order to keep flying. Prime.

And they've probably been doing that for years. Why didn't anyone catch on?"

His mother shrugged. "Space is a large, dangerous place. Ships disappear." She accessed *NightHawk's* memory. "Yep. El Dorado lost a loaded fuel ship six years ago. That's billions of planetaries worth of fuel ore."

Andrew wiggled his eyebrows. "Of course, once they started to raid Freighty's territory they had moved into the big leagues and didn't know it."

Toni grinned. "And we're the big league enforcers, are we? Flattering."

"That seems to be the story." Natalia eyed both of them. "I guess we'd better live up to our reputation."

Andrew flicked his fingers in a shooing motion. "I'm not worried. The new gestalt and the new ships are prime. We'll handle them."

Natalia opened her mouth to speak, and then changed her mind about a lecture. "All right. Get on it. Research this destroyer, cross-reference with lost ships; you know the drill. Assume that most of the resources of the victims have been available to the pirates, including crew, auxiliary ships and armament. Tomorrow we'll make a preliminary gestalt with the Auxiliary Flight Crew and do some strategic planning."

Andrew flipped her a salute. "Sure enough, Captain. Right on it." He sauntered out the door, Toni and Nzinga straggling behind him.

The crew split up, and Natalia retired to her chart room, where she leaned back in her chair, hands behind her head. *Something's wrong, here, but I can't say, 'You're not worried enough,' to a crew this experienced. Or else I'm getting paranoid. NightHawk, am I getting paranoid?*

According to your latest psych evaluation, you are operating within three percent of your norm. Three percent les paranoid, as it happens.

When was my last psych evaluation?

I am not allowed to give you that information Ma'am, for fear of skewing the results of future assessments.

Can you give me a ballpark?

Regulations require a psych evaluation of every ship's commander at least once a week.

Prime. It's not me. It's the crew. Please access crew psych reports. Any anomalies?

Nothing that stands out, ma'am. Crew morale is high and tension is low.

How low?

Five percent below norm during this stage of an operation, ma'am.

Does that bother you?

I am unsure how to answer that question, ma'am. In normal circumstances, calmness is a quality to be fostered in a crew on a mission or long journey.

It is. But too much of any trend is suspicious, and a trend in a direction I don't expect is doubly so. Do you consider this mission to be normal circumstances?

Most of our missions over the past few years have been outside the experience of humans. Perhaps the crew has become accustomed to this situation.

Fair enough. I'm at the point where I don't want them to get accustomed to anything. I want them on edge, ready for any twist fate is going to throw at us.

I read you loud and clear, Ma'am. I will continue to monitor the crew's readiness level, and inform you the moment anything changes.

Thank you, NightHawk. She had a sudden thought. NightHawk, your new communications protocols allow you to communicate with the barwolves. What kind of communications do you get?

Mostly visual and emotional.

The same as you get from the crew?

Visual is clearer. Emotional seems...hazier.

So you're not getting as strong or clear signals in the emotional range.

That's accurate, Ma'am.

Good. Please access recent conversations about levels of barwolf communication.

Accessing...yes. I see what you're getting at. Patches is inexperienced with our powers, and could be feeling too confident in our abilities. This could be feeding back to the human crew...

...which could cause the humans to feel more relaxed, thus signalling to the barwolves that everything is under control...

Emotion: humour. At which point we go into battle in a haze of joy and good cheer. Not funny.

18. SCIENTISTS!

Natalia was working in the chart room when rising voices on the bridge distracted her. Pete Kanaka sounded hot under the collar.

"I don't care if it was in the rules or not. You don't do that to one of your allies."

Fraser's deep voice carried a hint of laughter. "You assumed I was an ally, did you?"

Ah. The never-ending round of battle games the crew indulged in. She quite approved; it kept their minds sharp. *As long as it doesn't cause crew interaction problems.* She listened more carefully to see how it played out.

"Lieutenant, you tell him. It's not smart to double-deal your friends. After a while nobody will team up with you."

The First Officer's measured tones undercut the tension. "It is true, Charlie. People don't forget quickly when they've been taken advantage of."

Fraser laughed. "He's just upset because he had a week's galley duty riding on the outcome."

Karaka's voice took on an aggrieved tone. "That had nothing to do with it. Don't make me out to be a sore loser. I'm just telling you it's a bad idea, that's all."

Then, to her surprise, Alwyn's voice drifted in. "Say, Pete, weren't you telling me last week something about winning a session by making alliances with three different enemies, and then sitting and watching them beat each other up?"

"Yeah, what of it?"

"The same game?"

"Yeah." The Master Pilot chuckled. "Got out of three hours of radio monitor duty with that trick."

"And Joe, just yesterday, didn't you insert three platoons on B'Kosa's flank by persuading her you were headed for an attack on Lundeen, but then you took her unawares?"

"Umm...yeah."

"I don't see the difference from what Charlie did."

"But he cheated...well, not really cheated, but..."

"So, you just learned something new. It's a game of both strategy and diplomacy. Diplomats cheat. Nature of the beast. You have to be aware of the shift from one phase to the next."

"Yeah, but..." A disgusted snort. "Yeah, I guess."

"Well, there you go."

There was silence, and then footsteps — a long, relaxed stride — came down the corridor. As Blaney passed the chart room door, she motioned him in and pointed to the chair. "That was the 'Cast the First Stone' lesson from the New Testament."

"Sort of." He took the chair reversed, arms folded along the backrest. "You know, the interesting thing about ancient religious texts is that the ideas they talk about resonate deep in the human psyche. It's why so many of the stories recur all over the world."

She regarded him. "Do you spend a lot of time thinking about stuff like that?"

He shrugged. "Keeps me from being bored when I can't sleep."

"Oh, do you have trouble sleeping?"

The side of his mouth curled slightly. "Yeah, all my ideas keep me awake."

She allowed a small smile and went back to her tablet. Then she looked up. "Why did you step in, anyway? They're always arguing about their games."

He shook his head. "They had stopped talking about the game and were getting into personalities. I don't know about this bunch, but in a lot of groups, being a sore loser is a bad brush to tar a man with. Joe was really bothered."

She nodded. "And it's pretty frustrating to argue against a guy as big as Fraser. Especially when he's in the right."

"Was he?"

"Oh, sure. Charlie's such a nice guy, he never has trouble getting allies in the games." She grinned. "Do them good to remember he's got a brain as well." She lowered her tablet. "And I know why you did it."

"Do you?"

"Yep. You've decided on your role in the crew. You're going to be the guy with the moral high ground. You have no military authority, so you're going to be the one that voices the group opinion. The judge."

"Do you approve?"

"It's not up to me to approve or disapprove. A good captain doesn't mess with the social interactions of the crew. Unless they're screwing up, in which case I wait until it spills into their performance, when I have the right to act."

"But until that time, you foster good crew dynamics to keep them together."

"That's right. And since now I know you're aware of it, I'll be counting on you to swing your weight in the right direction when it's needed. Like you just did."

"You're welcome."

She looked up at him from under lowered eyebrows. "Don't make light of it. It could save your life some day."

He rose. "And now the uppity newcomer has been put back in his place, and all's right with the ship."

She jumped up and stepped towards him, placing a hand on his arm. "Alwyn, I don't want to put anyone in his place, especially you. I'm sorry I said that."

He patted her hand and turned away. "I'm not sorry. That was you, being a good captain. Which will probably save my life some day."

With a grin over his shoulder, he sauntered off down the slideway, leaving her to wonder what had just happened.

* * *

When she entered the mess that afternoon, Andrew and Alwyn were sitting at the smaller table, staring off into space. They were too far away to understand, but every once in a while one of them would murmur something, and the other's face would register a reaction.

She smiled to herself and ignored them, pouring a coffee and checking the snacks bin for a muffin.

After a while the action became more pronounced, with Andrew moving around in his seat more, frowning. Finally he slapped both hands on the table and turned to stare at Alwyn accusingly. "That was sneaky."

The scientist raised his eyebrows. "You concede mate in thirteen moves?"

"Fifteen...wait a minute." The boy's shoulders sagged. "Yeah. Thirteen."

Natalia smiled. "3-D chess?"

Andrew shrugged. "Yeah."

"And he beat you?"

"Five times in a row."

Natalia frowned. "But he doesn't have an augment."

"He does it from memory."

Natalia faced Alwyn. "That's pretty impressive."

He shrugged.

She grinned at Andrew. "You'll have to cheat. Try him against you and Chakka in gestalt."

"You don't get it. That was all of us. He just beat *NightHawk,* Chakka, and me."

Natalia regarded the scientist. "Now, that's very impressive."

He shifted in his seat. "I just have an affinity for patterns."

"That's not what he means, Mum. He means he's a flipping genius, and his intelligence is off the scale, and that's why Freighty put him on this mission."

Natalia frowned at her son and turned to Alwyn. "How do you feel about someone talking as if you're not in the room, explaining what you really mean?"

"Not a problem."

"It isn't?"

"I'm used to it. Cultural characteristic."

"Oh? What culture?"

He didn't skip a beat. "Inuit."

She glanced at him. Again the humorous curl of the lip. She shrugged. "Well, who am I to question a cultural trait?"

"I was adopted." He sighed. "To make a long story short, I was born in the town of Iqaluit in northern Canada. My parents died in an accident, and I was raised by what Christians would call my godparents. The concept doesn't exist in that culture. I was their *tiguak,* I suppose. Adopted non-relative child."

"The term 'tiguak' comes from the North Slope Alaskan Inuit language, Inupiaq."

"I'm stretching, *NightHawk.* There simply is no word for the concept in Inuktituk, the language of Nunavut, the district I come from. Like some African tribes don't have a word for 'snow,' for some reason."

"Point taken."

"And in Inuit culture, it is considered very bad form to praise yourself. You are expected to sit modestly by and blush as your friends tell everyone about your wonderful deeds."

Natalia nodded. "I like these people more and more."

"But I seem to have maintained a streak of my ancestors' European egotism. So I have to manipulate my opponents into lauding my superiority." He mimed tipping his hat to a grinning Andrew. "But he's wrong. What I said was exactly what I meant. I am not a genius by standard measurements. I'm more like an idiot savant, or, to be more politically correct, gifted. My abilities are not measurable by standard tests, because they range greatly. As Freighty told you, my main talent is recognizing patterns. Hence the skill at chess. Freighty has boosted my abilities in my chosen field of study." He glanced around the lounge. "For example, you have a stress pattern in the hull," he pointed, "right where that bulkhead is attached. I suspect it will be skewing the PermaSkin readings in that area.'

"Really?" Natalia pulled up the specs for that section of the hull and opened her augment. *Lundeen, will you look at this layout?*

He answered from the engine room. *You mean that minor stress anomaly? Is it important?*

Could it be the source of that astigmatic blip in the portside PermaSkin view?

Give me a moment.

She nodded to Alwyn. "Lundeen is checking. The PermaSkin suturing process isn't perfect, so we have minor optical anomalies all over the hull. We cope with them by programming, but every little hitch like that takes computing time, and that slows our reaction."

"Sounds logical."

"You knew that already."

He grinned. "I had no idea."

Lundeen came back on. "Yes, ma'am. Stress at that point would cause that glitch."

Alwyn spread his hands. "See? No super-geniuses here. Just us folks."

"Do you know what we should do about it?"

He shook his head. "I just find 'em. Can't fix 'em."

Natalia folded her hands on the table. "Look, Alwyn, I'm sorry to subject you to an interrogation when it makes you feel uncomfortable, but this is how the Commandos work. We need to know everything about each other, because our lives may depend on each other at any moment."

"I understand. And I'm the new boy, about whom you know nothing."

"Including why Freighty sent you on this mission.'

He gave a rueful laugh. "About which I'm almost as much in the dark as you are."

"Really?"

"I hardly know what the mission is. Piloting this revolutionary new spacecraft, obviously. I'm not a pilot, and I'm not a physicist."

"But you do have some kind of natural augmentation."

"You could term it that. I can hear your communications and respond with ideas and images. Actual words are harder."

"You're doing fine with the crew. All we have to do is figure out how you fit in with the mission. Knowing Freighty, it will be painfully obvious when it occurs, and we'll all be kicking ourselves that we didn't see it beforehand."

"Fair enough. And in that vein, do you have any more questions?"

She shrugged. "Sure. Anything else that you think is important that I know? You've given us your main strengths. Any little weaknesses we have to watch out for? Any Achilles' Heel?"

"Did you know I'm claustrophobic?"

She glanced around the tiny mess hall. Besides Andrew, no other crew were present. "Didn't they treat it before they sent you into this environment?"

"Treated, but not a hundred percent successfully."

"Have you had any recent attacks?"

"Once in a while, but the coping skills they taught me have always worked. So far."

"I see."

"I don't like it spread around. There's always some ass who wants to use it to bring me down a peg towards his neanderthal level. Then things get embarrassing because I really do have no control over it. It's a phobia, and put in certain circumstances, I panic."

"Keeping in mind what I said a moment ago, should I know the circumstances?"

He sighed. "It's like this. The village I grew up in had its share of idiots and bullies. I was small, smart, and the wrong skin colour. The traditional show of dominance, at least with these dolts, was to pin the victim on his face, often in soft snow. Once they found out this would make me panic, they took special pleasure in submitting me to the practice. So, if I'm held in a prone position with my face down and my breathing impaired, I panic."

"I don't think any of us would find that a particularly pleasant experience."

"Yes, but I react sooner and more violently. It's all in my psych report."

She nodded. "Which I need to find time to read, and nobody besides myself and Jones has access to. Thanks."

He returned the nod. "I won't say it was a pleasure, but I'm glad we got it out of the way." His eyes slid to Andrew.

She shook her head. "When Andrew is in gestalt with *NightHawk,* he virtually is the ship. He has access to everything, so Space Arm doesn't have a security classification that applies to him."

The scientist grinned. "Really? That's interesting. Same here."

Andrew's eyebrows shot up. "They can't find a way to measure you, so they can't restrict you, hey? Prime."

"That's right. I am on my honour to recognize the dangers of knowing things I'm not supposed to know, and keeping my ears closed and my mouth shut."

The ensign slapped his hand on the table again. "And now we know why you're really on this mission to the far reaches of space..."

"...to keep me as far away from all their sensitive material as they can."

They all chuckled, and Andrew got up to leave. Then he stopped. "Oh, one thing I've been meaning to mention, ma'am. You know all the ship-joining configurations we practiced? There's one we missed."

"Yes, I know. The Ship Busters are blocking *NightHawk's* ventral hatch. That bothering you?"

He shrugged. "Just thinking ahead, ma'am. The ventral hatch came up in a couple of scenarios we ran through."

"That's been niggling at me, too. Will you hang on a moment? *Lundeen, will you join us in the mess, please?*"

On my way, ma'am.

When the Chief Engineer was seated with them, Natalia laid it out. "Andrew has just reminded me that the Ship Busters are an unknown factor. We know how to deploy them, but they're rather unwieldy to manipulate in close proximity."

"Not to mention dangerous." Nelson grimaced.

"That's right. But once I think about it, there could be any number of scenarios where we might want to dismount them and move them to another configuration or another ship."

The engineer nodded. "We did modify the ventral docking clamps slightly to accommodate them under acceleration. They were tested in space dock, and suit all specifications."

"Right, but now we're not in space dock, we're in space, and we need to be sure of everything. Let's give ourselves until tomorrow to think up some exercises that will test our ability to maneuver the weapons with the slivers and *Diablo,* and at the same time recheck our ventral docking system."

She looked around the table, received three nods, and dismissed them.

19. AIR LEAK

As Natalia expected, the practice maneuvers went without a hitch. To start with, Fiona and Fraser went on EV to assist with the docking, but after a couple of runs, the crew demonstrated the ability to remove one of the ShipBusters, fly it out to either *Diablo* or one of the slivers, and dock it again by remote.

The trouble came when the Red Slab docked in place of the Ship Busters at the ventral airlock.

Natalia briefed them before the exercise started. "Listen up, now. Alison, you're in charge of the ShipBusters. Keep them on steady decel with the rest of us, and keep them out of the way."

"Aye, ma'am."

"Auxiliary gestalt, you're responsible for Red Slab."

Emotion: eager willingness to succeed.

"Pete and *NightHawk*, you just keep her steady as she goes. Questions?"

"Do you want me anywhere special, ma'am?"

"No, Mr. Blainey. You're on observation in the Auxiliary Bridge as usual."

"Aye, ma'am. I'll stay out of the way."

She thought she detected a note of disappointment in his voice, but this was not the place to deal with it. *"All right. Alison, disengage on your own time."*

ShipBusters disengaging in five...three, two, one, action. Buster One away. Buster two away.

After a brief pause, the pilot came on augment again. *Busters clear of operational area, ma'am.*

"Thank you, Major. Auxiliary Bridge, the exercise is yours."

Aye ma'am. Red Slab approaching ventral airlock.

She watched on the viewscreen, pleased at how gently the slab, still holding deceleration, slid into contact with the mothership. Barely perceptible jolts channelled through the space frame.

Red Slab connected, ma'am. Umbilical attaching...attachment complete. Pressure rising...

A yellow light flashed on her viewscreen just as *NightHawk* jolted her with a warning.

Air leak, ma'am.

"Hold everything. We've got an air leak. NightHawk, run Diagnostic Protocol 37. Engineering, what do you see?"

124

Lundeen came on the com. *"Introducing smoke now. Give it a moment to reach that line...yes, there it is."*

On the viewscreen a faint trace of smoke sprouted from the point where the ship's umbilical attached to Red Slab.

Natalia scanned Protocol 37 in her augment. "Continue with pressure testing."

Ma'am...

"Not right now, Alwyn. We're in the middle of an emergency protocol."

But ma'am, there's a pressure...

"Not now, Mr. Blainey. Stay off this channel."

...Aye, ma'am.

She refocused. *"Have you done your readings, Mr. Lundeen?"*

"Aye, ma'am. No particular danger. We've pinpointed the source, but there's no obvious cause."

"Listen up, now. We will abort this exercise. Auxiliary team, disengage Red Slab. Major Rowell, bring Buster One in, and hold Buster Two alongside. Specialist B'Kosa, would you return to EV and remove the umbilical fitting, pursuant to Protocol 37B?"

Aye, ma'am.

Proceeding with 37 B, ma'am.

"Alison, as soon as she's finished dock the other buster."

"Aye, ma'am

In less than half an hour, the scan was complete and the second bomb was once again nestled into *NightHawk's* belly.

"Thank you, everyone. Not a successful operation, but a very smooth response. Department heads meeting in the mess in fifteen minutes." Then she switched to Alwyn's private channel. "Dr. Blainey, could you meet me in the chartroom now?"

Aye, ma'am.

She was sitting at her desk when he entered, and he stood, looking uncertain as she stared up at him. "That didn't go exactly as planned."

He looked puzzled.

"A lesson nobody thought to teach you. When we're in the middle of an emergency protocol, we follow it to the letter, with no improvisation. Do you understand?"

He shrugged. "I understand in general, but I could see..."

She shook her head emphatically. "This is the military, Alwyn. There is no 'but.' If you distracted someone in the middle of an emergency procedure and they missed a step, it could kill us all."

His shoulders sagged. "Yes, I understand."

125

She regarded him. "But now I have time to listen. What did you observe?"

"Observing the force lines in the titanium seal, it seemed to me that there was a pressure differential on the wrong side."

"Can you explain...no, don't waste it on me." She rose. "The next part of Protocol 37 is the debrief."

He gave her a twisted smile. "Into which I will not insert my distracting influence unless asked."

She responded with a similar grin. "You're catching on."

She led the way to the mess, where *NightHawk* had posted the next steps of the protocol on the main viewscreen. She went through each step, and each member of the crew gave the appropriate responses.

Which were all negative.

She looked around the table. "So, as far as you can see, there's nothing out of place, nothing wrong."

Everyone shrugged, with the exception of Alwyn, who fixed her with an unblinking stare.

She shrugged as well. "And since our military protocol has let us down, we now turn to our civilian support. Dr. Blainey, I gather you have an observation."

"Yes, ma'am. The titanium gasket that seals the join. The pressure differential was on the wrong side."

"And you knew this because..."

"When a gasket of any sort is sealed, the pressure of the support flange squashes the ring slightly at the spot where the air is trying to leak out, thus making the seal. If it's rubber, anyone can see it. With metal, it's harder to see, but it's there. In this case, the pressure was on the back of the flange, as it should have been, but the face of the seal was not under pressure. So it didn't seal."

She glanced at Lundeen.

"Metallurgy 201, ma'am. The question is, why wasn't there any pressure where there was supposed to be?"

"Well, let's take a look at it. *Fiona, is that fitting warm enough to handle?*"

Coming now, ma'am.

The Engineering Specialist brought in a bundle of insulating foam, placed it on the table, and unwrapped it. The fitting was a simple threaded hose end ten centimetres in diameter. Mist formed on it immediately. "I wouldn't touch it with bare hands."

Lundeen nodded. "Fine. Will you take the tungsten seal off, please. We need to look at it."

Fiona reached out with gloved hands and eased a shiny metallic piece off the end of the hose and placed it on the table. It resembled a short hunk of pipe with a flange sticking out around the middle.

"Wait a minute." Lundeen peered closer. "Where's the positioning mark?"

She picked up the ring and turned it over. "There doesn't seem to be one."

The engineer nodded. "I don't suppose it matters. It's symmetrical."

"No it isn't..." All eyes turned to Alwyn, who raised his hands in defence. "Sorry, Nelson, but it isn't symmetrical."

The Chief Engineer frowned and stared harder at the ring, fishing a micrometer out of his coverall pocket. Fiona held the fitting out, and he measured it carefully. Then he dropped his hands to the table with a snort of disgust. "The flange is half a millimetre off centre. If you put the ring in backwards, the pressure would come on the shipside edge of the flange, not on the outside, where it's supposed to be."

"So the seal was put in backwards?"

"All the evidence leads to that conclusion. That flange was replaced in a routine refit..." he accessed his augment, "...two years ago. There is supposed to be an "o" on the outboard side of the flange, but the new part didn't have one. Probably someone put it in backwards. And the proof is simple." He reached out carefully and, juggling the piece of frigid titanium in his hands, reversed it and put it in place. Then he nodded to turn the meeting back to Natalia.

She, too, nodded. "Take it back out and put it on, Fiona."

"Aye, ma'am." She re-wrapped her parcel and departed.

"Any chance it's been damaged?

"That's titanium, ma'am. If there had been any undue stress, I'm sure Alwyn would have seen it."

Once again all eyes turned to the civilian. "Right as rain, ma'am."

Natalia slapped her hands on the table. "Fine. Let's take two hours for lunch and reset, and we'll try it all again."

Blainey raised a hand for attention. "And I should apologize for breaking into a military protocol. I have some learning to do."

Lundeen grinned. "But you had already solved the problem, hadn't you?"

"Well, yes."

The engineer nodded. "It isn't whether you should break in; it's when. Our standard rule is if there's going to be broken equipment, injury, or loss of life, you interrupt."

Alwyin grinned. "That's interesting. We have the same rule on racing sailboats. You never step in and do somebody else's job unless equipment or people are endangered. Then it's to hell with egos, and make it safe." He glanced at Natalia. "And I know there's more than egos at stake here."

She created a small smile, then dismissed the crew.

She strode back to the chart room, keeping a calm face, but inside she was seething. *He's got this mission mixed up with a sailboat race. He was fitting in with the crew so well, I stopped worrying. So I just got my wakeup call. Until I find a place for him, I'm going to have to keep him in line a little better.*

She threw herself into her chair and slammed her heels onto her desk. *And if I'm honest, he was fitting in with me so well, I let my guard down there, too. Well, I got my eyes opened in that respect. Damn! Another dud.*

* * *

Over the next few days, Natalia kept an eye out for Alwyn, but he rarely intruded into the operating gestalt, even of the Auxiliary Bridge.

Then she noticed that he wasn't around the ship as much as previously. Not that she was trying to notice, but she was used to seeing certain members of the crew in certain places, and Blainey didn't seem to be spending much time in his usual haunts.

Then one afternoon she was passing his cabin door when it opened, and Patches stepped out. One glanced over one's shoulder, and Natalia felt *NightHawk* receive the request to close the door. Then one afforded her the leg-touch, plate scratch ritual.

Emotion: Question?

Image: Patches and Blainey playing with a ball.

That image had become the common symbol for any interspecies recreation. *Emotion: humour.*

Image: adult barwolf moving through forest, barwolf cub following and copying every move.

"Oh. Training,"

Emotion: agreement. The barwolf turned and meandered away down the hall, and Natalia continued about her own business.

20. THE FUTURE

But the problem continued to bother her, and finally she came up with a partial solution. She pulled Andrew aside the next day. "Something has been bothering me, Andrew, and this latest problem brought it up again. We have yet to find a place in our operations for Dr. Blainey. He's been assigned to the Auxiliary Crew, and you're the augment expert. I'd like you to focus on figuring out what he can and can't do in the gestalt, so we have an idea of his strengths that we can use to place him."

"You want me to run some tests on Alwyn?" He stared at her in surprise.

"Whatever you need. We have to tie him down to something. Otherwise, as has already happened, we have a loose cannon rolling around on deck that could be a distraction at a fatal moment."

"I see what you mean." He still looked doubtful. "I'll talk to him."

"Whether you tell him or not, find out what he's good for."

Andrew nodded slowly. "I can't see treating him like a guinea pig. I'll talk to him."

"You do that. Dismissed."

If he was surprised at the abrupt end to the conversation, he didn't show it, merely saluted. "Aye, ma'am. He turned out the door.

Then he spun and stuck his head back in. "You and Alwyn having a tiff, Mum?"

She gave him her best scowl. "What do you mean by that?"

He slouched back inside, grinning. "What it sounds like. You've been giving him a rough time, lately, and I haven't noticed you spending any time together." He regarded her and shook his head. "It's a small ship, Mum."

"Well, since this seems to be a mother-and-son conversation, how are you and Toni getting along these days?"

He pulled up the chair and sat down. "Setting aside your obvious change of topic, I suppose now would be a good time for a chat."

"Do we have something to chat about?"

"Yes. Toni and I have been discussing the future. Mainly what's going to happen when she doesn't re-up for another tour."

"I know about her deal with Freighty for Nzinga's future."

"Surprise, surprise, Freighty's plans seem to mesh very neatly with ours."

"And when that happens, I have learned to be very careful."

"Don't worry. I've been watching you deal with him for years, and I've known him even longer. But despite that, our best plan is to part from the military and take up our positions on the Board of the Freighty Consortium. "

He held up a cautioning hand. "Oh, we won't go until after the Proxima Centauri problem is solved. We wouldn't leave you in the lurch."

"Thank you for that. So, what do you plan?"

"Well, I had a chat with Freighty face-to-face, and I've been on the blower with the University of Mars. Once my PhD is through, I'll be continuing my augment research. The obvious place is Arborea, where most of my subjects, or partners as the case may be, are located."

He rubbed his palms on his jeans and looked at her sideways. "Downplanet is also the best place to raise children. Apparently if they spend the first five years of their lives in gravity, their bodies develop more naturally."

She took a moment. "So am I likely to be a grandma soon?"

He shrugged. "Once the Centauri mission is over, we'll start working on it. And there's more."

"Why am I not surprised."

"It has to do with Toni's auguar research. The only way to get new subjects is to create them, and the only two adult auguars in the Barnard System are Nzinga and Chakka. Nzinga's augment suppresses her breeding cycles, but it's an easy fix."

"Another reason to set your operations downplanet. We do not want to go through an auguar mating session on a small ship."

"Precisely. So we have begun the approval process with Space Arm admin and the Auguar breeding boffins for the genetic match. I'm not too worried; Freighty and I have already done the prelims."

She leaned back in her chair. "So what we're looking at is some time in the next couple of years, you two are going to leave the military at take up residence on Arborea and work on auguars and gestalts for Freighty."

"And for the University of Mars. I'll be Project Head. Joachim will be my first graduate student. Morissa will be guest lecturer and on the Board of Directors. Toni will be a research assistant, but I think she'll be taking a degree as well."

"And they're going to let you run it because Freighty will finance the lot?"

He grinned. "Not a chance. Space Arm and Mars U want their share of the pie, and that will cost them. It'll probably be a three- way split. Oh, sooner or later they'll want to start a branch university, and then they'll send in the bureaucrats."

She laid her hands on her desk. "Well, I'm glad to see you have it all tied up so neatly. It sounds like a very workable plan..."

"...I know. Until suddenly it isn't." He stood. "You taught me well, Mum."

She looked up at him, suddenly aware of how tall and adult he was. A shot of cold gushed down her spine at the thought of losing him.

"Come here." He grabbed her hand and hauled her to her feet. "You've still got us for a year or so." He enfolded her in those long, strong, arms, and for once, she just let it happen. Then she pushed him away.

"What was that all about?"

"I dunno. You were just looking sort of forlorn, and I thought you needed it."

He started out, but then turned back. "And we can talk about your tiff with Alwyn another time."

Then he was gone before she could respond.

* * *

She gave Andrew a week, and then found him alone in the Auxiliary Bridge one day. She stepped in. "How's progress with Dr. Blaney?"

"Doing fine. You want a report?"

"If you have anything ready."

He shrugged. "It's rather informal. I can tell you right now. But shouldn't he be here?"

She considered. "You've told him what you were doing?"

"Yes. Like I said, I didn't want to treat him like a lab experiment."

"How can you expect to get any good data from a subject who knows he's being tested..." She waved a hand. "Fine. Let's invite him in." *Dr. Blainey, a quick word in the Auxiliary Bridge, please?*

Be right there.

The engineer soon appeared in the door. Noticing their casual seating, he perched sideways on a quad accel couch. "What's up?"

"Andrew is updating me on his progress in finding places for you to fit in." She held up a hand. "It's a formal report, but he wanted you to be present, so you knew what was going on."

"I appreciate the thought. "

131

"I'm not so sure, but all right, Andrew. Go ahead."

The ensign glanced at each of them, his brow furrowed. Then he collected himself and started.

"Given that this is a military ship, having a crewmember who does not understand military procedures could be considered a disadvantage, and in an emergency, even a detriment to proper function. So I looked around for a competitive situation where I could gather some data on Alwyn's usefulness to a team exercise. The answer was easy. Gestalt Volleyball."

"You're using a volleyball game to gather data on a subject who is aware of the test. Where is the scientific part of this?"

Andrew started to speak, then shook his head.

The engineer leaned forward. "It seems to me that..."

She turned to him. "Dr. Blainey."

He stopped and regarded her.

"I believe we have discussed this. We are considering a scientific question, here, and as the subject of the test, it is not your place..."

He shook his head gently and raised a calming hand. "With all due respect, ma'am..."

She registered a frown on Andrew's brow and reconsidered. "All right, Alwyn. You're a member of the crew and you deserve your say. What objective data do you have for us that applies to this situation?"

"Thank you, ma'am. You have mentioned in the past that part of my value to the crew comes from a fresh, outside viewpoint. In this case, I have noticed that nothing happens on this ship that is not beneficial to its military nature."

"Nothing?"

He shrugged. "An example." He accessed the ship's com. *"Sorry to bother you, folks, but I need some data. How many people aboard have a novel in their private database?"*

Three positive responses.

"Right. How many have read one of them in the last month?"

Only Alison gave a positive. He thanked everyone, and the com faded. "New crew member. Not indoctrinated yet. *What kind of novel, Alison?*

It's a murder mystery. I'm rather enjoying it. It's one of those where the writer lays out the clues to the readers at the same time as the detective finds them. You've actually got a chance of solving it yourself.

He grinned. *"Ah. Mental exercise. Problem solving. Thanks, Alison."* He turned to Natalia. "Partially indoctrinated."

She sighed and faced Andrew. "So, Research Specialist Collingwood. What scientific purpose is served by your volleyball game? Besides the obvious gestalt practice."

"I didn't think to use it until you gave me the assignment, ma'am, but one thing we haven't been able to do is test the relative power of a gestalt in any quantitative way. There are no units, no norms, nothing testable. So I fell back on the lazy teacher's assessment trick: have a contest and give the prize to whoever wins."

"And what did this shortcut reveal to you?'

"An interesting fact. When we play the game with teams anywhere near fair, the one with Alwyn always wins."

"So he's a star volleyball player. And the military application is...?"

"That's just it. He's not. He doesn't contribute anything special that I can tell. He's just part of the gestalt. It's merely a statistic and open to interpretation, but there it is. He's a factor in the winning team. Everybody already knew it, without any testing. If Alwyn and Patches are on the same team, nobody will play against them."

"And your conclusion?"

"Dr. Blainey performs some as-yet-undefined function in any gestalt in a competitive situation."

"And where does this go, next?"

"It's beyond my area of expertise, so I plan to consult a specialist. I will appraise Patches of the situation and ask what one suggests."

"I see. Well, I gave you an assignment, and you seem to be making progress. Keep me up to date, please." She nodded, politely she hoped, to Alwyn and returned to her chart room, where she sat staring at a blank viewscreen, going over recent events and wondering if she had been completely professional.

* * *

But now that she was aware of it, Blainey was spending more of his time with the barwolves, often pulling a chair over near their area in the mess hall and communicating with them. Considering this to be a significant change of behaviour, she felt it her duty to discuss it with him.

Not wanting to be too formal, she waited until she found him alone in the mess one afternoon. There she casually slipped the idea into the conversation, hoping not to elicit a negative response.

She seemed to be successful, as his answer came easily. "You're right. I've changed my focus. You know how you talk about reviewing your orders and trying to figure out what's expected of you? Well, once Andrew started doing those tests I started to consider my possible usefulness and how I had been trying to assimilate with the crew. And the reversed flange incident demonstrated that I was going about it the wrong way."

She considered. "You were trying to fit in with the crew. And that was wrong?"

"Correct. I was trying to develop the military mindset that you all have. Now I realize that in the time available, I have no possible way of developing an attitude and an outlook towards duty that you people have spent most of your lives learning. So, I shouldn't be trying. There is so much more opportunity for success with the barwolves. Nobody else is any more tuned in to them, although you auguar trainers have a head start with communication through imagery.

"I laid this out for Patches, and one agreed wholeheartedly. We have been working on a two-being gestalt. It works very well in a different way. It's not very powerful or wide ranging, because there's only two of us, but it's very intense, because of the lack of distractions."

"Any applications showing up?"

"Not a thing. But if Patches wants to spend ones time on it, then I think it's up to me to accept ones guidance, don't you think? We expect the barwolves to follow our lead on everything else. It's only fair to give them a chance in their field of specialization."

"Yes...yes, I suppose you're right." The more she thought about it, the more pleased she became. "You're the only human on the crew who's likely to excel at this, and you're right about Patches. One is a specialist in augment communication, brought on the mission for that exact reason, If one chooses to work with you, there's a good reason for it."

He smiled. "Great. Then I have your blessing to continue?" He turned towards the door

She snorted. "Don't let's bring religion into it. That would really complicate things."

He turned back, his hand on the doorjamb. "They do have a religion, you know."

"What?"

"Well, not like most human religions. But what can you call the contents of their worldwide gestalt? Remember fifty or so years ago some philosopher came up with the theory that augmentspace was humanity's new metaphysical world?"

"Vishnuva Faridabad? He was a fake. A Fantasy novelist who got caught up in his own fantasy. He was completely discredited."

Blainey raised his eyebrows. "You can't discredit an idea that has merit, no matter how you treat the person who first thought of it. If you compare augmentspace, and cyberspace before it, with the metaphysical worlds of most religions, there are a lot of similarities, both in the nature of the space and in the needs it fulfills for its believers. Barwolves use Otherwhere communication for their metaphysical space."

She grinned up at him. "That's pretty philosophical for an engineer."

He shrugged. "Just remember what the first two letters of PhD stand for." He slapped his hand on the doorjamb, regarded her a moment, then spun into the corridor and strode away.

She sat there a moment, mulling over what he had said. *Well, maybe not such a dud after all. But I'm still going to have to watch myself. He's just...so...different.*

21. METASPACE

Natalie made three forays into Faridabad's theories of augmentspace, but then realized that, unless she had Alwyn to bounce her responses off, it wasn't much fun. *Dammit, I'm used to having him around.*

Then she realized she was bored. *How can I be bored? I'm commanding a state-of-the-art spaceship, connected with an alien species driving a futuristic battle machine, and we're headed into our first battle. I've got a million things to do. I'm not bored. What the hell's wrong with me?*

"*NightHawk*, I'd like to access your mental health program."

Program accessed, ma'am.

She outlined her problem. "What does that indicate to you? Am I depressed or something?"

Indicators have flagged a minor ennui, yes. Nothing beyond normal swings of emotion.

"But look at our situation. How can I be bored?"

May I access Protocol 17-B, ma'am?

"Why would you like to do that?"

Because it deals with areas of the human emotional makeup that aren't usually needed by a ship's ArIn.

"Such as..."

Falling in love.

"What? I'm not falling in love!"

That's probably true.

"Then why do you have to access that section?"

Because you aren't. And you haven't. Ever since you joined this ship, you have lived a monastic life. Andrew was a step in the right direction, but that's a different sort of love. What your psyche is telling you is that you aren't perfectly balanced. Sort of like Pete Jager.

"You start comparing me to Pete, and I'm really getting worried."

The ArIn chuckled.

Pete has a weakness in his self-image, probably due to a lack of female attention at an early stage in his life. He tries to make up for it through his piloting, which is right on the edge of acceptable at times, but a great asset in military situations, so he isn't considered a risk. Many pilots exhibit the same tendencies. But the lack is still there.

"You're saying I have a similar weakness?"

Not a weakness. Just a normal human need, which you are not allowing yourself to fulfill. Thus there is an imbalance in your self-image, which no amount of success in all the other areas of your life will counter. According to 17-B this is a common problem with the upper levels of the command structure. They call it the 'loneliness of command,' and individuals are expected to find their own solutions.

"And the usual solution...?"

As I might have mentioned before. It would help if you just got laid."

"And that's the solution provided by a two-billion planetoid ArIn project and a service-wide psych protocol? I don't think Space Arm got its money's worth."

Don't worry, it's not that simple. What you really need is male companionship at a personal level. The sexual aspect would be useful but not essential.

"And the danger that it might distract me at the wrong time? As in, just before an important battle?"

To give you and Space Arm your money's worth, here is my conclusion, backed by analysis from 17-B. Given the otherwise balanced nature of your personality, the most extreme result of such a liaison would be that you end up in a permanent relationship. Which, by the way, would solve the whole imbalance permanently.

"Hmm. That ties it up rather neatly, doesn't it?"

I'm only an ArIn, ma'am. I leave the nuances up to humans. In my experience, they can find a way to screw up the most simple of situations.

"Well, thank you for your input. I'll do my best to keep from killing us all in a fit of girlish pique."

My self-preservation protocols thank you, ma'am. And on behalf of the crew...

She chopped her hand down. "And you can now turn off protocol 17-B. Chat time is over."

Aye, ma'am. Back to business. Shall I send the victim to you?

She frowned. "I will arrange my own trysts, thank you. Go navigate the ship or something useful."

She was rewarded by dead air. As she picked up her enterpad, she reflected on that final exchange. *It was familiar somehow...Andrew!*

137

Dammit, that ArIn has been around Andrew too long. It's starting to act like him, and I'm responding the same way. I really need to normalize my relationships.

* * *

With the rather uncomfortable feeling that she was completing a homework assignment, she wandered past Alwyn's cabin the next time she had a free moment. *To be honest, the next time I could create a free moment.*

He was lying in his bunk, and looked up from the viewscreen he was reading. "Hey, Natalia. Come in and pull up a chair." Then he glanced at her again. "Or should I be standing and saluting and saying, "Reporting for duty, ma'am."

She flopped down on the only other chair in his compact room. "No, good call the first time. I've been reading Web theology, and wanted to toss some ideas at you."

"Fine." He swung his legs over the edge and reached out to tap a cupboard open. "Would a touch of Scotch serve to lubricate the mental wheels?"

She grinned. "Not in the middle of the afternoon." She craned her neck. "But if that's a bottle of Talisker I see, we could re-schedule."

"Some other time, then." He arranged his pillow against the wall and leaned back. "We're talking Faradabad, are we?"

"No, I'm past that. When you look into his theories, they're pretty shallow. I have to agree with them, but I don't think they'll help much with the barwolves."

"Probably true. After all, most religions created their metaphysical worlds based on a database consisting mostly of myths and legends. They're much skimpier about present events."

"But with the barwolves, it's real-time. It's all happening right now." She snapped her fingers. "They're living in re-ti and in their metaspace at the same time."

"Perhaps."

"I know that's pure speculation. We don't even know what happens to their Otherwhere presence when their body dies. I just assumed it would die as well. Maybe it doesn't, because it's so enmeshed in their mindspace."

He nodded. "Likewise, as Faridabad reminded us, each modern human has a huge presence in augmentspace. If we die, we may be gone, but all that information is still there."

"Scary thought. Can you imagine what damage someone could do with your data?"

"Not mine." He shook his head. "I'm signed up with an Afterwards Service. My name has a metacode embedded in it. The day my death is official, every scrap of me on any and every server disappears. The only data left will be what's in the personal logs of specified people and organizations."

"Including Freighty?"

"He doesn't have much. He only met me a year ago."

"But what if he wanted to find out more?" Her mind made a jump. "Say, doesn't that make you wonder about the Mariel construct? You didn't know her from before, but she has certainly changed."

"She's a work of art. When I first met her it took me a few minutes to figure out what was wrong."

"A few minutes? In a social situation, I doubt if most people would ever notice."

"You think Freighty has accessed her augmentspace data."

"He must have. She was a member of a very powerful family. There would have been a lot of data." She frowned. "But now that I remember, it was all hidden."

He smiled. "They're rich enough to afford what everyone wants: privacy."

"Until Freighty gets interested." She nodded. "Yes, that would explain it. He accessed her metadata and loaded it all into the construct."

"And unless you want that sort of thing happening to you after you're gone, you sign up with an Afterwards company and have yourself scrubbed clean. Unless, of course..." he shook his head. "Not sure you want to do that."

"Do what?"

He winced. "My takeaway from this conversation is that Freighty has a lot of communications capability. If I really wanted my data secure, and if I happened to be a member of the...what do you call it? The Factory 4-80 Manufacturing Consortium...?"

"You're suggesting I get Freighty to take care of the security of my personal data after I die."

"I don't think I am. You're in a very delicate balance, keeping your duty to Space Arm and humanity in equilibrium with the obvious benefits of having the most powerful being in this part of the galaxy on your side."

"Yes, a move like that could put me even more into his power, couldn't it?"

He grinned. "Unless you take the other option, which is that he is so powerful you never really had any choice. In which case you might as well enjoy your advantages."

She frowned up at him. "Do you remember all those folk tales where the devil sends his emissary to tempt someone? Untold riches and power in exchange for their soul?"

"Emissary of the devil?" He held up his hands in defence. "Wait a minute. I knew we were having a bit of a rough patch. Let's not go overboard."

She grinned. "No, I suppose not." Then it just felt right. *Now is the time to ask.* She became serious. "Is that what we're having, Alwyn? A bit of a rough patch?"

"You're asking me?"

She thought about that. "Why wouldn't I ask you? You're the other person involved."

"There's nothing wrong with asking. I just didn't expect it."

Where the hell is this conversation going? "Now you're telling me you don't expect me to do the right thing." She raised a hand to stop his answer. "I'm not trying to pick a fight. I'm just trying to understand your thinking. It doesn't sound as if you have a very high opinion of my decision-making ability."

"Natalia, in almost everything on this ship, and in almost everything else you do, you are the Captain, with a capital 'C.' You think ahead, you know what's going on, you have earned the right to make the decisions. You're even good at knowing when you shouldn't be making a decision."

"And now you're going to explain the 'almost' part."

"Like any other human being, no matter how much in charge you are, there are aspects of your life where you are not better qualified, talented or informed to make decisions."

"I'd be a fool to argue with that. And in this specific case…?"

He shrugged. "I don't know you well enough to be sure, but as an experienced observer of the human race, I'd say you were struggling."

"With what?"

"With how to fit me into your ship and your life." He hurried on to forestall her response. "You can delegate the job of fitting me into the ship to Andrew, who is well-qualified for the task. But…"

"And what makes you think I want to fit you into my life?"

140

"All sorts of things, many of them too subjective to be dependable for proper scientific use."

She frowned. "You're trying to use scientific principles to decide on our interpersonal relationship."

He grinned. "Thus disqualifying myself for the job, too."

"Great picture. Two grown adults with all the interpersonal skills that come with maturity, no further ahead than two teenagers on a first date."

"Well, I wouldn't go that far."

The idiotic turn of the conversation got to her, and she wiggled her eyebrows. "How far would you go?"

He jumped to his feet. "All right. When you start harassing me with bad humour, you've overstayed your welcome." He bowed to her and gestured towards the door.

She had no choice but to leave, saving face with a regal inclination of the head and a small smile.

Certainly not a dud. I really have to be on my toes, here. But now I have another chore. "Andrew, you busy?"

Depends. Is it my mother or the captain calling?

"A little of both. I'm headed for the chart room."

At which point I become too interested to refuse. Be there in a moment. Soon as I finish recalibrating Diablo's Otherwhere sphere.

"Which I know you are not doing. Get over...ah, there you are. Come in and sit down." She sat at her desk.

"Aye, Captain Mum, ma'am." He parked himself backwards in the chair, rested his arms across the back and his chin on his arms. "What's up?"

"I was just having a chat with Alwyn, and the Mariel construct came up. Everybody noticed how lifelike she's become."

"Yes. She's great, isn't she? Freighty and I have been working on her programming off and on. You know, when I can find time in a life made busy by my Mum and my captain bossing me around."

"So you know about her Web data."

"It was my idea."

"It was?"

"Yes. Freighty and I have never been completely happy with the way the Collingwood family just dropped out of my life, so he went looking. Once he started understanding the way augmentspace and the Sol Webs are configured, it wasn't hard to find them. They're just as powerful as ever, perhaps moreso. And we don't like the idea of them having all that data on Mum's past. And mine, of course."

"I can see why that would bother you."

He grinned. "So I asked Freighty to go in and delete her. He can do it, you know."

"Yes, Alwyn brought me up to speed on that technology."

"We didn't want to make a fuss or draw attention to ourselves, so over the past two years he's been quietly closing files. One here and one there, no particular order. As far as we can tell, they haven't even noticed she's gone."

"But sooner or later they will notice."

"If they were nice people, they might never come looking for her, and would never know. It's more likely they'll want her data when they come up with a plan to use it against me. When they find out it's gone, they'll try to figure out how. They won't be able to, and that will serve as a message to them. If we can do this to her files, we can do it to theirs. If they have any brains, they'll realize they're out of their league and quietly drop it."

She stared at her son for a moment. "So you've figured out a whole cyberattack that will be triggered by them, repelled by you, and over and done with when, basically, nothing happened."

His grin turned smug. "Nicely put."

"You two are dangerous. You realize that?"

He gave a downward smile. "Nah, Freighty's not dangerous. You've got him too well trained. I'm the dangerous one. I'm young and stupid and wasn't brought up right."

"So now this is my fault."

He frowned. "What's your fault? Has the famous Natalia O'Rourke finally made a mistake?"

She sighed. "Yes. Adopting you on the premise that I could do something about your sense of humour." She waved a hand. "Go stick your head in an Otherwhere sphere or somewhere useful. I've got a ship to run."

He got up and left, but then he peeked back around the door jamb. "I passed Alwyn's cabin on my way here. He was whistling." His voice went sing-song. "I know what that means."

He was gone before she could find something to throw at him. She sighed and dragged her mind to considering the coming battle.

142

22. NOW YOU TELL ME

Natalia gazed around the crowded lounge of the *NightHawk*. "I herby declare this strategy session open. Any and all ideas will be considered." She scanned the eager faces. "Here's the situation as I see it.

"We can't sneak up on anyone. Coming out of Otherwhere sprays a blast of electromagnetics all over the spectrum. We only have a general idea of their sensing capabilities, but I suggest we come out far behind the enemy on full decel. If we put *NightHawk* in the lead blasting merrily with the Greens docked to her, we can have *Diablo* and the Reds in full stealth behind, and the larger ship's emissions will disguise their presence. From that point we come in on a normal decel until we're within attack range and speed, and play it from there."

Andrew was shaking his head. "We don't have enough information. What about a fast flybay, then come back and get them for real?"

Natalia thought about it. "I'd like to, but we don't have time to play around like that. Our stealth capability is our best weapon, and if they caught even a whiff of the sliverships the first time through, they'd be looking for them the next time, and our surprise is over."

"I guess. So it's a one-shot deal."

"That's how I see it. We'll toss it around now, and then the Auxiliary Assault Team can run it through their gestalt while the rest of us do our jobs and fly the ship."

They held a loose scrum after that, not really trying to pin any plan down, just looking for all the factors they would consider later in the gestalt. When the ideas began to run out, Natalia sent them all away to their duties.

As the meeting was breaking up, she got her nerve up for something she had to do. "Alwyn, can you spare me a moment?"

He shrugged. "My time is your own." Then he regarded her face and his smile disappeared. "Certainly, captain."

She nodded and beckoned him to follow her.

When they were in the chart room, she pulled her chair out from behind her desk and sat. "Close the door, will you?"

Again that piercing look, then a nod. He reached out and pushed the "close" button, placed the other chair facing hers and a little closer than usual, and sat in normal fashion. "So. Personal?"

Taken aback, she paused. "...ah, yes. Personal. We need to set a few things straight before we go into battle." She held up a finger.

NightHawk, could I have a com blackout here? Captain and Dr. Blainey's personal logs only."

"As you wish, ma'am."

She faced Blainey again. "I know this might sound mysterious, Alwyn, but..."

He smiled. "No, not at all. I understand."

"You do?"

"Of course." He waved a hand at the door. "That door is usually open, but now it's closed. You had me do the honours so I wouldn't feel trapped. You make sure I know we have privacy. You're making me as comfortable as you can for what you're about to tell me, because you're not sure how I'm going to take it."

She raised her eyebrows. "And now you're telling me all this in order to make me feel more comfortable?"

He smiled. "Considerate of us, isn't it? Now we can have the conversation that we both knew was coming."

She sat back, folding her arms. "And now you're just showing off."

He held out open palms. "Not at all. Go on. Is it a prepared speech, or are you doing it ad lib?"

She frowned. "It's not a speech at all, Dr. Smarty Pants. If you're so good, you tell me."

He gave an upside-down smile. "Aha! A challenge. All right, if it will make you feel better, here's how I see it."

He leaned back and looked at the ceiling. "You and I have a developing personal relationship." He glanced at her. "Not something that happens to you often, I would suspect. Loneliness of command and all that. Witness our recent disagreement, which seems to have disappeared into smoke lately. That means you want to proceed with caution. I thank you for the consideration. Space Arm very specifically does not regulate interpersonal relationships, but that doesn't make it easy for senior officers to interact with their crew. Yes, I looked it up, a fact that you would know..." He raised a palm to stop her protest, "...but you don't interfere with your crew's personal lives as long as *NightHawk*, who listens to everyone, doesn't note a security issue. How am I doing so far?"

"Not bad for someone with no military background. I can't wait for the next bit."

He shrugged. "This part's not so easy. I have to assume that you want to go ahead with a serious relationship, or we wouldn't be having this conversation. We'd just wait till the mission was over, hop into bed, and say good bye when circumstances changed. But you want more than that, and you don't know how I feel about it, whether it can happen, and how it will work out if it does happen." He shrugged, holding out open hands.

Then, before she could answer, he straightened and held up a finger. "But, having tricked me into saying it all, you have strategically removed yourself from any wrongdoing or inappropriate advances to a subordinate. That was very clever. Does Space Arm give you training in that sort of thing?"

Natalia grasped this new line with relief while she regained her aplomb. "Nope. I'm a natural. And I don't get much practice, either."

He smiled. "I understand. I have no military experience, but I can see how it goes. At some time in the near future you might have to make a choice between my life and the survival of the ship or the accomplishment of the mission. Emotions just mess up your ability to do the right thing."

She shook her head. "That sort of scenario is for cadets at the academy. Assuming any choice is that black-and-white shuts down creative thinking." She sat straighter. "But you've been playing your own game. You did all the talking, but it was all about me. What if you're right? I still don't know about you."

"Am I right?"

"Oh, no. You're not going to get past me that easy."

"Yes I am. Tit for tat. Now you have to tell me all about me."

She eyed him. "If you're trying to persuade me that this whole thing isn't such a good idea after all, you're making great progress."

He laced his fingers together and regarded her. "You're procrastinating. Talk."

"Fair enough." She straightened in her chair. "Short and pithy, if not sweet, here it is. There are two possibilities, and I'm taking the charitable one. You wouldn't have put all this thought and research in unless you were considering a relationship, and you wouldn't have laid it all out unless you agreed." She tossed her hands up. "That's it."

"And the uncharitable choice is that I'm playing some other game, and that's not worth considering."

"Exactly. Do we have a deal?"

He stood. "Right. No hanky panky until the mission's over. After that, all bets are on the table, all possibilities to be considered."

She stood and held out her hand to shake. "Deal."

He held her hand a moment. "It will be a pleasure doing business with you."

She brushed by him and opened the door. "Whatever that means."

He winked and strolled out, sauntering down the slideway towards the habitat ring.

She returned to her desk, feeling more comfortable than she had in years. Then she sat, frowning. *Is this those damned barwolves? Well, I don't care...no, that could be them, as well.*

She pulled up a document on her viewscreen. *What can't be cured...*and she went back to work with a smile on her face.

* * *

Now it was getting close to battle time, and barwolves or no, the crew's tension levels were rising. Augment sessions became intense, and finally they worked out their attack.

"Here's the recipe, folks. We approach as we always knew we would. *NightHawk* front and centre, *Diablo* trailing behind on full camo. The sliverships will spread out early and come in full stealth from six different directions, each one heading for one of the outlying ships. Their intention is to disable those ships and then stand by. We're all in decel, so once their engines are shut down the derelicts will drift ahead of the battle and soon be out of play.

"Since this is a police action, I will talk first, threatening to use the ShipBuster. They will not surrender. They'll put up their barrage and send out their missiles. Our forward deflectors and PermaSkin will handle the shrapnel, and our ArIns will send their missiles right back where they came from.

"The one weak point in our plan is the ShipBuster. It has several different points of attack, but the classic method is to sneak it into the enemy's drive plume. It works like many parasites; it crawls up the exhaust against the heat and pressure until its ablative tiles wear off, at which point it explodes, causing a reactor overload. The timing is crucial, because at the beginning you might be able to set it off or shut it off on command, but once it's in that maelstrom communication is iffy."

The Chief Engineer grinned. "Sounds elegant. What's the problem?"

"It has no camouflage, and they have a lot of smaller ships out there. It has its own ArIn, which is the best new Space Arm tech, and it should be able to avoid them. Our best bet is to create as much noise as we can. Once the Buster is in place in their drive plume, they won't dare touch it, if they ever see it."

She grinned. "Then we'll call them up for a very different conversation. Comments?"

Thoughtful frowns were all she got.

"Right, then. Take that away and pick at it. We'll tear it to shreds tomorrow and come up with the real plan." She stood. "As it is, prepare for Otherwhere exit in three hours."

23. BOARDING PARTY

They came out of Otherwhere in a blaze of glory and a bit of a bump, but not enough to interfere with navigation. Once they were on course, the slivers joined to make a single ship, and *Barwolf One* and *Diablo* tucked in beside *NightHawk* closer than any other three ships on decel would dare. The drive plume from the bigger ship's deceleration spread around them all, obscuring them electronically. Experimentation soon proved that Otherwhere communication was unimpeded, so they were able to keep a close eye on their adversaries. Natalia called a meeting on augment.

"Just as we expected. We have one old destroyer, four outriders under their own power, and it looks like three smaller ships moored on the Florrie's ventral deck. The rest of their fleet must be runabouts and shuttles, berthed inside the mothership. Comments?"

She got a flash from Engineering. "Yes, Chief?"

Those ships originally had four main shuttles, armed with .50 calibre machine guns and whatever rocketry they felt useful fitted on side racks. They were designed for boarding, so they have all sorts of grapples and cutters on exterior arms.

"Could they pierce PermaSkin?"

Doubtful. And if they got that close, we have about a dozen different ways to shut down their whole ship.

Emotion: agreement. "The closer we get, the more information we'll have on their armament. Mr. Jones, what do their communications give us?"

The First Officer was sitting in his station beside her, so he spoke aloud as well as through the augment. *"There's a lot of chatter, ma'am. Very unmilitary. The captains of the outriders seem to have a lot of independence, and they argue about everything."*

"So the leadership is fragmented. That's to our advantage. Any idea of their plan?"

"Well, that's the good part, ma'am. They seem to think their battle com is secure, so we know everything. They assume we're one ship and we're going to do strafing runs: through, around and back to the attack. Their standard form is a big hexagon with the outriders, Florrie at the centre and the shuttles spread throughout."

"But there's only four outriders."

"There must be two more available, because I heard the word 'hexagon' three times."

"Probably the ones moored to the mothership. Continue."

"They travel slower than their prey, and as it approaches they hit it with their com interference and a barrage of ordnance, mostly shrapnel. No commercial vessel has enough shielding to withstand that, so the victim is crippled before the battle even starts. Her only escape is to accelerate through if she still can. Nobody is stupid enough to come anywhere near the big ship, but whichever way the opponent tries to dodge, the two nearest outriders close in and bracket her. They must have kept these seven ships because they have the best acceleration. Then the piranhas attack from all sides, board any way they can, and take over."

"Andrew, how does that match with our battle plan?"

Her son answered from his post in Barwolf Control. *Pretty well, ma'am. The Slivers can go wide, miss the shrapnel, and come in under camo to nullify the outriders. Then Diablo drops the Ship Buster into position, and you start negotiating. We like the news about the outlier captains. They'll be happy with the Ship Buster, because it doesn't threaten them. Divide and conquer.*

Others chimed in with smaller details. The crew feeling was optimistic, but Natalia wasn't quite happy. "I think it's a good plan, but I hate to count on just one attack."

Lundeen clicked in. *A multi-pronged approach is better. Especially with our communications superiority.*

Andrew attracted her attention. *Ma'am, the alternative that came up most often in gestalt was a boarding party. Especially with an auguar. It's too big a ship to take over the whole thing without attacking the control room, and I can't see doing that with the number of crew on board. But Nzinga or Chakka could certainly cause a lot of trouble.*

"Toni, What do you say?"

Emotion: confidence. Nzinga has never done a re-li penetration, but she's been ready for some time.

Emotion: total agreement. Fierce desire to attack.

Natalia laughed. "That was easy. Who do you want to take with you?"

Emotion: uncertainty. "We need to know more about the mission, first. How are we getting onboard? What can we do when we get there?"

Natalia frowned in concentration. "Reality rears its ugly head. But at least we know where we're going. Let's keep an open mind and see what comes up."

Andrew and Chakka came in together. *Emotion: fierce desire to attack.* "I suppose you won't be interested in the Andrew Cunningham Patented Reverse Entry?"

"I don't see busting in like that. *Diablo* and Alison have one main job: dropping the ShipBuster as close to its target as possible. Then they're free for another assignment, and your trick is hardly her style."

Yeah, and it makes a mess on the PermaSkin. Last time I had to go downplanet and scrub all the soot off by hand. Best way in is on one of their own ships.

Toni sent agreement. *I can see that working. We use Diablo's stealth capabilities to capture one, then waltz in through an open door and disappear into the maintenance tunnels.*

"Do you know anything about the maintenance tunnels?"

"No, but we have the specs. Give me a few hours to study."

"I'll leave it with you, then. Figure out our best approach to inserting a small boarding party." Natalia closed the com.

24. MOLE

As the little fleet got closer to the enemy, tension slowly rose, despite the calming effects of the gestalt. Natalia was studying an old file on space battle tactics when her augment gave her a polite nudge.

Image: old-fashioned telephone ringing.

Natalia opened her augment. *I don't know where you found that image, Patches, but here I am. What can I do for you?*

Emotion: strong need. Image/idea. Whole crew.

You want a full gestalt? Why?

Image: old-fashioned telephone ringing. Captain answering, listening closely.

Natalia shrugged. *Emotion: agreement.*

Andrew?

Aye, ma'am

Patches wants a full gestalt. We're getting a message from somewhere.

Right on it, ma'am.

Natalia had thought she had used the full powers of the gestalt, but under the control of One who Merges, it became a whole new experience in focus. As the various members were added, her consciousness began to spread, first throughout the ship, then out into surrounding space. The images were clearer, the thoughts swirling around easier to access. She found it simple to pull her son's mind out of the mix.

So this is how the pros do it.

He responded with a wash of awe and a single image of a pile of Martian rock crab dung, complete with the usual accompanying reek.

Couldn't have said it better myself.

She returned to the main gestalt. *Question?*

In response, the view shifted, zooming through space and into the ship ahead of them. Down in the dimness a light flickered. The image firmed and grew as the gestalt focused in, drawing closer. They became aware of a misty swirl of minds, dominated by one that came through clearer and stronger as they concentrated. She got the impression of a male of middle age, tired and discouraged.

Awareness dawned. *Emotion: surprise, fear, suspicion. What the hell! Who is this? Where are you?*

Natalia took charge of the communication. *I'll be the one asking the questions, sir. Take it as a given that I am outside your vessel and close enough to do her serious damage if you don't cooperate. Now, answer*

151

your own questions. Who are you, and what's your position in this operation?"

Emotion: grim humour. Well, ma'am, everybody on this God-forsaken tub knows something's going on, and your image feels exactly like a Space Arm officer, so I'll take that as a given. I am Chief Engineer John Anderson of El Dorado Corporation. I was in transit back to Mars from El Dorado 12 six years ago after doing some design alterations, when the ore carrier I was travelling in was taken over by these assholes. Since then I have been doing my damnedest to maintain this pile of junk sufficiently to keep us all alive, but not well enough to be an effective fighting unit. And to avoid getting myself terminated because of my ineptitude. If you're an agent of the Bridge Crew, I guess I'm done, but I'm so tired of this I guess that's okay with me, too.

Natalia switched to the *NightHawk* gestalt. *"What do you think, folks?"*

Emotion: truth.

Patches is right. He believes everything he's saying.

"Any indication of other augment activity onboard, Andrew?"

Not at this distance. Especially not in gestalt with each other, which we'd pick up for sure.

"Fine."

She contacted Anderson again. *All right, Chief Engineer Anderson. We believe you. I'm Natalia O'Rourke of the Reconnaissance Sloop NightHawk, and we're out here looking for this lot.*

Emotion: extreme relief. Manager Ludge spoke of you in the highest terms, Captain. I'm putting myself and my people under your orders as of this moment.

Thank you, Chief. Can you give me an outline of the personnel involved here?

Sure thing, ma'am. The ship's crew consists of those who were already aboard when the original mutiny took place, combined with passengers and crew off captured ships over the years. Needless to say, the two groups may overlap some, but in general they don't get along.

There are five classes aboard. The Bridge Crew are the original gutter scrapings who took over the ship years ago. Just below them are the Pilots of the attack craft. These two groups live high on the hog, take all the luxuries and the good food, and demand instant obedience from everyone else. The next layer down are the Marines. That's what they call themselves, anyway. Plenty of ex-military among them, to be sure. They earn their positions through their action in the boarding parties, but their main function is policing the rest of us.

Beneath this aristocracy are the functionaries who pretend loyalty. We call them the Toadies, and we're always very careful around them. Many are crew from the captured ships who have gone over to the enemy. Some through force, others through selfishness."

Natalia thought that over. *So none of those you mention can be counted on for any help.*

Emotion: uncertainty. I'm sure a good number of the Toadies will go with whoever seems to be winning. Counted on? No chance.

Numbers?

There are about twenty Bridge Crew. That can change with the shifting power politics. Fifty or sixty pilots, depending on recent action.

That's a lot of pilots.

There are a lot of vessels. They have a swarm of runabouts and shuttles off the captured ships. There's six or seven main attack boats, the newest and fastest of the captured vessels. The others were sold outright or sent back to the scrap yards in the Asteroid Belt.

Six or seven? You don't know?

Six at the moment. Depends on which ones are functional. I try to control that as much as possible, too. Don't know why, really.

Fair enough. It will be useful now. Think about ways to disable another couple in case I ask you. And the rest of the crew?

The pilots and bridge crew have their women — some willing, others not. They've been out here almost ten years, so there's a slew of little kids running around. About a hundred Marines, more or less well armed. Lots of obsolete equipment, but recent ships have carried modern hand weapons. No idea how many Toadies, because who knows where to draw the line? But the vast majority of us are slaves. It takes a huge number of trained people to keep this beast and its spawn operating, and a lot of drudges to keep everyone fed and all the machinery maintained.

It's a pretty rough life. The Bridge doesn't care what happens to us. Crew and passengers from a captured ship are just shoved into the Hold, and we sort out who's useful and put them to work. The others manage however they can. Our numbers have been rising, but the Bridge won't give us any extras, so we all make do with less.

Hmm. And that's a great recruiting tool for the upper classes. Make life unbearable for the loyal Planetary citizens, and the scum rises to the surface.

Precisely.

What kind of an organization do you have?

A fairly loose one with nebulous objectives. A Captain's Council with no ships to run. We worry about survival, mostly.

Weapons? Training?

Emotion: rueful humour. As far as training, whatever we came on board with. We have a few weapons stashed, but not many. Not worth the risk, and what would we do with them, anyway?

How about take control of the ship after the upper classes run out on you and leave you to die?

...I'm thinking about that. What do you have in mind?

Nothing I'm likely to pass along, yet. You pretty well have to believe I am who I say I am. On the other hand, I have no such confidence in you.

Agreed. You're in the pilot's couch. Say, what is it with this gestalt? I'm feeling...mars apples! Do barwoves really exist?

Image: One who Merges tapping engineer's leg.

Emotions: confusion, wonder. Yeah...um, pleased to meet you, too.

Engineer Johnson, I'm going to consult with my crew. Will you stand by?

I've been waiting for you to show up for six years. Another hour won't make much difference.

Natalia pulled the gestalt away from the enemy ship. *"All done, Patches. You can shut it down. Everyone, I want a face-to-face in the lounge. Diablo crew, I'll put you up on the big viewer."*

She felt a great sense of loss as the gestalt faded and disappeared from her mind. *"Whew! That could get addicting".*

And I handed in my thesis last month!

Emotion: humour. "Think post-doctorate."

Think the rest of my life.

"That might work, too".

She strode into the ship's lounge and sat at the head of the table, regarding her team. "Well, what do you think?"

Toni nodded slowly from the screen. That makes a difference. With allies on the crew, a boarding party will be much more useful. Who should I take?

Natalia considered. "How about you, Nzinga, Jager and Patches? Jager will fly the stolen craft. Pete, you've got a ton of hours on various ships, haven't you?"

The Master Pilot grinned. "Please don't bring up my misspent youth, ma'am."

"Fine. If they've got a lot of shuttles buzzing around, it will be easier to get lost in the crowd once we've taken control of one. We'll do a personnel transfer before the attack and put the boarding party on

Diablo. We'll be in gestalt through the whole snatch. Pete has an eight point five augment, so he can match the rest of you. With Patches to help, it ought to be smooth. We can use availability of specs and pilot experience as part of the criteria for our choice of which ship to nab. The moment we choose our target, Pete starts researching the specs."

Pete's blond head came up. "Pick a more modern one, because there will be more automation."

Right. Andrew rubbed his chin. *And one with a military background, because that will make it easier for Nzinga to break the ArIn's security programming. She has a file on historical Space Arm cyphers.*

"Once we have control, we'll put our party on board and resume maneuvers as ordered by the pirate command. Then we'll dock as close to Engineering as we can, and join forces with Johnson.

She pulled in the rest of the gestalt. *Johnson, are you there?*

Ready and waiting, ma'am.

We're thinking of a boarding party. There's a fighter hangar down at the stern, very near Engineering. Is it functioning?

That's where some of the older ships come in because they need the most maintenance. We've got...let me see, twelve operational right now, one that might be able to fly, and three junkers for parts.

That's a big bay. Room for one more?

What kind of ships do you have?

We don't know yet.

Pardon?

We don't know which ship will be carrying our crew. We'll let you know. How much control do you have over that hangar?

Nobody pays it much attention. I have a strong enough force here to overwhelm the guards, and our techs wander in and out freely.

Good. Please stand by. Are you in your office on level 23, corridor K?

...ah, yes, I am. You know this ship pretty well.

I have the specs. You might do an inventory of any serious modifications that have been made since the ship was decommissioned.

I can do that easily, ma'am. There haven't been any. Only stuff that has broken down and been jury rigged.

Something that's likely to fail at an inopportune moment might come in handy.

I'll keep that in mind as well.

Thanks, Johnson.

She phased out of augment and went back to her crew meeting.

"New problem, folks. There's no way we can use a Ship Buster on that many civilian hostages."

Lundeen was thinking. "Can we set it off close enough to their stern to shut down their reactors and leave the rest of the ship in livable state?"

"Do you want to decide what that distance would be?"

The Chief shrugged. "Isn't that what our gestalt is for? Solving difficult problems?"

She sighed. "We can work on it, but I don't like it."

What about a bluff? Andrew stared down from the viewscreen. *We tell them we're going to set it off. They jump ship, leaving the hostages behind. Then we don't set it off.*

Natalia shook her head. "They'd never believe we would do that, and it's a pretty poor bluff when you have nothing to show if you're called."

They sat in silence, minds churning.

"Well, I must say, this is rather interesting."

All faces turned to stare at Alison, who was grinning at them.

Natalia frowned. "What is?"

"Watching a gestalt work outside the augments."

"We do this all the time. It feels natural, just tossing ideas around. So what?"

"You've solved your problem already. You just haven't put it together yet."

Andrew pointed out of the screen at her. *Right. We tell them we're going to put a Ship Buster up their bunghole. They say, 'You wouldn't dare.' We say, 'yes we would,' and set off our blast outside the danger range, but close enough to give them a real shaking. Then we get Johnson to fake a reactor meltdown. Once the perps evacuate, the hostages take over onboard, and we mop up the rats that jumped ship.*

Natalia jumped back into full gestalt, Patches a second behind her, and they reached out to the enemy ship again. *Johnson, can you fake a reactor meltdown?*

How persuasive do you want? I can start a real one and hope to shut it down later.

That's a little more persuasive than we dare try, Johnson.

Believe me, ma'am, most of the slaves on this ship would willingly take the risk.

Let's hope it doesn't get to that stage. How about persuading a panicked bridge crew who are too busy looking to their own skins to check properly?

Emotion: humour. Oh, I can do that easily.

Good. Stand by.

Standing by, ma'am. Don't take too long. Word is going around there's something big coming up. The atmosphere on this ship is clogged with fear, anger, and who-knows-what. Word of your presence is bound to get out, and who knows what will happen then.

I can imagine. Everyone on your Bridge Crew knows when we'll be dropping in. They've been monitoring our decel for hours. O'Rourke out.

She opened the full com. "Andrew, bring *Diablo* alongside. Major Rowell, get over to *Diablo* and prepare to load one ShipBuster. B'Kosa and Fraser, you're EV for the operation. Everyone else, brush your teeth and comb your hair. The Commandos provide nothing but the prettiest corpses. Battle stations in one hour." Then she faced the screens again, watching her quarry glide closer.

* * *

Captain O'Rourke's attack squadron rolled into place, holding perfect formation, all eyes on their screens, all augments tuned for anomalies. At two hours to contact, a swath of jamming filled the usual com channels, and their target burst like a stirred wasp nest, with hordes of small craft issuing from all sides. The outriders moved more sedately to their expected positions on the capture net and the small ships filled the space between. Closeup views showed the barrels of the destroyer's standard ordnance swivelling into position.

"They've got six big ships out like we expected, ma'am. There's a seventh still moored to the ventral deck. We can assume she's out of service."

"Until suddenly she isn't. Thanks, Mr. Jones, we'll keep an eye on her." Captain O'Rourke checked the position of her ships. *Barwolf 1, the moment I begin talking to their command, you can take out your targets. Then report in and stand by.*

Image: barwolves pulling down prey with a great splattering of blood.

Easy on the damage. We want those ships to have functional life support.

Emotion: reluctant agreement.

Patches, this is the first time your people have done this, and I stress the need for absolute discipline.

Emotion: fierce determination to succeed.

That sounds better. "Mr. Jones, please make contact with our adversary."

"Opening Battle Chanel 45, ma'am. Handshake accepted."

The bridge of an obsolete Space Arm destroyer came up on the viewscreen. It was like watching an old holosaga, right down to the sharply-dressed, stiff-backed blond spacer with the short haircut glaring at her. "Who the hell are you, and what are you doing?"

She nodded politely. "Captain Natalie O'Rourke of the Planetary Community Scoutship *NightHawk,* sir. I might ask you the same. And I should warn you, 'Minding my own business' is not an acceptable answer to the second question. I perceive a certain number of vessels in your vicinity that are otherwise considered lost in space. Can you explain that coincidence?"

He snorted. "I don't really think I need to answer any questions from you and your dinky little Scout. Your best bet is to turn tail and get your butt out of here. Space Arm is good at that."

"You need to think ahead, sir. Space Arm knows you're here. Your little operation has gone bust. Surrender now, and nobody gets hurt."

"Since you're the one likely to get hurt, I suppose you would like that plan."

Bingo. Got a match. He's Anders Gunnarson, former head of security for Nordic Arms Manufacturing Consortium...yes...under investigation for involvement in the Aryan Return Movement, but disappeared before charges could be brought. Taken off the "Most Wanted" list after 7 years, as mandated by PC legal policy.

Thanks, Adrian.

"Well, Mr. Gunnarson, it seems your reputation precedes you. The Planetary Community judiciary has some questions they would like to ask you as well. Please stand down your weapons and present yourself at an airlock, prepared for transfer. Then we'll deal with the rest of your crew."

The handsome face in front of her twisted into an ugly scowl, and his hand reached forward, closing the connection.

Natalia left their battle com open. "Well, we know what we're dealing with. Now, he'll shoot a couple of tons of shrapnel at us. Once it bounces off, we'll call him again.

Incoming, ma'am. Four Exocet ShipMount 391 missiles...they are now reprogrammed to match his exhaust signature. Light armament contact in four minutes.

The viewscreen showed the missiles curving back towards their source and a frantic burst of small weapons fire destroying them.

Incoming in 30 seconds... in ten...five...three, two, one, contact.

A rattling like hail on a tin roof was accompanied by a blurring of the outside view, then *NightHawk* soared serenely through clear space again.

"Open the channel again, please, First."

"Aye, ma'am. Captain Gunnarson is on."

"We've got the antique mementos out of the way, Anders. Let's move on towards modern reality. I direct your attention to my ventral airlock. That rather large shape you see attached is called a ShipBuster. I'm sending you the specifications on a channel I'm sure you monitor..." she nodded to Jones "...but I'll give you the free tour now. I could just blast it at you and blow a hole in your ship. However, it's more elegant to send it up one of your exhaust ports. If I'm lucky, I detonate it at exactly the right point, it overloads that reactor, and your whole ship blows up. If you're lucky, I wait too long and it explodes in the reactor itself, taking off the back end of your ship, but spreading the reactive contents all over space before it has a chance to destroy itself. With a ship your size, a full half of your crew might survive. Check the specs. You'll see what I mean."

Again the snarl. "Thank you for the information If you think you can get that big hunk of metal anywhere near my ship, you're delusional." Again, he abruptly cut off the com.

Natalia turned to her battle com. "*Diablo,* please start your run."

"Aye, ma'am." Alison's voice was steady as a rock. "Commencing course 95, 104, 236. Full camouflage."

"Barwolf one, report."

Eager desire to please.

"Andrew and Patches, keep them under tight control. This is all new to them."

"Aye, ma'am."

Eager desire to please.

Soon Alison's voice came over the battle com. "There are more shuttles and auxiliary craft out here than we bargained for. I'm having trouble keeping out of everyone's way."

"Keep us informed, *Diablo.*"

"Aye, ma'am."

Emotion: success! Image: Target 3 floating in space.

Emotion: congratulations. Well done, Barwolf 7. Please move to decoy maneuvers for Diablo.

Emotions: pride, compliance.

NightHawk, what do we have on Target 3?

A mining exploration vessel belonging to Rio Tinto/Shenhua, ma'am. Versatile and maneuverable, but not fast.

Emotion: success! Image: Target 6 floating in space.

Emotion: congratulations. Well done, Barwolf 6. Please move to decoy maneuvers for Diablo.

Emotion: compliance.

Emotion: question?

Target 6 is the old 'Eclipse VIII,' ma'am. A luxury yacht converted to interstellar travel. Had some important people onboard when she went missing five years ago. Glad we got that one. Fastest of the lot, although vulnerable to conventional ordnance.

"Thank you, NightHawk. Keep the reports coming."

Aye, ma'am.

"Major Rowell, please report."

No better, ma'am. I'm twisting back and forth, but not making much progress.

"We now have two slivers running interference for you, more to come."

I can use all the help I can get.

Targets 5 and 1 disabled.

"Thank you. Slivers go and help Alison get through. Boarding party, progress report, please."

One moment, please, ma'am. Report coming up.

"Take your time and do it right. But not too much time. Alison's not happy."

Okay, ma'am. Here's our ride. Image: small mining exploration vessel.

"What the hell is that?"

Emotion: humour. It's a small mining exploration vessel, ma'am.

"I can read the specs as well as you can."

Pete's choice, ma'am. Small, innocuous, and versatile. All those sample-retrieval tools have grapples and lasers on them. Much better armed than most. It's also right on Diablo's course. If Alison would set a course, that is."

"*Diablo,* time for phase two. Dump your cargo and switch control to Major Jones. He can handle it from here."

Aye, ma'am. Control of the ShipBuster to Mr. Jones. There's no one near at the moment, so with any luck when the bomb comes out of our camo no one will notice.

Andrew jumped into their conversation. "Alison, before you drop, can you get Nzinga to insert this file into its guidance system?"

"Got it...file added. What did we just do?"

Emotion: humour. "Look out your forward screens ten degrees up and twenty-five degrees left of your course."

All eyes focused on that small portion of space,

Specialist Fraser called in. "Florie is retargetting, ma'am." He sent the view from his gunsight. Sure enough, several of the main cannons were changing position. Then they all spewed flame; their tracers and the lines of plasma from three projectors converged just ahead of *Diablo.* There was a small puff of light at that point, then nothing.

"Contact from the *Florie,* ma'am."

"Put him through, Jones."

The destroyer's bridge came up on the viewscreen, with a close shot of a leering face. "Well, that wasn't much of a show, was it? Your famous ShipBuster was more of a fizzle."

Natalia pretended to heave a deep sigh. "I think if you check my hull you will see that I have a spare. I believe I'll hold onto it and deliver it myself."

The sneer turned to a nasty chuckle. "Do join us. I can't wait."

"Not much longer, then, *Florrie. NightHawk* out."

Natalia opened a direct contact to Andrew. *I don't know what that was all about, but couldn't you give a person a hint beforehand?*

Sorry, ma'am. There wasn't time. Chakka and I just came up with the idea.

"Which was?"

Emotion: humour. We switched FOF ids with the nearest enemy vessel. Their programming is completely elementary. Now he's blown up one of his own shuttles, he thinks he's destroyed our bomb, and the ShipBuster has a Friend id.

Remind me to give you a medal later. Next time try to warn me.

Aye, ma'am. We will endeavour to think up genius moves to save the day at a faster rate.

Don't waste time. We need a way to make sure that missile gets through.

On it, ma'am.

161

Target 2 disabled. Sliver B-5 headed for camo duty.

"Thank you, B-5. Alison, time to board your target."

Approaching now, ma'am. Nzinga's in their electronics. Shutdown accomplished...boarding party away.

Several clangs of abused hull metal came over the com, then silence.

Single pilot subdued.

Fine. Stand by for a diversion.

Pete is firing up the drive again. He'll use the time to get acquainted with the controls.

Jager here ma'am. Piece of cake. I spent months driving one of these little beasties.

That's great, Pete. Stand by for recall to the mothership.

Target 4 Disabled. All slivers routed to camo duty.

"Thank you, Patches. Mr. Jones, report."

"I'm having trouble getting the bomb through, ma'am. Their small ship screen has pulled over to this side, and I don't dare close with any of them for fear they get a visual."

"All right. Then we'll aim *NightHawk* over to the other side of the net and pull them away from you. *Course change, Mr. Karaka. Here's the coordinates.*"

"Changing to coordinates 95, 105, 237, ma'am...new course assumed."

While this conversation was going on, there was action on the barwolf side of the gestalt. Now the emotions peaked

Emotion: frustration and anger!

Andrew took control of the gestalt. *Take it easy, there, Barwolf 7. We'll get through.*

Emotion: determination to succeed.

Keep working on the camouflage, everyone. You may target any ship in front of the bomb. Just take out their drive and sensor capability.

Image: Barwolf 7 and ShipBuster blasting into the drive plume of Florrie and explode.

A shock of horror drove through Natalia. *Emotion: strong negative! Patches, that sacrifice is not necessary. We can break off our attack and no harm done!*

Emotion: doubt.

Emotion: STRONG NEGATIVE! That doesn't matter. This is a time to obey orders!

Emotion: subjugation. Image: Patches touching Captain's leg.

Andrew came through. *All right, Barwolf 7. Break off and return to the fleet.*

Emotion: fierce desire to succeed!

Emotion: STRONG NEGATIVE! Barwolf 7, break off. I repeat, break off!

Andrew's aura took on a desperate tone. *He's not breaking off, ma'am. Patches, what's going on?*

Emotion: helplessness. Image: barwolves in frenzy.

Captain, he's got a 40% chance of making it through, but...

I get it, Andrew. He's gone off the deep end. We'll have to cope. ALL HANDS, ALL HANDS, this is an emergency. If we don't get Barwolf 7 through to accomplish his mission, he's likely to take it all the way and blow the ship. Otherwise, we'll have to detonate prematurely and waste his life and the bomb. Andrew, put all the slivers on his course. Shut down every ship that comes near.

Aye, ma'am. A series of rapid images passed back and forth in the barwolf gestalt, and the slivers abandoned their previous courses and zoomed straight for their compatriot.

Soon the viewscreen showed a tunnel of dead ships, its forward end moving straight towards the stern of the enemy destroyer.

"Damn. He can't miss that."

Sure enough, drives began to light up in the enemy swarm, their courses aimed ahead of the Space Arm penetration.

"Pete, now's your moment. You couldn't have a better diversion."

Aye, ma'am. Simulating engine malfunction. Heading for mechanical bay.

Natalia switched channels. *"Johnson, are you there?"*

Right here, ma'am.

You've got a Caterpillar DS-25 Mining Explorer heading into your repair bay with engine problems. Sending you its FOF code now.

Got it, ma'am. Ready to receive.

She switched back to the battle. *"Report, Andrew."*

Mission accomplished, Barwolf 7. Switch detonator to my command and disengage.

Emotion: desire to kill.

Emotion: negative. Emotion: satisfaction. Well done, Barwolf 7. Return to Barwolf 1 for new assignment.

Emotion: fierce desire to kill.

"Patches, Andrew, this one's up to you. If you can't control him I'll have to detonate the bomb prematurely. I can't risk that many lives."

Emotion: confidence.

A rush of warmth and joy surged through the barwolf gestalt, along with images too fast for humans to read. Gradually the resistance in the frenzied barwolf faded.

Success, ma'am. Barwolf 7 has disengaged.

Emotion: extreme worry.

What's wrong, Nelson?

That took too long. The bomb is too close to the ship. If we don't blow it in the next thirty seconds, it moves over the threshold for a real reactor overload.

Can't we slow it down or call it back?

It only has Space Arm communication, and the destroyer's drive plume is interfering with reception. The only way to call it back is to shut down his drive."

"NightHawk to Florrie. We've got an emergency, here Gunnarson. Our ShipBuster is in position, but it's too close. It's going to explode in twenty-two seconds if we don't send a cancel code, but we can't get through because of the ionization in your drive plume. Please shut off your B drive immediately, and we'll cancel the command to blow."

The handsome face took on a nasty smile. *"So the little Space Arm captain is getting worried, now. Well, I'm not falling for your lame ploy. I already blasted your baby hand grenade to smithereens, and now I'm getting set to do the same to your ship."*

Natalia slammed her hand on the arm of her accel couch. "That wasn't our bomb, you idiot! We switched FOF codes with one of your own ships. The bomb is there! Shut down...Oh, you poor fool..."

The view lurched and fragmented as a huge shock wave hit *NightHawk*. The view settled, revealing broken images of people flying in every direction on the enemy bridge. Then the com went blank.

On the main viewscreen the Florrie was hidden by a bright blast of light, soon covered by clouds of expanding smoke and debris, rapidly dispersing. Then NightHawk's PermaSkin visual filters cut in and showed the destroyer tumbling slowly away, end over end. Her stern plates hung warped and broken, and all three exhausts spewed ionization of all colours. Streams of debris showed where atmosphere still rushed out through the holes. Shapes recognizable as human figures cartwheeled away through the expanding cloud of rubble.

"Johnson, report, please. Engineer Johnson, are you there?"

A faint groan escaped the augment. *I'm here, ma'am. That was a bit more than I expected."*

"Well, it was more than we expected, too. What's your status?"

Just checking now, ma'am...there. All engines off line. Emergency power is functioning. Hull pressure firm in 90% of the ship. Doesn't seem too bad, yet.

"Monitor Reactor B closely, and initiate an emergency shutdown if you haven't already. Status of the other drives?"

A and C are showing a lot of red and amber lights, ma'am. Automatic shutdowns in progress. I'll move over to B and see what I can do. Of course, none of these safeties have been upgraded for years.

"Where's my boarding party? Nzinga and Toni could be a lot of help."

They could? I'll have them brought along from the mechanical bay...oh. I think this must be them...

Boarding party on duty, ma'am. Nzinga's already deep in the electronics of Reactor B. You can leave this to us, ma'am.

"I'll be happy to do that, Major Jacobs. We've had a slight hitch, but the rest of the plan rolls as scheduled."

Aye, ma'am. Working.

Natalia nodded to Commander Jones, who gave her a thumbs up.

"Captain O'Rourke calling Anders Gunnarson. What is your status now, Captain?"

After a long pause, a blackened face appeared on the screen. Blood ran down the captain's pale forehead, and his left cheek was swollen. His appearance matched the string of profanity that spewed from broken lips. "*...you bitch, you bombed me! You took half my stern off!*"

She shook her head. "I told you I couldn't stop it without your help. May I assume you are ready to surrender your ship?"

He straightened, a grimace twisting his face. "No, I am not ready..." His attention was diverted off to his left, and he listened to a garbled message.

Natalia's own battle com chimed. *Ma'am, this is Toni. We've got a big problem."*

"*Right with you, Major.*" She turned back to the screen. "It seems we have some develop..." but the view was of an empty bridge.

"Okay, Toni. Give it to me straight."

The major's usual steady voice held a quaver. *This reactor is toast. The safeties are all fused and broken, and Nzinga says they can't be replaced soon enough, even if we can find spares. Johnson says we're heading for a meltdown.*

26. MELTDOWN

Natalia glanced at the viewscreen, still connected to the *Dirty Florrie*. *Well, that explains where they went. A meltdown with near a thousand souls on board. Lucky if half of them survive. And it's all my fault. I never should have let a barwolf near that ShipBuster. Damn! What am I going to do?*

She wrestled her thoughts to the present. "Prime. How much time do we have?"

Toni gave a mental shrug. *Could be hours, could take a day. There's some kind of cycle going on. Forces build up, then the automatic safeties that still work shut them down. Five minutes later, it starts all over again. But it's stronger every time.*

"So, put Nzinga on beefing up those safeties."

She's trying, but she's not a nuclear power engineer. She and Johnson are pooling their talents. It still looks pretty nasty.

"Let them do their work. You look around. What's happening?"

The Captain called down for a report. We didn't have to exaggerate too much, believe me. The slaves down here are a pretty together bunch. They're running around, but their movement has purpose. No idea what's going on in the rest of the ship.

"Keep in touch."

Aye, ma'am.

"Lieutenant Jones, what's going on out there?"

"The smaller ships and shuttles are powering up and streaming back to the mothership, ma'am. They're congregating around the nose."

Natalia allowed herself a wry grin. "An easy guess what that's for."

"The rats packing up their portable loot and hotfooting it out to the smaller ships."

"Which they don't realize are non-functional. Good. Once they're out of the way, we can concentrate on our real problem."

She opened full battle com. "Listen up, folks. Strategy meeting." She waited until her augment showed her that everyone was online. "Here's the situation. The *Florie's* B reactor is going into meltdown. The Bridge Crew and their friends are abandoning ship. Let them go. Our every effort is to stop the destructive cycle that is building. I want everyone in battle gestalt. We'll station the slivers in a circle around the *Florie's* hull aft, so they're as close to the reactor as possible, and latch on magnetically. With her tumbling like that, *NightHawk* and *Diablo* have to stand clear. Lundgren and B'kosa, you match up with

Johnson and pool your knowledge. Andrew and the rest of the Auxiliary Bridge, you join up with the Slivership gestault. We'll start using you for analysis and data gathering, but if there's a chance we can do something physical, I want you available. Your tricks in that volleyball game might turn out handy for controlling mechanicals we can't access. The rest of *NightHawk's* crew will lend their augments and their hands wherever needed. Fraser, you're in charge of defense. Any threat from outside, and you break in on whatever I'm doing.

Aya, ma'am. Eyes up and out.

Patches, do you have that?

Emotion: agreement. Image: crew joined in one large gestalt but subdivided in teams.

"Excellent." She sent a private message. "*Alwyn, I'm trusting you to find a place to fit in, because I have no idea.*"

Emotion: humour. Neither do I but don't worry. You'll know if it happens.

Emotion: agreement.

"Johnson, what's going on? What do you need?"

What you said, ma'am. I need data on the inside of that reaction chamber. Half my readouts are blown or obsolete. From what I can tell, the situation hasn't changed. We have building pressure, magnetic oscillation and sub-atomic activity. They peak every five minutes. Then, for some reason, they fade, then build again. But it's gradually getting stronger. For all I know, it will keep building until it blows.

"Andrew, get on it. We can use our own capabilities re-ti, and the barwolves can access the Otherwhere spectrum. Major Rowell, bring *Diablo* alongside *Florrie* as close to the B reactor as you dare to assist the barwolves."

Aye, ma'am.

"Carry on. Johnson, you're calling this game. Feed us information."

Right you are, ma'am. Notice that the flux is building now. Here it comes. Pressure up, radiation levels up. A bunch of other forces going wild. There...that's about the top. Now those safeties or whatever cut in and down it goes. Comments?

This is Chief Engineer Lundeen here, Mr. Johnson. Chakka and I are monitoring your electronics. We don't see any evidence of safeties. Nzinga?

Image: reactor disengaged from electronic system.

See what I mean? Can you show us these safeties?

Sorry, Chief. I was just assuming they must be there, because of the cyclical nature of the problem. I'm not familiar with any extras the military put on their machinery.

Well, as a working hypothesis, I think our evidence, or lack of same, trumps your assumption.

I'm willing to go with that. So, why does the problem go away?

I have no idea. Let's watch the next one. Patches, what are you getting in Otherwhere?

Emotion: frustration. Image input rising and falling, rising and falling like waves.

Alwyn suddenly burst into the gestalt. *Waves! Captain, put me through to Nzinga.*

What?

Pattern. Natalia, there's a pattern!

Emotion: enthusiastic approval. Nzinga front and centre, please.

Emotion: eager desire to please.

The engineer's augment voice steadied. *Nzinga, I need to see what's happening in that reactor. Feed me everything you've got. Now!*

Without waiting for orders, the whole gestalt reoriented. *That's it. Andrew, follow me.*

Natalia couldn't understand what the two of them were observing, but Andrew's feel in the gestalt changed to one of intense concentration.

Watch that level there. See how it's rising? It's a recurring pattern. It happens every five point oh seven minutes.

Andrew sent a negative. *But the surge we've been getting is stronger than that.*

Here's why. When it builds to a certain point...right...now, quick. Look at that level.

Where?

Way over there.

Got it. Now it's peaking as well. Here it comes...now they're both dropping off.

That's the pattern. The engineer sent a simple image of two wave forms on a graph. *Those two waves are on different frequencies, and every five minutes their peaks come one after the other. The one that is last peaks about every five point oh two minutes, so it's catching up, and they're getting closer together. In a few cycles, they're going to coincide perfectly, and we might all be toast.*

Emotion: fear and determination. They can't be allowed to join!

Natalia surveyed her resources. *Andrew, Lundeen, what do we do?*

168

The Chief Engineer made a helpless gesture. *NightHawk can exert electromagnetic force, but I don't know what to use it against. Andrew, can you use your augment to control it?*

Yes, but I'll need help. The plasma mass is suspended in the centre of the reaction chamber electromagnetically, but it's oscilating. Will it help to keep it away from the walls?

Most definitely. See there...?

Andrew's presence swelled in the gestalt. Natalia fed him support, and she could feel Patches realigning the members.

All right, folks. Time for the shielding we've been using all along. Apply it to NightHawk's electromagnetic field, just like we did in the ball game. Slivers should deploy their force weapons inward. We'll control them from here. Start at low power, and if we get positive results, feed us more. I don't know how it's going to work until we try it, but we have to keep that plasma from breaking out!

It was frustrating, not being able to see what was going on, but Natalia threw all her power into the general gestalt. After a moment of strain, the pressure eased.

When Alwyn's concentration relaxed, she pushed in. *Andrew, what's going on? Is it still five minutes before the next one?*

Correct.. That was the strongest one, yet. If Alwyn hadn't been there to tell us where to focus, it would have been hard to handle it, and the next one will be stronger.

Alwyn, any ideas?

Like I told you before, Natalia, I just spot 'em; I can't fix 'em. Sorry.

You and Nzinga keep scanning. We need a solution. Everyone else give them support. Andrew, Chakka, we need a council of war. About three minutes long.

Emotion: attack!

Yes, I know, Chakka. That's your reaction to everything...

No, no, Mum. He's right. What we're doing now is completely defensive, and the waves will just keep coming, closer and closer together, until finally they overwhelm us, the plasma hits the wall and blasts through. We have to do something to interfere with one of the waves. All we have to do is change the frequency of either one and break the pattern.

What if we change it in the wrong direction, and they coincide immediately?

Good point. We have to concentrate on the faster one and slow it down. That will slow the rate they're closing, giving us more time to act.

Can we change them?

Emotion: disappointment. They're caused by huge swings of radiation in the reactor. Nothing we can do physically can affect that.

Okay, can you find a third factor that is supporting one of the main waves?

I don't know. Alwyn?

Emotion: frustration. Do you know how many waves in the electromagnetic spectrum are bouncing around inside that shielding?

Can you find something that affects one of our two main drivers?

Give me a moment.

You have about three and a half minutes. Everybody, new target.

Blainey's concentration faded from her awareness as he focused on his task.

Pressure's building. Anything, Alwyn?

One possible. I don't know the functions, but there's a separate flow...see, that one there, that seems to fluctuate at the same time. Chief Lundeen, do you recognize that?

It's something in the cooling system. Yes, that would work. If we can change the temperature of the coolant up or down it will advance or delay the surge that's causing one of the waves we're experiencing.

Natalia felt a wash of relief, but she kept it to herself. *Prime. Which one is it?*

Emotion: helplessness. I have no idea. I can barely sense the waves you're talking about.

Andrew, you keep everything under control like last time. Alwyn, do what you can to figure out how the coolant system fits into the pattern. Everybody ready? It's building...

Once again the inferno in the reactor core blazed, and the whole crew threw their minds into the task of holding it down. Natalia felt a draft of different minds, and it threw her for a moment. Then she realized that Patches was reaching out to the augments aboard the destroyer, weak as they were, and adding them to the mix. Encouraged, she renewed her efforts to support the failing engineer.

How's it going, Alwyn?

Emotion: desperation. I'm having trouble keeping track of it. It's just a faint echo, getting lost in all the other patterns. I have to concentrate. Concentrate...

Hold on, man! We're all with you.

Emotion: despair! I can't follow! I can't find it anymore.

Andrew, we need your help here. Can you follow him?

I think I see it, Alwyn. Hold on...

Suddenly the engineer's concentration collapsed. His body drooped, and tears streamed down his face. *I lost it. I couldn't keep it up any longer.*

She tore her mind out of his sorrow.

Andrew, any luck?

Not this time. I'm getting a handle on it now. Next time we'll get it...

She registered his hesitation. *...or what?*

Three or four more cycles and we won't be able to hold it.

So we have two more cycle to solve this.

Lundeen's presence intruded. *Leaving us only five minutes to get out of here before the reactor goes. We can't get far enough away in five minutes.* He didn't mention the crew who were on *Florrie*, three minutes hard run from the nearest airlock

Natalia thought rapidly, trying to keep from tapping any of the gestalt's power away from its fierce concentration on the tasks at hand. *But we might get far enough away that we'd probably survive.*

NightHawk would possibly survive. I have no idea about the specs on Diablo or the Sliverships.

Andrew, do we have any chance at all of solving this?

A reasonable chance, if we can get back to the point we lost it last time. Alwyn, I got the impression that the temperature is connected to the plasma balance, which is the wave that is peaking first.

I...think you're right, but I'm not sure. The other wave has something to do with pressure.

Natalia broke in. *We don't have time for more observation. We go with that opinion. That means we should try to up the efficiency of the coolant. If we drop the temperature of the plasma, it will stop catching up. Problem solved. What do you think, Nelson?*

And if you're wrong, let's change the temperature enough that it makes a jump and comes in way quicker when the pressure wave is still coming.

She turned to the engineer, collapsed on the accel couch next to her. *Emotion: question?*

He turned his wan face over towards her, the teardrops still wet on his cheeks. *How can I say no?*

As she gazed at him, a great yearning filled her. She wanted to put her arms around him and protect him. She wanted...

Mother! Not now!

What?

You're broadcasting through the whole gestalt with enough power to distract everyone. Focus that energy on something useful!

She gave herself a mental shake. *All right. Listen up, folks; this is how it's going to go. Patches, I hope you can understand this. I want the NightHawk gestalt, just the three of us, split off and assigned to supporting Alwyn. He has to keep going this time. The rest of you are under Andrew's command. He knows what to do. Lundeen, any spare energy you have goes up and out. I want you worrying about our possibility of escape. Everyone got that?*

Image: spaceship, auguar, and Captain holding Blainey tightly. Crew forming a spearpoint thrusting at a blazing fire. One engineer with head up, looking around.

Couldn't have said it better myself, Patches.

Lundeen suddenly blasted into the gestalt. *Up and out! We're not thinking, folks.*

What?

We're so caught up in trying to solve this ourselves, we forgot our main ally. Johnson, are you in here with us?

Right here, Chief. I don't really understand what's happening, but I caught something about the cooling system. I'm at that panel now. What do you need?

Good man. How much control do you have over it?

We're way past temperature levels where it could make any difference, so I never thought to try.

We don't need much. If you could increase the efficiency by about ten percent, that would be enough to change the frequency of the plasma cycle.

It's running at 110% rated capacity at the moment.

Crank it to full military override. That reactor is going into shutdown the moment this is all over, and nobody cares if it ever works again.

Core cooling system is now in emergency override. I've just dumped all the refrigerant from the precooler tanks in at full pressure. We'd be seeing an immediate drop if the damned reactor wasn't already gone far beyond the most optimistic parameters. Let's hope these military outfits are overbuilt more than the commercial ones I'm familiar with...there we have it. Temperature dropped half a degree...

Natalia broke in. *Keep your foot on the pedal, Johnson, and keep it to the floor. Everyone, we're coming up to the next cycle. This is the big one, folks, so don't save any energy for later. If we don't hold this time, there won't be a later to worry about.*

The wills of the crew solidified like a sheet of PermaSteel, and the NightHawk prepared for the next encounter in what could be her final battle.

Natalia threw her energy into the gestalt, reserving a tiny amount to monitor the image of the inside of the reactor in Alwyn's mind. The pressure was building as usual, the plasma levels following very close behind now. She could feel it beating against the wall of *NightHawk's* electromagnetic forces. It was strong this time, and she could feel the fatigue eating away at the crew's consciousness.

Patches...

Grim agreement. Somehow the barwolf tightened one's hold on the other minds, welding them more firmly together. The pressure continued to build, but something was different, Natalia couldn't tell what...

...And then the pressure began to fade. The plasma was still building but its peak was slow in arriving. It rolled by under them and was gone. The gestalt eased.

Emotion: relief.

Lundeen and Blainey were still communicating. *All right! The frequency has changed...*

The crew held their breaths as the engineers calculated.

...estimated new frequency, fourteen minutes.

A burst of cheers erupted, to be killed by a weak thrust from Johnson. *We've got a leak in the cooling system, Chief Lundeen. Nothing serious, but we have to shut it down, only for a minute or two, to do some rerouting. Otherwise we'll have radioactive water spraying all over the place.*

Go ahead, Johnson, although I doubt if it's going to matter. In fact, maybe you should leave it shut down. If our last trick turns out to be only temporary, going in the opposite direction might work. That okay with you, Alwyn?

These are huge forces, but in delicately balanced patterns. Anything could work.

Emotion: laughter. You're giving away engineering secrets, Blainey. If it doesn't work, hit it with a hammer. Sometimes it does the trick.

Natalia knew they needed the release, but now it was time to focus. *Back on duty, boys. Johnson, your cooling system seems to have done the trick. The frequency has changed to every fourteen minutes. But we need it working again to separate the frequencies more. So get it fixed ASAP and up and running again at whatever level it can handle. We've got another conjunction coming up in...nine minutes. To your posts, everyone.*

The sense of dismay washing through the gestalt reminded her of her training sessions back in the Academy. She cranked the volume on the ship's com and the augment channel and spoke in both. *"I know. Getting back up for the next battle after you thought you won the first one is the hardest part. This is where we discover what we're made of. You thought you gave your all last time, right? Well, you didn't. You're Commandos, and you have reserves you never knew were there. Remember the bear in the bush. Now we find out how fast you can really run."*

Emotion: laughter. Emotion: fierce determination.

Blainey slipped out of gestalt and leaned over to speak to her. "The bear in the bush? Is that something to do with the Pope being Catholic?"

"Nope. Different joke. I'll tell you later."

"Great motivation, Captain. Now I'll be doubly sure to survive, waiting to hear the punch line."

"Ah, I'm a clever one, aren't I?"

She slid back into the gestalt, and he was right there with her.

Andrew jumped immediately into communication with Alwyn.

Pressure level coming up. What are you seeing?

Cooling system is back on line. Pattern's changed. Just a moment. Plasma coming up slower, I think. Lundeen?

Plasma definitely slower. The pressure's on schedule. There it comes...

Dig in, everyone.

There was an intense silence in the gestalt. No communication was needed. No one had to be told when the pressure peaked and began to fade.

Andrew broke in. *Here comes the plasma now. We don't know what's going to happen, so be ready for anything.*

Nothing happened.

Plasma fading. Pressure fading. I think we did it. Alwyn, did you get a handle on that? What are the new frequencies?

I'll need one more cycle to be sure, but I think we're looking at the next conjunction in...about twenty minutes. Lundeen?

Twenty-one minutes, forty-seven seconds, give or take. The coolant system's had a bit of a rough go, though. We better get this thing shut down long before then, Johnson.

Roger that. I'm working on it now.

Once you get used to the gestalt, you'll find Nzinga invaluable.

She already is. She's about the most beautiful thing I've seen in six years.

Emotion: regal acceptance.

Toni took charge of the gestalt on the destroyer. *Now that we have time, we can get in there and work with the safeties that are functional. Leave us a couple of the slivers to help with moving stuff around.*

Natalia sent approval. *The boarding party can go play in the reactor. We have some very unhappy pirates floating around far too near for comfort. Greens Two and Four stay with Nzinga and Patches. The rest of the Sliverships, I liked that pushing technique we used in the reactor. Can we use that to boost the disabled outriders a few thousand kilometres, and then bring back any shuttles and runabouts that are drifting around?*

Andrew pulled his team back into gestalt. *Right you are, ma'am. One large snowplow coming up.*

And while you're at it, can your crew do another sweep through each ship's electronics and make sure they're not going to get their propulsion systems restarted?

Wilco, ma'am. Leave them life support but not much else?

You catch my drift. Away you go.

Aye, ma'am. All right crew, here's the trick...

Natalia glanced across to the right-hand couch, where Alwyn lay, looking exhausted. She reached over and covered his hand. "Well, that's what it's like in the Commandos. Feel like joining up?"

He twisted his hand to grasp hers. "It would take some getting used to."

She jumped up, accessing the ship's com. "*NightHawks,* debrief in the mess. Jonny, double grog ration."

As they made their way towards the habitation ring, she discovered that the slideway was wide enough for two people if they walked very close together and in step. It helped to have an arm around the other person.

When they were seated and the mugs were full, Natalia gazed at her crew with pride, framing how she was going to put this. But she didn't get the chance. Alwyn gazed at her, his head tilted. "Is the battle over, Captain? Have we stood down?"

"Umm...the battle isn't officially over until the away team finishes. But the crew on *NightHawk* is standing down for the moment."

"Okay, now you can tell me about the bear in the bush."

Natalia glanced around at the crew, who were watching her with knowing smiles. "It's an old line the sergeants use in Basic Training. They wait until everyone's completely exhausted, and then they say, "All right. A bear just jumped out of the bush at you. Let's see how fast you can run.""

175

Alwyn chuckled. "I thought you were talking about the other 'bear in the bush' joke. You know; you don't have to outrun the bear. Just the slowest member of your party."

They were old lines, but the laughter was a great relief, and a gush of humour rolling from the barwolf gestalt suggested that their species had similar jokes.

27. TIDYING UP

The away team returned to *NightHawk* three hours later, dirty, tattered and tired. Toni reported to the captain in the chart room, where she was watching the old destroyer as it gradually lost its random spin. Natalia gestured towards the screen. "Somebody got the steering thrusters working."

Jacobs peered at the *Florie*. "No shortage of well-trained people onboard. They'll be more comfortable, now. The spin gave a strange wobble to the gravity that was quite unsettling."

Natalia nodded towards the chair. "How did it go?"

The major shook her head, collapsing into her seat. "That place is a nightmare. I don't know how a spaceship can create so much dirt. There's barely enough lighting to see where you're going, and half the corridors are sealed off as unsafe due to electrical hazards."

Then she grinned. "But that Johnson is no slouch, and he has talented people working for him. He had some proper equipment in good working order stuck away in secluded corners. The moment the reactors shut down, they cranked up their own generators. No problem with heating, because there's plenty of excess hot water in the holding tanks. So the first thing they did was light up the kitchen, raid the fridges and plan a feast. They were just sitting down to eat when we left."

"Any word on the B reactor?"

"He says with the overstressed cooling system it'll take a couple of days to get the temperature down to the point where they can check it out. No obvious damage, though. Once we got control of it again, we vented a bunch of plasma into space, and that helped a lot."

"Well, your team did a good job over there. Get cleaned up and hit the mess. You're about three drinks behind the rest."

"I know. Pete didn't even stop to wash his hands."

"Your group is all off duty for the next twelve hours, so relax."

Toni grinned. "Music to my ears. But I need to spend some time with Nzinga. I think I've got competition."

"Johnson? I caught some of his comments."

"Mutual admiration society. They work well together. He's a bright guy, and she feeds him better information that he's ever had before."

"That's fine. I've just used the barwolf communication gestalt to connect with Freighty's Pony Express system, and sent in a preliminary report to Space Arm at Jupiter Base. We're not that far from Sol anymore, so we'll have a response in a few days. There's no hurry. Our job now is to get these people settled and as comfortable as possible. They're not exactly out of the woods, yet."

She waved a hand. "Go on, get out of here. You're officially stood down."

Toni tossed a tired smile over her shoulder and staggered slightly as she cleared the doorway.

Natalia sat, staring at a blank viewscreen, her mind awhirl. *I never should have done it. It was too dangerous. I never should have let an untested alien anywhere near a ShipBuster. I never should have even tried to get the damned bomb anywhere near that many innocent civilians. Why did I do it? It seemed so right at the time.*

A sudden thought struck her. *Was it the barwolves? Did their confidence in me make me too confident in myself? No, I can't blame anyone else. I screwed up, and Admiral Mira is going to chew a strip off me a mile wide.*

I'll have to discuss it with Andrew first, though. He's the expert, after all. The thought gave her comfort.

And I'll bounce it off Alwyn, as well. He'll give me the outside viewpoint. That idea gave her a whole lot more comfort than it really merited, but she tucked it away carefully anyway.

Then she returned to her work.

The slivership had reunited and tucked in beside the *Florrie* to facilitate communication. Natalia called up Johnson on regular ship's com.

He answered from the Chief Engineer's cabin, a place of bare metal walls and functional furniture. But his face had lost its haggard look.

"How are things going over there?"

He answered with a chuckle, rubbing his stomach. "I'm afraid I rather overindulged at dinner. Best meal I've had in six years. Just sitting around, now, resting the body and exercising the mind. Do you have any suggestions for the future?"

"You might want to get one of your reactors back online. It will take Space Arm vessels about forty days to get out here and stop, then another ten to catch up to you. It takes a while to get an expedition like that organized. You'll be here two months, minimum. If you can manage some decel, it will shorten your stay."

The engineer gave a knowing smile. "I think we can manage."

"You do? I thought you were in pretty rough shape over there."

"We were. But the motivation of the crew has changed considerably. Now that their efforts are directed towards their own comfort and convenience, it's amazing how the infrastructure is shaping up. I'm a little worried about the Bridge Crew staging a coup, though."

"You don't need to worry about your former owners coming back. Their ships' propulsion systems have all been permanently disabled — at least, without parts from Sol — and they're clumped together twenty thousand kilometres away. If you get any decel at all you'll increase that. We left them only their steering thrusters. If the criminals want to get together, exchange crews, meet for pirate parties or whatever, they can do as they like. Space Arm will pick them up, then repair the ships and return them to their owners. And they better behave themselves."

"Why is that?"

"Because we're all doing 0.012 light speed right now. If Space Arm doesn't come and get them, they will sail right through the Solar System and out the other side into infinity. Our best guess is that Space Arm will send a tug to decel the Dirty Florrie and ship it to a breaker's yard in the Sol Asteroid belt, where it will be scavenged and scrapped for real this time. They will probably also send two passenger ships: one to bring hostages back to Sol and one to go on to Barnard, because a good number of you are immigrants on their way out."

"That sounds great. I haven't got my head around the problems we're going to have. Any ideas?"

"First thing to do is start a census. We need data on everyone, including any deeased, so we can send messages to loved ones, spouses, lawyers, that sort of thing. Before we leave, we'll upgrade your com system so you can communicate directly to Sol. You're going to be out here quite a while longer, so have patience."

"Oh, we've got patience. We've all proved that."

"What about the threat of a takeover from inside?"

The engineer shrugged. "There were a lot of weapons left behind, and we collected most of them. We know who we can trust and the ones we can't, and the rest will go along as they always have. As you might guess, there's been a bit of social upheaval. The few thugs that weren't lucky enough to get to an escaping ship will stay in lockup for the duration. The Toadies will find themselves working for their grub and air. Most of the rest of us will continue with our old duties. I'm looking into the feasibility of starting the A reactor again. We've got tonnes of fuel, and our auxilliary generators will be hard pressed to maintain minimal gravity as well as heat, light, and the other basics. Now that I know the schedule, we might as well start the C reactor and get some decent decel going again. The farther we get from those goons the happier I'll be."

"How's the food supply?"

He gave a wolfish grin. "If everybody's willing to exist on what most of us have been eating for years, we can last as long as the sunlamps in hydroponics have power. Plus the Bridge Crew's freezers were pretty well supplied with goodies from the ships they caught."

"Have you thought about evidence gathering?"

"That's going to be a thorny problem."

"It will be obvious which side most of the citizens of your little world belonged to. But for some in the middle, there has been coercion and all sorts of excusable reasons for people's actions. I have no explicit orders from Space Arm, but I do have some advice."

"Anything that will help."

"I assume you understand the legal system. Do you know anything about its history?"

"Not much, but I can search the data bases."

"There was an old idea that lasted a thousand years or so before modern technology made it obsolete. It was called "trial by jury.""

"I've heard about that. Highly subjective, from what I learned in school."

"True, but in a situation where the crimes have mostly been on the social end of the scale, a formal session of some sort could straighten a lot of things out while everyone's memories are fresh. I strongly suggest that you don't make any statements of guilt or innocence. Just collect data in an organized and public way, to hand over to the Space Arm lawyers when they show on board. Use a jury to decide which facts to save, who really needs to be locked up."

The engineer mused awhile. "Yes, it could short-circuit a lot of revenge-taking if people knew something official was being done. Thank you Captain. I'll get working on it. You know, we even have a couple of lawyers. They'll be happy for something to do, and I imagine they won't charge too much."

"On the topic of money. Official policy is to return private property to individuals who can be identified, and then divide the profits from the sale of any leftover assets equally between the victims. Part of your job is to try to figure out who deserves what. We have precedents in the Barnard System. If the legal system of a small democratic group of people makes reasonable decisions, as long as they don't counter standard Planetary Community rules, those decisions will stand in general court."

"Democratic. That's already been a problem."

"In what way?"

"Think about it. We have the captains, crews and passengers from sixteen ships in here. They have banded together in predictable ways."

"Tribal."

"In some cases, yes. I think you could say we have a functioning oligarchy. They call themselves the Captains' Council. Not that there was much for them to do."

"Where do you fit in?"

"I'm the boss of Engineering. I'm a tolerated member of the Council, but they don't all trust me, because I had to work with the Bridge Crew."

"It sounds like they need a bit of guidance. Do you want me to come over?"

He grinned. "Do you need an invitation? You're pretty much in charge, the way I see it."

She shook her head. "Space Arm has no reason to direct your people in any way, as long as nobody is breaking any laws. You are a group of Planetary Community citizens, and you are basically in charge of yourselves. However, I should come over to make sure that everything is legit and aboveboard. Will you arrange a meeting?"

"Why don't you come over about on nine hundred? Rumours are flying, and I want to make sure everyone knows you really exist. You can give them official word what's happening, which will settle them down. We'll gather in the main mess hall for that. Then you can meet with the Captains' Council for the nitty gritty."

"Sounds like fun."

"I'll try to scare up some fancy decorations."

"Just make sure there's sufficient light for them to see us."

"Who are you bringing?"

"I thought Patches plus Chakka, Nzinga and Toni. The barwolves are a reality they will all have to face sooner or later, and the auguars have a calming effect on aggressive sorts. Any problem with that?"

"Don't worry. All is in hand."

* * *

Captain O'Rourke showed up in the *Florrie's* main mess hall the next morning, stared out at the mass of gaunt faces confronting her, and changed her mind about what she was going to say. *These people don't need rules and discipline. They need hope.* And in the back of her mind, a little voice was prodding her. *They shouldn't look so grateful. I just about killed all of them.* She squashed it as not useful at the moment: to be dealt with later.

But while she paused, Nzinga strolled to a table in the front row and rolled over at the feet of a six-year-old boy, exposing her underside for a rub while Chakka manipulated the viewscreen camera to zoom in on the pleased response.

When the amused chuckle died down, Natalia stepped forward. "Thank you for that introduction, Nzinga. I'm sorry if you have missed out on your tummy rubs lately. We've been rather busy with serious matters. Chakka, may I...?"

The auguar panned the camera back to the captain, and she took a deep breath. "You folks have been through a rough time. It's getting better, but it will take work to set you up in your new lives. Space Arm will probably send two passenger ships: one to bring people back to Sol, one to go on to Barnard carrying those who are outward bound. Once you have some kind of organization, you should do a census. We need to know what each of you wants to do: on to Barnard or back to Sol.

"We're also in the process of setting up communication with Sol. As you might expect, when your ships went missing, they were declared lost. This is going to cause all sorts of trouble for the people who are heading back towards Sol, because you are all officially dead, and trying to put your life back together will be full of snags. Those headed for a new life in Barnard will probably have a better time of it, because your closest family, friends and belongings are here with you. In any case, the Planetary Community will give you all the legal help you need. Those of you who are ship's crew and employees of Interplanetary corporations are probably pretty wealthy right now. My ship's ArIn tells me that lost spacers are considered to be still on the payroll until they are found. I don't imagine you've been spending much of your wages recently. Life insurance and compensation payouts are going to be a real tangle. Again, you'll get lots of legal help."

"Which brings me back to organization. You have been functioning as ship's crew for the past years, which is a hierarchy. You are no longer in that situation. According to Space Arm policy, you are a group of Planetary Community citizens, under the aegis and restrictions of the PC. Which was democratic, last I heard.

"The citizens of Barnard System have worked out some details you'll be interested in. Here's how it goes. Any group of citizens cut off from the control of the Planetary Government are expected to create their own democratic organization to the best of their ability. Any legal decisions made by this ad hoc government will be honoured by PC courts, as long as none of the actions are counter to PC laws."

She noticed heads turning to each other uncertainly.

"What that means is, if you make any decisions that are not arrived at democratically, the moment you step off this ship they will be null and void, and if any of those actions are counter to PC law, you will be liable to prosecution."

She waved a negating hand. "Nobody in the government back home wants to do that to people who have been through such an ordeal as you have. I'm just suggesting that you access the legal sections of your ship's memory and act accordingly while you're waiting for rescue."

She waited until the buzz of conversation died down. "I'm now going to meet with your Captains' Council to give them any guidance they need, and they will communicate with you."

She glanced at Johnson. "I must remind you that the Captain's Council has no legal position. You are a democracy, and you can form any kind of government you like. The Council has temporary executive function during the transition, and that's all."

Johnson stepped forward. "We don't really know much more than that, folks. But you can start thinking about the future, something we haven't had much chance to do recently. And I'd like you to show your appreciation for the Space Arm squadron that Captain O'Rourke brought out to save us."

Natalia's face warmed as a roar of applause and shouting filled the room. When it didn't show any sign of abating, she nodded, waved, and motioned Johnson to get her out of there.

Emotion: awe. Image: ocean wave pouring over Captain, smothering her.

Emotion: complete agreement.

Emotion: pleasure. Image: Queen Nzinga on throne with multitudes at her feet.

Toni reached down and cuffed her auguar on the shoulder. *Emotion: amused disgust.*

As they left the noise behind, Natalia spoke aloud. "Now we come to the real job."

While Johnson introduced the team to the men sitting around the Officer's Boardroom table, she scanned the group. Then she turned to the engineer, a question on her face.

He gave her a grim smile. "Sixteen ships captured, only nine officers here. Two were murdered during the takeover of their ships. Five thought their own personal safety and comfort were more important than sticking to their responsibilities."

"I see." She regarded the captains. Mostly young middle age, alert and well dressed. All a little gaunt, their faces lined. "Well, gentlemen, here we are. You have heard my speech about democracy. How does that strike you?"

Quick glances passed around the table, and then one older man cleared his throat. "Captain James Bennet of the *Saint Bernadette*. Very reasonable, with a couple of reservations."

"As long as they have nothing to do with people not having the ability or knowledge to make decisions for themselves, I'd be pleased to hear them."

The silence spread and lingered, while the captains looked at each other again.

"Look, I know this is hard for you. You don't deal with democracy on your ships. It's not possible. But this is not that sort of situation. You don't have a ship's crew, here. You have a society." She waved a hand in the direction of the mess hall. "Look at those people out there. A superior cross-section of humanity, well educated and well trained. Your crews are the best spacers humanity has produced. Any emigrants were carefully vetted. If the dregs of humanity that almost destroyed Earth in the Twentieth Century could create democracy, you should be able to."

Bennet nodded slowly. "That does shine a different light on the matter. We have been ruled by a dictatorship for years, and only survived by maintaining the discipline that carried over from our ships. It's hard to let that go."

"I understand. But you can." She smiled. "This is where you find out how good a captain you really were."

He frowned. "Why is that?"

"Because if they still follow you now that they no longer have to, you've been doing all right." She became serious. "Believe me, gentlemen, now that the common enemy is gone, the tribalism that kept you going could now break you apart."

A younger man down the table raised a hand. "First Officer Hiebert of the *Nimitz*. I'd like you to explain that, ma'am."

She regarded him. "How have you dealt with inter-crew conflicts? Bar fights and the like."

He straightened. "We dealt with them very firmly, believe me."

"Did it stop them?"

He glanced around the table. "A certain amount of rivalry is to be expected…"

"Which means that to some extent you condone this activity in your crew because it helps to weld them together as a unit, right?" She nodded. "Tribalism. Us against them. Loyalty, even honour."

There were puzzled nod of agreement around the table.

"And now the enemy is gone, but "they" are still around. There is no need for loyalty to a ship that you will never see again." She paused to meet their eyes. "You are the leaders. You have brought your people through a harrowing time. It's very difficult to discard all the old fears and responses and lead in a different direction. But how well you adapt is going to make the difference between a very reasonable two or three months' wait and a ghastly one."

She held up open hands. "I'm not giving you any orders. What happens inside this ship is no longer Space Arm's problem, unless you break Planetary Community laws." She paused. "Or the laws that you, as a democratic society, create to govern your existence here. You have problems to solve that may not even be mentioned in the statutes. I'm sure you have a far better idea than I do of how to deal with them."

She rose. "So I am going to turn this meeting over to you. My ship's ArIn will record it, but my last charge to you is to create some kind of governing system for this group, to keep its PC citizens safe. Once you have created the body, I strongly suggest you turn control of the ship over to them. Do you have any questions before we go?"

Toni chuckled in the augment. *That threw them.*

I want them to be sure that they're on their own.

Emotion: barwolf humour. Image: captains punching at empty air.

That's right, Patches. They don't realize how much they depended on their common enemy. I'm not going to provide a new one.

Captain Bennet stood as well. "I think someone ought to officially thank you and your crew for our rescue. We will all be forever grateful."

She smiled. "Just part of the job, sir."

He glanced down at the barwolf and the auguars. "And please thank your allies for us as well."

"No need. They understood everything that was said."

"Oh…well, that's fine then."

Emotion: barwolf humour. Patches approached the man, staring up into his eyes. Then she reached out and touched his leg.

With a hesitant hand, he stretched down and touched the front of her shoulder armour.

Emotion: satisfaction.

The captain stared at Natalia with wondering eyes.

She nodded informally and turned to lead her group out of the room.

Image: Captain Bennet striding over grassy fields, the other captains following. Many humans streaming behind.

Emotion: agreement. Couldn't have said it better myself.

Natalia glanced to Patches, then to Toni. "Well, team, I guess you've done what you came for."

"I imagine so. That's a good bunch, in there."

She shrugged. "What I said earlier applies to them as well. They're the best of the best. They'll do all right."

Image: wide platform held up by many people. In the middle, eight captains holding up a smaller platform. On the smaller platform, Captain Bennet alone.

Image: Similar, but humans are standing in a complex mechanical environment, run by many other humans, all looking to Chief Engineer Johnson, who stands to one side, his eyes turned to Bennet for instruction.

Natalia laughed. "You two just pictured modern human society in a nutshell. Let's go home."

* * *

Once the *NightHawk* and her little fleet was decelerating again, preparing to head back towards Freighty, there was one last, important task to accomplish.

Andrew stood in his mother's cabin doorway, regarding the two who lounged side by side on the tiny sofa along the bulkhead. "Well. Here I am. What's happening?"

"Come in and sit down, son."

He sat on the bunk. "You two look cosy."

"Do we?"

His smile became smug. "Yep. Have to say, you do."

"And what have you to say about that?"

He frowned as he regarded her. "Speaking as the sole representative of the rest of the family?"

"Let's say you were. What then?"

"Hmm…I'd say I was being presented with a *fait accompli*. I'd say I wasn't being given any choice at all in the matter, because you've made up your mind already, and when Captain Natalia O'Rourke makes up her mind, her resolve is such that sometimes not even she can change it."

"You have got that exactly right. This is nothing at all to do with you, young man. This is a personal decision, for me alone to make. Do you follow?"

He stood. "Oh, yes, ma'am. You have made your desires clear." He stood, snapped her a salute and made a perfect about face, but as he strolled out, she detected a loud snicker.

"I could have used a little support there."

Alwyn did not look perturbed. "First lesson in blended families. Never take sides."

"An expert in blended families, are you?"

"Grew up in one. I was the one blending in, and I can do it again."

"We'll just have to see about that."

He leaned closer. "Is that the plan?"

She put a hand on his shoulder. "Do you want it to be?"

"Already you're doubting my commitment. What about you?"

She tightened her grip. "The whole damned ship knows exactly how I feel."

He shrugged his arm out of her grasp and slipped it around her. "I guess I'll have to work on my communication skills, then."

THE END

If you enjoyed this book, do the author and other readers a favour and go to your favourite retailer and post a review. Even a rating and a few words is great.

ABOUT THE AUTHOR

    Brought up in a logging camp with no electricity, Gordon Long learned his storytelling in the traditional way: at his father's knee. He now spends his time editing, publishing, travelling, blogging and writing Fantasy, Sci-Fi and Social Commentary, although sometimes the boundaries blur.

    Gordon lives in Tsawwassen, British Columbia, with his wife, Linda, and their Nova Scotia Duck Tolling Retriever, Josh. When he is not writing and publishing, he works on projects with the Surrey Seniors' Planning Table and is a staff writer for <indiesunlimited.com>

MORE FROM GORDON A. LONG

www.ingramcontent.com/pod-product-compliance
Lightning Source LLC
Chambersburg PA
CBHW070513260626
47161CB00004B/1537